Other Jersey Shore Mysteries by
Beth Sherman

DEAD MAN'S FLOAT
DEATH AT HIGH TIDE

A JERSEY SHORE MYSTERY

DEATH'S A BEACH

BETH SHERMAN

AVON BOOKS

An Imprint of HarperCollins*Publishers*

This is a work of fiction. Names, characters, places, and incidents are the products of the author's imagination or are used fictitiously and are not to be construed as real. Any resemblance to actual events, locales, organizations, or persons, living or dead, is entirely coincidental.

AVON BOOKS
An Imprint of HarperCollins*Publishers*
10 East 53rd Street
New York, New York 10022-5299

Copyright © 2000 by Beth Sherman
Library of Congress Catalog Card Number: 99-96770
ISBN: 0-380-73109-6
www.avonbooks.com

First Avon Books paperback printing: May 2000

Avon Trademark Reg. U.S. Pat. Off. and in Other Countries, Marca Registrada, Hecho en U.S.A.
HarperCollins ® is a trademark of HarperCollins Publishers Inc.

Printed in the U.S.A.

WCD 10 9 8 7 6 5 4 3 2 1

For my parents,
Glenda and Victor Sherman

Thanks for your love, encouragement,
and support and for introducing me
to the works of Agatha Christie
at the tender age of eight

Acknowledgments

I'd like to thank the usual suspects: Dominick Abel, Trish Lande Grader, Johanna Keller, Andy Edelstein, and Jessie Rose Edelstein. For their invaluable help and expertise, my thanks to Margaret Caldwell-Ott, a consulting forensic anthropologist with the New York City Medical Examiner's office, and Helen-Chantal Pike, author of *Images of America: Asbury Park* (Arcadia Publishing). Special thanks to the following folks in Ocean Grove, New Jersey: Mary Hughes, Phil May at the Ocean Grove Museum, Linda Meaney, Ray Huizenga and Harriet Ellner at Century 21, Carol Aitken at Adventures in Video, and Diane and Pete Herr at the Ocean Vista, who documented the big storm.

Chapter 1

When tackling home repairs yourself, decide if the project is something you can handle. Make a list of the tools and materials you'll need. Formulate a step-by-step plan and go over each step in your mind. Give yourself plenty of time. Now, roll up your sleeves and get to work.

Home Repairs Without the Hassles:
A Beginner's Guide to Fixing
What Ails Your House

It rained for four straight days, and then it rained some more. Waves crashed against the shoreline, rolling under the boardwalk, making the gray planks ripple like piano keys. The surf surged forward, spilling past the dune grass and across the street until it lapped hungrily at the doorsteps of the houses on Ocean Avenue. The wind gusted up to eighty miles an hour. It was the middle of October, and the Jersey Shore was bearing the brunt of the worst storm in years. In Oceanside Heights, roads had flooded. One of the piers collapsed and floated away. Trees and lampposts toppled over, downing some power lines. Schools closed, people boarded and shuttered up everything they could. You could practically hydroplane down Main Street.

On TV, solemn-faced weather forecasters talked about "hurricane force winds" and "significant beach erosion." The governor declared a state of emergency. A local radio station played the Rolling Stones's "We're on the Eve of Destruction" every hour on the hour. The men who hung out in the back of Moby's Hardware said it was worse than '92, when Seaview Pathway was so badly flooded the fire department had to rescue people by boat. The newspapers dubbed it "The Storm of the Century."

Anne Hardaway called it a mess.

When the rain finally stopped and the sun slid bashfully above the horizon, looking almost ashamed at being away for so long, Anne uttered a long, loud sigh of relief. There was nothing like an off-season northeaster in October to make you wish you lived someplace else. Someplace dry and secure. Like a duplex in Philly or a ranch in Wyoming.

Of course, the rain was conducive to work. There was nothing else to do but sit at her computer and type, unless you counted worrying about whether she should have had flood insurance. Or how much longer the lights were going to stay on.

The morning it finally stopped raining, Anne got out of bed, put on a pair of pink fuzzy slippers, and padded downstairs. Across the boarded up front door lay four giant sand bags. The bags were supposed to keep the water out. So was the blanket over the door. They hadn't worked. Rain had seeped in through the windows, soaking the towels she'd piled underneath. The pastel rug in the living room was soggy. Wallpaper buckled in the dining room. The roof leaked. Part of the aluminum siding had peeled off and snapped sharply in the wind, like a wayward silver cookie sheet.

Anne raised the damp window blinds and looked across the street. For days she'd peered out and seen nothing but rain, slashing down in torrents. Now, she gazed at where the beach had curved against the sea. It was gone. Vanished, like a cruel magician's trick. Water replaced what had once been sand, as though the ocean had gobbled up the beach in one great gulp. She'd never seen anything like it in her life. A shrunken strip of dune, sea grass washed away, the boardwalk a long stretch of broken driftwood littered with debris. The bulkhead had disappeared. The only trace of the fishing pier was a few scattered pilings jutting into the air like the arms of a drowning man.

In the middle of her front lawn was a bench, still attached to a half-dozen boardwalk planks. Mounds of sand covered the grass in the yard. Shingles had blown off the roof and one of her white shutters had landed in a boxwood hedge. There were patches of rust around the window frames—another bad sign. The air in the house smelled of mildew.

She stared at the destruction for a while, trying to take in the magnitude of it—the sheer brute force. The cat rubbed itself against her ankles, then leaped onto the window seat and pressed its nose against the glass. He was black and white, old, fat, with only one eye. His name was Harry. She'd had him two months—a mercy adoption. Either take the cat home or let him face euthanasia at the Wee Care Animal Shelter. She wasn't really a cat person, but she was trying.

During the worst of the storm, Harry had cowered in a basket on the kitchen floor, hiding his face as each loud clap of thunder shook the sky. Anne had fed him extra Purina and hoped the northeaster hadn't traumatized him. Each night, she let him curl up at the foot of her bed, on top of her mother's eiderdown quilt. Evelyn would have had a fit. Her mother hated cats; besides, she'd been allergic.

Now, the cat watched intently as Anne went over to the thermostat on the wall and set it to sixty-eight degrees. After a few seconds, she heard the reassuring click. Thank God. The oil tank was okay. The pipes hadn't burst. Still, she'd better take a look.

Steeling herself, Anne opened the empty linen closet in the first floor hallway and lifted the trapdoor leading to the basement. She hadn't wanted to look in the basement all week, on Grandma Betty's theory that what you didn't know couldn't possibly hurt you. Grandma Betty was pushing ninety, and refused to go to the doctor. Period. But she continued to live at home, by herself, enjoying good health while her friends died or got carted off to nursing homes, so the theory was working just fine, thank you very much.

Anne walked carefully down the steep concrete steps, peering into the half-dark. The cat stayed at the top of the stairs, looking at her like she'd lost her mind. The smell was worse down here, dank and fetid. When she got to the bottom of the stairs, she stopped and rolled up the cuffs of her gray sweatpants. It seemed like an unnecessary precaution. No puddles to speak of. No ankle-deep flooding. No miniature lake.

Her house was over a hundred years old, a pale yellow Victorian "cottage" with a wraparound porch, deep bay windows, and gingerbread on the facade. It was the house she'd grown up in, her parents' house, and sometimes she still thought of it that way, even though both her mother and father were dead. The basement was small, what real estate agents called a partial "Yankee" basement—measuring fourteen by eighteen feet. At one time, it had had a dirt floor, but in the mid-seventies, her mother had hired someone to put down wood boards.

Anne pulled the chain on the naked lightbulb and looked around. Same old mess. Milk crates, paint cans, shovel, spare tire, sled, her purple Schwinn bike with psychedelic flowers on the wide vinyl seat. Leaves had slid beneath the outside door, crinkling up and dying. The boiler looked okay. She took one step forward, brushing a cobweb off the low tin ceiling.

So far, so good. These old houses were built to withstand the weather. Hadn't she made it through Hurricanes Andrew and Gloria and the northeaster of '92? She took another step and a third, trying to tread lightly. On the fourth step, the wood suddenly gave way, and she pitched to her knees, falling through the planks to the dirt floor below. She reached out and touched the rotted, broken wood. The boards were wet, spongy. She pounded her knuckles against them angrily.

Damn it, she said to the empty room. Damn, damn, damn.

Chester Higgins surveyed the basement one last time and shook his head. His expression was mournful, like someone close to him had died.

"How much?" Anne said, from her perch on the stairs.

Chester scratched his head. He was pushing seventy and wore tan coveralls with Acme Builders printed in black script above the breast pocket. "You got yourself a real predicament here," he said, lifting the brim of his Acme cap to reveal a pair of bushy white brows.

Anne sighed. Her slippers were slimy with dirt. "Just give it to me straight."

Chester cleared his throat. "You best put down a concrete floor. That's four, five thousand easy. And your walls will need to be repointed. So you're looking at another eight grand."

"What's the grand total?"

Chester peered around the basement and appeared to be calculating. "I'd say we could do the job for $12,500."

Anne did some quick calculating of her own. She had exactly $3,439 in a money market fund and another $200 in her checking account. Half her advance for *Home Re-*

pairs Without the Hassles: A Beginner's Guide to Fixing What Ails Your House was still winging its way to her in the mail. And she'd just spent the rest of her savings having Dr. David Chilton create a bridge to replace a missing tooth that had been knocked out two months ago when an irate person who'd murdered two women had punched her in the mouth. Her cheap-but-crummy health insurance didn't cover assault with a right hook. So she'd had to pony up, in full. In another couple of weeks, she faced a mortgage payment, the tax bill, car insurance, electricity, and heat, which would eat up a big chunk of her dwindling bank balance. Not to mention her leaky roof, torn siding, missing shingles, and the sandbox in the yard.

"What if I wait a while?" she said hopefully.

"Not a good idea. It's way too damp down here. Heck, it's too darn wet. And you've got cracks in the walls. Lots of cracks. Worst case, your foundation starts to shift. And then . . ." Chester shrugged. "You wouldn't want this old place to come tumbling down around you."

Anne looked at Chester Higgins. He'd stuck a tooth-pick between his lips and was chewing on it thoughtfully. She could call around, get a couple of other estimates. But what was the point? Acme had been in business forty-five years. Like it said on Chester's blue Ford pickup out front, they did "quality work for less."

Anne gazed at Chester's work boots, which peeked out from beneath the warped planks. He was right. The walls were cracked. The floor had rotted. It was wet down here. The basement was an unofficial disaster area. She'd have to come up with the money, one way or another.

"When can you start?"

Off-season in Oceanside Heights. The tourists had all gone home, and with them the historical house tours, parades, flea markets, sidewalk art shows, craft fairs, book sales, and concerts that enlivened the Heights in the summertime. Between May and August, the tiny town swelled to three times its size, and people from all over the country came to stroll the boardwalk, admire the quaint Victorian architecture, and attend services in the Church by the Sea, the largest Methodist church on the entire eastern seaboard. But after Labor Day, the crowds faded away and "God's own acre," as the locals called it, returned to normal.

Half the town breathed a collective sigh of relief. The other half cursed the cyclical nature of their lives and set about making up for lost income. Innkeepers took second jobs, donning suits and ties for desk jobs at AT&T, Bell Labs, and U.S. Life. Some of the restaurants and antique shops closed for the winter, their owners departing for warmer, more populous climes. Each year, there was a rhythm to the changeover. The pace slowed, and people took time to linger over second cups of coffee, settling into familiar routines, unfazed by camera-toting outsiders. But the northeaster had upset the seasonal tempo of the town.

As Anne walked along the beach the morning the storm ended, she saw that the northeaster had hit the Church by the Sea hard. Several of the stained glass windows had been smashed by the pounding of the breakers and parts of the roof had blown off. The big white cross, paid for by an egomaniacal director in exchange for permission to film the church in his latest movie, was tilting at a precarious angle. On Main Street, there was a flurry of hammering, plastering, and mopping as cleanup crews swung into action. People were out videotaping the damage, chronicling tar paper and shingles torn off roofs, a missing car door, the sand that piled up in mounds. Three boats were piled in a heap by a downed streetlight. The wind had blown out windows. A garbage can roosted in a tree. The grand opening of the new Oceanside Heights Museum was four days away and the town looked like a disaster area.

Meanwhile, the local news media was out in force, chronicling the destruction. A young, skinny photographer from the Landsdown Park Press was photographing a dove-colored Queen Anne house, whose gingerbread porch had splintered in two. On the corner of Main and Pennsylvania Avenue, a perky twenty-something reporter in a shiny yellow slicker was thrusting her microphone under people's noses, and asking them to talk about the impact of the storm for News 12's evening report.

Anne sidestepped the reporter and continued on her way. What was the point of moaning about her basement on the six o'clock news? She was thirty-eight years old, and she'd lived in the Heights all her life. By the time dinnertime rolled around, everybody in town would know the extent of the damage and how much it cost to fix it. That's the way the Heights operated. Gossip traveled even faster than an angry northeaster.

She crossed the street, skirting puddles the size of kiddie pools, her sneakers so wet they squished when she walked. On the curb, she stamped her feet and caught a glimpse of herself in the side-view mirror of a rusty white Pontiac. Not a pretty sight. Her red hair stood out from her head, like an unruly mop. Her normally fair skin was pale. There were faint circles under her deep blue eyes. From what, she wondered. Lack of sleep? Worry? Too many deadlines, not enough time?

In four short hours, Jack was coming to spend the weekend, and she looked like something Harry the cat had dragged in. Personally, she ranked dead birds and mice right up there with plagues and locusts, when it came to stuff you wanted to avoid.

Thinking about avoidance brought her back to Jack Mills. The last time she'd seen him was seven weeks ago on a hotel balcony in Venice, overlooking the Grand Canal. He'd ordered room service and the waiter had wheeled out a bottle of Chianti and two plates of spaghetti carbonara. As they ate, the streetlights went on, casting a soft lavender glow on the water in the canal. The setting was picture perfect. Jack had taken her hand and begun talking about the future. Their future. How great it would be. And that's when she'd started to tune him out, to wonder if the water in the Grand Canal was as dirty as everyone said, if Venice was really sinking, and if it was, whether they could save it in time. *I need time*, she'd told Jack. *I love you, but* . . . Well, that was the problem. There were too many buts.

She liked living alone, not having to answer to anyone else. She liked knowing that if she didn't feel like cooking for a week or doing the laundry or making conversation, it was perfectly okay. Living alone meant having your freedom, having it "My Way," as Sinatra would say. She'd been dating Jack for a little over a year, seeing him a couple of times a month, talking on the phone several times a week. It worked for her. It worked fine. If it ain't broke, don't fix it. Hell, even Chester Higgins would agree with that.

Besides, Anne didn't know if she could live with Jack, or if she even wanted to try. Yes, Jack was fun to be around. And sexy and charming and caring. But he liked running the show, being head honcho. She knew what he was like at work. She'd seen contractors and builders and plumbers sent packing because they'd made some small mistake, rubbed him the wrong way. That attitude carried over to his personal life, too. If the wine wasn't to his liking at a restaurant or he got a little lost on the way there, Jack acted like it was the end of the world. Maybe it was his perfectionist side. Maybe it was because he didn't seem to know how to relax. Whatever. It seemed only a matter of time before she began to irritate him, before he flashed her that warning look that signaled he was going to get mad. Not explosive mad. But sharp-tongued and sarcastic, making every minor setback into a major catastrophe.

Still, there was something about Jack she found hard to resist. Part of it was physical. When she looked into his cornflower blue eyes, she felt her insides start to melt. He had a great build and a wicked, sensual grin. Each time he put his arm around her, she wanted to stay there for hours, soaking him in. It didn't hurt that he was loving and funny and incredibly smart. And that he understood her better than most people did.

And now, Jack was coming down. Distracted, she stepped straight into another giant puddle and felt cold water creep up her ankles. Forcing the matter from her mind, she sloshed into the Mini-Mart and stocked up on staples: Lucky Charms cereal, frozen waffles, a dozen powdered donuts, eggs, Pepperidge Farm pizza-flavored goldfish, peanut butter cookies, Diet Coke, strawberry Jell-O. Not exactly the healthiest choices, but hey, a girl had to eat. Luckily, she jogged three or four times a week and her metabolism was still good. Yet she had noticed with some uneasiness that her jeans were getting a little snug.

By the time she got home, she was thoroughly soaked. Chester's pick-up was still parked in the driveway. Even though he was swamped with work, he'd told her he wanted to get started on the basement right away. From the way he said it, Anne got the feeling her house was about to come crashing down around her if the wind blew hard enough. She let herself in through the back door, kicked off her sneakers, and plopped the groceries down on the kitchen counter.

Tearing open the package of cookies, she wolfed down several of them and started to put the rest of the food away. She looked up to see Chester standing in the doorway.

"I got something to tell you."

Anne stood on her tiptoes and shoved the Lucky Charms into the cabinet above the refrigerator. "It's going to cost me more than you said, right? Honestly, Chester, twelve grand is bad enough. If it comes to more, you better stop work. I'll just have to take my chances."

Chester shook his head. "That's not it," he said dolefully.

"What then?"

Chester shuffled his feet uncomfortably. "There's a body down in your basement. Stone cold dead."

Chapter 2

> *The do-it-yourselfer must have the following tools: a claw hammer, pliers, a toolbox saw, flat-headed and Phillips screwdrivers, a staple gun, a utility knife, an Allen wrench, and a 3/8-inch variable speed reversible drill.*

"What?"

"There's a dead body buried in your basement," Chester repeated.

Anne stared at him in disbelief, searching for signs that he was joking. But Chester didn't appear to be blessed with a sense of humor. And as far as she knew, he didn't drink.

"Well, not a body exactly," he amended, scratching his collar. "A skeleton. Buried under the dirt in the cellar. The rain must have loosened it up a bit."

"Uh huh," Anne stammered, trying to digest this mind-

11

boggling piece of information. Her mouth had dropped open. She made an effort to close it.

Bad enough that the basement was a total disaster area, that the yard was a wreck. Now she had to cope with buried bones. For a muddled moment, she linked the storm and the skeleton. Had the northeaster caused someone to die in her basement? But that was impossible. After a few days, they'd be flesh, not bones.

Anne followed Chester downstairs, hoping against hope he was playing a practical joke. Acme Builders: Quality work for less while you laugh. She picked her way carefully over the rotted wood planks to the farthest corner of the room, where Chester had begun working. His tools were lying where he'd left them. A half-dozen boards had been pried off, revealing a mound of loose damp earth.

Chester squatted down and Anne knelt beside him. He picked up a spade, plunged it into the dirt, and worked it back and forth. Anne heard a sharp *ping* and recoiled in horror. Lying there before her was a bony hand, the fingers long and curved and horrible.

"Oh, my god," she gasped.

"Rest of it's buried a little deeper. I could dig it up, if you like." Chester idly churned the dirt.

"No!" Anne shouted. Her heart was thumping wildly against the wall of her chest. This was bizarre, outrageous. A *Twilight Zone* episode in living color. She stared at the hand. From this angle, with the wrist protruding from the earth and the fingers reaching upward, it looked like the hand was trying to claw itself loose from its muddy earthen grave.

"No," she repeated, tearing her gaze away.

Chester sifted some loose dirt with his spade. "Going to have to dig it up sooner or later. Don't you think?"

Chester seemed unfazed by the skeleton. But then it wasn't his basement. Or his problem. "Sooner's fine by me," she told him. "Only we're not the ones doing the digging."

* * *

Detective Mark Trasker bent over the skeletal hand and emitted a long, low whistle. The cuffs of his charcoal gray suit brushed the dirt. His black leather shoes were caked with mud.

"Well, Hardaway," Trasker said. "Here's another fine mess you've gotten us into."

Anne managed a weak smile. She'd only known Trasker a short time. But she'd quickly come to appreciate his intelligence, his insights, and the effective, low-key manner with which he did his job.

"Any idea how it got here?" he asked.

"Not really."

Trasker looked over at her and raised a quizzical eyebrow. He was in his mid-forties, with skin the color of cocoa beans and dark, penetrating brown eyes. Full lips, broad nose, closely cropped hair. He dressed more like a businessman than a cop, and though he'd grown up in Trenton, his voice was completely devoid of a New Joizee accent.

"Why don't I believe you?"

"Gee, Mark, I don't know," she joked. "Must be a trust issue."

Trasker stood up and brushed off his cuffs. "Seriously," he said. "You've always got a theory or two up your sleeve."

In fact, she did have a theory. It had crept into her mind while she placed a call to the Neptune Township Sheriff's office, then sat on the front porch and waited for Trasker to arrive, staring out at the whitecaps flecking the gray Atlantic, the water now fifty yards from her front door.

Something to do with her mother. The body in the basement—connected to Evelyn. Her mother had died in 1989, of complications from pneumonia. But the disease that had attacked her mind and stolen her spirit for years before that was Alzheimer's. It had crippled her, ruined her, turned her into the town Crazy Lady, who pawed through the neighbor's garbage cans and set fire to the living room couch. Because of it, Anne's father had left them, moving fifteen miles away to a tidy rental apartment with shag carpet and vertical blinds. Gradually, the town had turned its back, not just on Evelyn, but on Anne as well. It was as though Evelyn's disease had spilled onto Anne, painting away everything happy and normal with a permanent, invisible brush.

The Alzheimer's was an irreversible blight, turning Evelyn into a stranger who did horrible, sad things—like taking her underpants off in public, driving her car into Grassmere Lake, accusing Anne of poisoning her. While Evelyn lay dying, she'd made Anne promise never to sell the house. It was Anne's home, the place where she'd grown up, her legacy. And now this. Did her mother have any knowledge of the body in the cellar? Not necessarily. The bones could have lain undisturbed for years, way before her parents bought the house in 1959. Still, it was awful. Living her life, eating, working, watching TV, while underneath the house lay the specter of death.

Anne pulled her sweater tighter around her shoulders. Outside, she could hear the autumn wind blowing gustily from the east.

She met Trasker's gaze without flinching. "I honestly don't know how a body ended up down here," she lied. A half-lie, really. She was wrong about her mother. She had to be wrong.

Reaching into the breast pocket of his suit, Trasker pulled out his cell phone and dialed. She listened to him giving directions, explaining to the person on the other end what needed to be done.

"The boys from Newark will be here in an hour," he said, after he'd clicked off. "Route 35's still closed."

"You want a cup of tea or something?" she asked him. Suddenly, she had to get out of the basement, away from the beckoning, bony hand.

"Vodka's more appropriate, considering the sorry state of your lawn," Trasker said wryly.

He followed her back up the stairs and into the kitchen, settling into a high-backed chair at one end of the oval pine table. The table wobbled a bit so she'd stuffed a cloth napkin under one of the legs to steady it.

She filled the kettle with water, set it on the stove to boil, and opened one of the cabinets. "You've got a choice. Jasmine or Sleepy Time."

"Jasmine's fine."

She plopped two jasmine teabags into two mugs and poured the rest of the peanut butter cookies onto a plate. He was studying her with those intense brown eyes.

"What?" she said playfully. "Do you think I had something to do with the skeleton?"

He smiled. Not long ago, he'd suspected her of murdering a washed-up actress on the comeback trail. But that was before she and Trasker had gotten to know one another. "Been there, done that," he said, matching her joking tone. "So," he said, waving his arms at the waterlogged dining room. "You going to spend the weekend cleaning up this joint?"

"Part of it. I have a friend coming down."

See? she told herself. A person who was planning a future with Jack would have referred to him as "my boyfriend" or "my significant other." "Friend" was pretty lame.

"What about you?" she said, turning toward him. "Did the storm affect you at all?"

"I live in a condo, further inland. Storm passed us right by."

A condo. That sounded right. Somehow she couldn't picture Trasker living in a house, worrying about drainage and burst pipes and whether or not the chimney was smoking.

She sat down opposite him, placing the cookies between them. "How do we go about identifying the skeleton?"

The corners of Trasker's mouth turned up ever so slightly. "We?"

"It's my basement, my corpse. I'd like to know who it is." She heard the defensive tone in her voice and smiled by way of apology.

"I don't blame you," Trasker said dryly, reaching for a cookie. "First thing they do is run some tests. Looks like the remains are human, but they'll make absolutely sure. Next, they'll determine the approximate age and sex of the victim, and the probable cause of death. Once we've got that, we do a missing persons check and hope to find a match."

Anne had to laugh. "You make it sound easy."

"Depends if we get lucky or not. They'll probably call in a forensic anthropologist who can estimate the time since death, the state of preservation, stuff like that."

"Could you do me a favor? Could you try to keep this out of the papers? I don't want the whole town knowing. Not yet."

"I'll see what I can do."

The kettle whistled, a high, keening sound that rattled Anne's nerves. Terrific, she thought. Next thing you know, there'll be ghosts.

Two police officers from the state medical examiner's office dug up the skeleton. The hole it had lain in was nearly two feet wide by six feet deep. The skeleton itself looked to be about five feet, ten inches long, and was a pale yellow color—intact, not in pieces. No identification. No wedding ring, watch, or jewelry. No clothes. Only the bones, elongated and prehistoric looking.

The ankle bone's connected to the knee bone. The thigh bone's connected to the hip bone. Watching them work, Anne couldn't get that silly jingle out of her head. When the cops turned the skeleton slightly to lift it, Trasker spotted the bullet holes—a chipped dime-sized entrance wound in the back of the skull and a larger exit wound on the right side of the head: probable cause of death. As far as Anne knew, her mother had never owned a gun and Anne couldn't imagine her using one. Score one for our side.

While they were digging up the bones she felt a kind of numb shock that made it seem like she was moving under water. She'd ask a question, like what were the soil samples for, then have to repeat it and concentrate hard on the reply. Trasker told her they would check the soil for things like metal fragments, hair, blood, cloth, rope, or insect casings.

"You okay?" he asked her. "You want to wait upstairs?"

She shook her head vehemently. "I want to see."

The skeleton had long arms and legs. Its teeth gaped in a wide ghoulish grin, as if mocking her. She watched them wrap it in a black body bag and lug it up the stairs, depositing it in the trunk of an unmarked blue van. Except for the years she'd been away at college, the two years she'd spent in a rented bungalow in Margate, and four summers at sleepaway camp in the Adirondacks, she'd lived in this house her entire life. When did those bones get down here? And how?

After the cops had left and she'd said good-bye to Trasker, Anne picked up the phone and called Helen Passelbessy. Helen was at work and from the tone of her voice, Anne could tell she was busy.

"Do you have a second? You're not going to believe this," Anne said, launching into the story. Helen was her closest friend. She lived at the other end of the Heights, near the marina, and worked as a loan officer at the Central Bank of New Jersey. She was sensible and level-headed, with a sharp sense of humor and a knack for putting a positive spin on the worst situations.

"You know what you should do," Helen exclaimed, when Anne had finished. "You should call up this store in New York City. I saw a story about them on the news. They sell all kinds of bones. I think somebody paid two thousand bucks for a skeleton they had in the window."

"I don't think I can sell the bones," Anne said, weighing the possibility anyway. "They're part of a criminal investigation. For all I know, the sheriff's office has to keep the skeleton around for years, as evidence."

"Oh," Helen sighed. "Too bad. Because if that store wasn't interested, I was going to suggest you contact some local med schools."

Anne pulled at the phone cord distractedly. "This whole thing is giving me the creeps. I can't believe these bones were moldering down in the basement for years."

"Is it possible they weren't?"

"What do you mean?"

"Could someone have planted the skeleton there recently?"

Anne considered the question. It seemed highly unlikely, but she'd run it by Trasker anyway. "I don't think so," she said doubtfully.

"Great timing, right? With Jack coming down."

"Jack. God, I wish he'd picked another weekend."

"Bring him by, okay? I feel like I haven't seen him in ages." Helen sneezed and blew her nose. "And try not to worry about the bones. They're gone now, good riddance."

Helen was right, Anne told herself. The skeleton was long gone. But it didn't help. She pictured the dirt hole in the basement. Telling Helen made the skeleton more real somehow. It didn't matter that they'd carted it away. Its presence still infected the old house, casting a pall on everything that was familiar, like a dark, invisible shroud.

After she and Helen hung up, Anne called her friend Delia Graustark. Delia wasn't home, so she left a nondescript message on the machine.

She put down the phone, went into the front room that served as her office, and turned on her computer. The screen confronted her, a dull blank. Mounds of dirt were scattered around the edges of the hole the cops had made. Chester couldn't pour concrete for a new floor. Not since the basement had officially become a "crime scene," complete with yellow police tape.

Anne stared at the screen until it began to blur. *Concentrate*, she commanded herself. *You have to get some work done.* She'd only been working on the home repair book for a few weeks. And the irony was starting to bug her. How was she supposed to tell people how to fix a leaky roof and repair drywall when her own house was falling apart at the seams? For the past seven years, she'd ghostwritten all kinds of self-help books, becoming an instant expert on everything from raising a nonrebellious child to organic gardening. She'd written about religion, exercise, soap operas, politics, house cleaning, career issues, how to get the man you want, how to dump the man you had, how to look healthier, how to get more sleep, how to have more money, and how to find inner peace. Most recently, she'd penned a tell-all by an egomaniacal actress—and nearly gotten herself killed.

But the home repair book irked her the most. For starters, she was all thumbs. She couldn't hammer a nail in straight if her life depended on it. Or open a window that had been painted shut. Or unclog the drain in the bathtub. The Unhandy Female syndrome, Jennifer Joan Klapisch called it. Jennifer Joan was planning to devote an entire chapter to the phenomenon in *Home Repairs Without the Hassles*. Which meant Anne had to translate Jennifer Joan's jumbled theories about how math anxiety and playing with dolls left girls "repair challenged" when it came time to use an Allen wrench.

Jennifer Joan lived in Cedar Falls, Iowa, and had her own radio talk show, syndicated in thirty-nine states, her own line of power tools designed especially for women (Anne's personal favorite was the powder pink drill, billed as "lighter, prettier, and sexier for today's powerhouse female"), and now, a book deal from Triple Star Publishing. Before Jennifer Joan founded Hammer Gals, her company that sent "handywomen" into homes across America, she was an unemployed actuary with a talent for fixing small appliances. Her husband had walked out and her bank balance was nil. Jennifer Joan's media kit pointed out these setbacks, using phrases like "indomitable spirit" and "old-fashioned resourcefulness" to describe the home repair guru, but Anne saw her primarily as a woman who'd spotted a niche in the market and moved quickly to fill it.

She leafed through her notes on repairing a storm-damaged roof. Jennifer Joan made it sound easy as pie. Or it would be if Anne could figure out the difference between fascia and soffits and how to apply roofing cement.

She could give back half the advance money when it arrived, but that would be dumb, considering how much the storm was going to cost her. Maybe she could get a tax deduction on some of Chester's repairs if she claimed it was research. *Yeah, right.* She got up from her desk, glanced out the window, and pulled down the shade. The front lawn depressed her. During the day, more driftwood had blown into the yard, and she hadn't bothered to clean any of it up. The bench still sat there, attached to planks that used to be part of the boardwalk. *Home sweet home.* The walls and floors were soaked, and she'd run out of fresh towels to clean up the mess. Rain had leaked into her bedroom closet, dampening her shoes and clothes. She got out her blowdryer and headed for the closet. It might not be a pink power drill, but for now it would have to do.

Chapter 3

After a storm, check for cracks or bulges in the foundation of your house. Cracked interior walls and sticky doors may indicate that the house is settling because soil has washed out from under the footings.

When Jack arrived, she was lying on the sofa, dreaming about clowns. In her dream, the circus had come to Oceanside Heights, pitching a huge tent next to the Church by the Sea. There was an old-fashioned side show, with a sword swallower and a bearded lady and a midget in a top hat and tuxedo. A marching band played so loud the music hurt her ears. Lions paced nervously in their cages, swishing their long golden tails.

In the center of the tent, two chalk-faced clowns in polkadot pajamas held megaphones to their lips and pointed high, high up in the big top, where a woman in pink tiptoed across a high wire. The aerialist swayed unsteadily, then regained her balance as she danced upon the wire. She was halfway across when the storm hit. Rain pelted the animals. The wind howled, and shook the wire. Anne saw the aerialist plunge to the ground, arms pinwheeling helplessly. Her scream tore the tent in two. One clown's white face had changed to bone, his eyes black and vacant, inhuman, ghastly in death. The tent swayed and collapsed, the pretty Victorian cottages melting into candy-colored puddles.

She woke with a start and saw him standing over her, smiling. Later, it occurred to her that she hadn't changed clothes or fixed herself up on purpose. Like this was a test. Love me or leave me. Well, she thought defiantly. This is what it'd be like if we lived together. You couldn't look your best all the time. It was physically impossible. Besides, most couples she knew worried more about their finances than their appearance or their sex lives.

"Hey, sleepyhead," he said, bending down and brushing his lips against her cheek. "I'm glad you're still in one piece."

She'd made him a key over the summer, something she would never have done if they lived in the same town and he had the chance to use it. But New York was sixty miles away, and the key was more a matter of convenience than a statement about the permanence of their relationship.

She shook herself loose from the dream, smelling the cedar soap he used, feeling his arms enfold her.

The thing about Jack was the way he'd gotten under her skin. From the time he'd showed up on her doorstep a year ago last July, she'd felt instantly attracted. Whenever she saw him after one of their long absences, she felt the same flurry of excitement and was smitten again. He looked great, like always. Tan dockers, blue cotton shirt, loafers. His country attire.

"I fell asleep," she said, wishing she'd had the chance

to brush her teeth, and change out of the sweatpants and baggy top.

"Can't blame you. Sorry I'm so late. Traffic was backed up from here to the turnpike."

He flipped on the lamp by the sofa, and she took a good long look, drinking him in. Those incredible blue eyes, the tiny mole on his chin, the way his dark hair shone when it caught the light. He was two years younger than she was, but seemed older, maybe because at work he was accustomed to taking charge, to thinking on his feet. He was independent, like her. He shared her love of baseball, sixties music, diners, and mystery novels.

Now, she sat back against the cushions and told him everything that had happened that day, including her suspicion that her mother was somehow involved. That was another thing she and Jack had in common: troubled families. His father, Troy Mills, was an abusive drunk. His older brother, Tigger, was an alcoholic who'd made one too many bad choices and had died alone, washed up on the beach across the street.

That's how she'd reconnected with Jack. He'd come back to town when Tigger drowned and Anne had helped him find out how his brother had died and who had killed him. It was an odd way to get to know someone— through death. Anne sometimes wondered what would have happened if she and Jack had met "normally," if they'd gone out on a few dates, asked each other the usual questions: hobbies, interests, background. Jack had grown up in the Heights, too. But he had little affection for it. Anne sensed he associated the town with his painful childhood. Jack had left town when he was eighteen and had never looked back.

She'd stuck it out and put down roots in the Heights. Although some people would always think of her as "the Crazy Lady's daughter," she'd come to love living at the shore. The ocean was as much a part of her as the air she breathed. She couldn't imagine living anyplace else.

"You're wrong," Jack announced, when she'd finished.

"About your mother, I mean. Do you know anything about the previous owners, or who lived in this house originally?"

"Not offhand. But I could find out. My dad researched it once. There are some papers around somewhere."

"In architecture school, I read about a couple in Indiana who found a bunch of buried bones. I can't remember if it was in the basement or the yard. Anyhow, the previous owner was a doctor. Had a practice in the house where he conducted illegal experiments. And he buried his clients who didn't make it. Could be the same thing happened here."

"I don't think so, Jack. What about the bullet hole? Doesn't sound like a routine doctor's visit to me."

She followed him into the kitchen and watched him peer into her refrigerator, wrinkling his nose ever so slightly. He went out to his car and came back carrying two grocery bags. "I thought you could use some extra stuff," he said, by way of explanation.

He'd brought herb-roasted chicken, rice pilaf, and a salad with eight kinds of lettuce from a gourmet shop near work. She didn't know whether to be insulted or grateful. They ate in the dining room, instead of the kitchen, and the food was delicious. It beat the macaroni and cheese she'd been planning to reheat.

It took a while to catch up. They usually spoke on the phone several times a week. But Jack had been busy working on a hotel in the financial district, and they'd talked less frequently lately.

"I almost came down early," Jack said, nursing a Diet Coke. He didn't drink alcohol, ever. One time, when she'd asked about it, he told her he was afraid to drink, afraid one beer would turn into two six-packs, and that he would wind up like his father and brother—a broken-down drunk.

"The pictures of the storm on TV were incredible," he said. "People being evacuated from their homes. Trucks submerged under water."

"That was a little further south." She drank the last of her wine, feeling better than she had all day. Safe, relaxed. Was this what living with Jack would be like? Gourmet meals, shared confidences?

"The meal was wonderful," she said.

"When you move to New York, you can eat like this every night."

Anne looked away. She wasn't ready to live in Manhattan. Not now. Maybe not ever. There was too much about the shore that she'd miss. But Jack always downplayed her concerns. He couldn't understand how anyone could resist the lure of New York. He liked to take clients to the top restaurants in the city. Anne hated those dinners. The women wore black, weighed next to nothing, and talked down to her. After the meal, the men smoked cigars and discussed the Dow and boxing and real estate investment trusts and a bunch of other things she had absolutely no interest in.

"Tomorrow, we'll get started on the house," Jack was saying. "I should be able to help you check the foundation and patch the siding. At least do a temporary fix, till you can get a construction guy in here."

"Hey, I'm not putting you to work."

"It's no trouble."

"Seriously, Jack. I'll take care of it. You're supposed to be relaxing this weekend."

He reached across the table and took hold of her hand. His touch was gentle, reassuring. He leaned forward and kissed her on the mouth. He tasted like basil. "Whatever you say. But I'm going to help you figure this skeleton thing out," he said. "Like you helped me. With Tigger." A shadow passed across his face at the mention of his brother. Even after a year, the pain was still raw.

He got to his feet and motioned her into his arms. Love, the great escape. Obliterating hurt, disappointment, frustration, pain. A balm on the wound. A quick fix. But no match for death. That body in the cellar, how many years had it taken to decay? Rotting quietly. Waiting,

waiting. It struck her that she'd had too much to drink. On the radio, Etta James was singing "At Last," her voice sad, throaty, aching with love. She leaned into Jack, rested her head on his shoulder. Jack wanted her to sell the house, move to Manhattan, and live in his two-bedroom apartment on the Upper West Side. His hand did things to her hair. She supposed it would be exciting to live in New York. An adventure. The anonymity of it appealed to her, the way you could walk down Broadway and be swallowed by the crowd. But she suspected if she lived there it would lose its appeal fast, that anonymity would soon give way to loneliness, that the teeming city would wear her down.

Why not have both? Jack would say. An apartment in the city and a weekend house at the shore? On paper, it worked out great. But the reality of it was that Jack skied in the winter and drove up to New England each fall for weekends of leaf watching and mountain biking. Spring was his busiest time of year when he often worked seven days a week. And the thought of just using the house in summertime, when the Heights was packed and you could barely swim or walk down the street without bumping into another camera-toting tourist, didn't appeal to her.

Upstairs, in Anne's bedroom, they undressed in the dark. Carefully, not hurrying, like there was all the time in the world. The only sound was the wind banging the loose siding against the house.

"I'm glad you're here," she whispered, as he pulled her close.

"Me too."

She *was* glad, suddenly. She liked living alone. But not tonight with the wind howling outside and the yellow tape marking the shallow grave downstairs. She closed her eyes and tried to blot out the image of those grinning spectral teeth.

Later, lying in bed, she lay on her side with her chest pressed against Jack's back, her arms folded around his waist. It was late. The wine had given her a headache. But she wasn't the least bit tired. She felt the rise and fall of his breath, traced his ribcage with her fingers, and was suddenly reminded of the skeleton again. She imagined the bones decaying underneath the house, the flesh slowly falling away, dissolving into the soil. Who had pulled the trigger? Was that person still alive, still out there?

She shuddered and held Jack tight, her left arm pressed against her body so his weight didn't crush it. Not the most comfortable position to sleep in, but she didn't much care. She shut her eyes, saw the bones, and opened them again.

Looking back, she wished she'd gotten to snooze a little longer on the sofa, before Jack had arrived. Especially since it was going to be the last sound sleep she would have for nearly a week.

Chapter 4

*To fix a squeaky floor, nail
the offending board down
tightly, so it can't move,
using a 2½-inch finishing
nail or a spiral-fluted
flooring nail with a partially
grooved surface for greater
staying power.*

Anne shifted from her stomach to her back, moving carefully, so as not to disturb Jack. One advantage of living together would be getting a bigger bed. Hers was full-size. When Jack was here, there was barely room to roll over. But tonight was worse than usual. She couldn't fall asleep. Her thoughts kept spilling out, like water shooting from a spigot. Her heart was racing, a full-fledged anxiety attack. She felt like she wanted to jump out of her skin. She turned and looked at the bedside clock for the umpteenth time. It was 4:39 A.M. And she hadn't slept at all. Her mind wouldn't shut down. Too many questions.

Like why her mother had bothered to put down wood

planks. In a way, it was unlike Evelyn. Her mother had always been neat but not clean, satisfied with surface tidiness—beds made up, countertops swept of crumbs, firewood neatly stacked. But underneath the beds, dust bunnies lurked. And many of the crumbs from the counter had landed on the floor and stayed there for weeks. You'd think Evelyn would have let the dirt floor alone. Anne tried to recall when the planks had been installed. Sometime in the mid-seventies. Her father had moved out by then. And Anne and her mother were living alone, like "roommates," Evelyn had said, like "two peas in a pod." Only by then, the Alzheimer's had struck and Evelyn's behavior had started to change. When Anne came home from school each day, she never knew which mother she'd find, normal Mom or Crazy Lady.

Evelyn had become obsessed with the house. She'd thought the neighbors were sneaking in at night and stealing things: the crock pot, her emerald brooch, sewing scissors, sanitary napkins. She'd taken to putting masking tape across the windows, tying a piece of string between the knob on the back door and a kitchen chair, in order to see if the door had been tampered with. One day, she'd rearranged all the furniture in the living room, dragging the good damask sofa onto the sidewalk with a *"For Sale Cheap"* sign taped to the back. Another time, she'd run a bath and forgotten to turn the water off until hours later, soaking the carpets so thoroughly the place smelled of mildew for weeks. She'd crayoned over the good Wedgwood china, boiled the curtains, and painted the ceiling in the master bedroom black. In the middle of all this, the dirt floor in the basement had disappeared, hidden beneath planks.

When exactly had that been? Anne wondered. She crept out of bed, jammed her feet into her slippers, and threw a sweater over her lavender silk nightgown. When Jack slept over, she wore Victoria's Secret lingerie to bed, instead of the usual sweats. She glanced at him, hoping he'd wake up and talk to her, but he was snoring peacefully under the covers. The cat had curled up on the rag rug next to the bed.

She tiptoed out of the room and flicked on the light in the hallway. Grabbing a long hook from the hall closet, she pulled down the short flight of rickety wooden stairs that led to the attic. She hadn't bothered to check for storm damage up here. Grandma Betty's theory again. What you don't know won't hurt you. Except this time, Grandma was wrong.

The dank stale smell was even worse up here. Some of the floorboards squeaked like crazy. When Anne turned on the light she saw that rain had seeped in through the roof, soaking everything—the walls, the floor, all the stuff stored in the attic. She did a quick survey of the damage: soggy old copies of *National Geographic*, waterlogged tables and chairs, newspapers so wet the print had run, dribbling down the paper like tears. Her mother's ivory satin wedding dress had yellowed to the color of buttercup on its dressmaker's dummy. Anne went over and ran her fingers over the damp frayed lace at the collar. The fabric was worn away in places, the satin thin as paper. She had meant to have the dress specially cleaned and packed away, preserved for eternity. Instead, it perched on its stand like a ragged, decaying ghost, a symbol of reproach. What would her mother have made of Jack?

Turning her back on the dress, Anne walked toward a black steamer trunk with rusty brass hinges. The top of the trunk was slick with water. When she threw it open, droplets cascaded down the sides. She sank down on the wood plank floor and peered in. She hadn't looked at this stuff in years, not since her father's death. Here were the buried remnants of her parents' life together: photos, records, ticket stubs, souvenirs from trips to Virginia Beach and Washington, D.C., matchbook covers, theater programs, and chips from a casino in Atlantic City. An old brochure stating the rules and regulations of Oceanside Heights: No alcohol. No driving on Sunday. Beach closed on Sunday. No bike riding on Sunday. No hanging clothes. No yard work. No playing in the street. No ice cream unless you ordered a meal first. On and on and on. Her parents had grudgingly adhered to the blue laws, parking their Buick Elektra in a lot in Neptune City each Saturday night and retrieving it each Monday morning. It was a tradeoff: a pretty Victorian house in a quiet safe community in exchange for sticking to certain outmoded religious restrictions.

Anne picked up a black-and-white photo in a silver frame. Her parents floating in a swan-shaped boat on Grassmere Lake. She glanced at the date. September 3, 1967. Her father was good-looking, in a studious way. Buzz cut, glasses, strong chin. Her mother was gazing at him adoringly, her hair flipping up at the ends, her eyes shining. If you didn't know better, you would think they'd been happy together.

She put the photo back in the trunk, face down. For the first two years after he'd abandoned them, she'd hated her father, refused to visit him in his new apartment, refused to meet the succession of girlfriends that popped in and out of his life with alarming regularity. She only relented when she was desperate, when her mother was spinning out of control so furiously that Anne had needed help. Her father's help. George Hardaway had arranged for a home health-care attendant and then had paid for his ex-wife to stay in a nursing home. A series of nursing homes, actually, because Evelyn kept getting kicked out.

Sometimes Anne subtracted the Alzheimer's from the equation of her parents' marriage and wondered if they would have stayed together without it. Hard to tell. Hard to say which came first, the fighting or the sickness, what was cause and what was effect. When her father died, she'd acted the part of the dutiful daughter—making funeral arrangements, cleaning out his apartment, even having lunch with his girlfriend *du jour*. Cheryl, Shirley, Shereen? Anne could never remember her name. Only that she was barely older than Anne herself had been at the time.

Rummaging through the trunk, Anne began to sort out its contents. Ashtrays, gloves, an old-fashioned wooden stereoptic machine with a postcard inside of the Atlanta, a grand Victorian hotel in the Heights that had been torn down years ago. She raised the stereoptic to her eyes and the hotel leaped out at her, resplendent in three dimensions. Had her parents ever strolled across its wide front porch, ever sat on the high-backed wicker chairs and gazed out at the ocean, making plans? When they courted, did they ever suspect things would end so badly?

She put the stereoptic down. It was drafty in the attic. Dirt streaked the hem of her silk nightgown. Instead of feeling tired, she was wired, jazzed. She pored through a pile of books. *I'm OK, You're OK. Fear of Flying. Jonathan Livingston Seagull. The Exorcist.* On the bottom of the pile was a burgundy book with a cracked leather cover. Anne picked it up. A diary. She vaguely remembered it being in the trunk, remembered seeing it years ago and deliberately not opening it, not wanting to delve into her mother's private pain. Now, she flipped through the first few pages, recognizing her mother's handwriting, her mother's scent, a lilac perfume Evelyn had applied to her throat and wrists each morning. The first entry was dated January 1, 1974. The last one was in August of the same year. Had she bought the book herself? Had George bought it for her?

Sitting cross-legged on the damp floor, Anne began to read, examining each passage carefully, poring over Evelyn's spidery scrawl. Her mother had known something was wrong. She had dutifully chronicled what she'd termed her "episodes"—lost keys, scorched brownies, missing hours she couldn't account for, the time she'd set fire to the clothes hamper. *I am slowly going insane,* Evelyn had written. *My mind is being eaten away by invisible carpenter ants who gnaw at the inside of my brain.*

Anne felt her stomach turn over. A lump formed in the back of her throat. During that first year, the doctors hadn't known it was Alzheimer's disease. They'd called it the "vapors," "female trouble," "marital stress," and had prescribed a host of pills that hadn't worked. Anne forced herself to continue. She read about her father's reaction, how George had tried to "fix" Evelyn as if she were a faulty electrical wire, how he had turned angry, silent, uncaring. *Why does he pull away from me? He sees me as a broken bird with torn wings. I need him more than ever, but the look in his eyes freezes my heart.*

She read about Evelyn's friends, how their initial support segued to indifference, to casseroles and baked goods deposited hurriedly on the back steps, to lame excuses about why they couldn't stay. The most painful passages had to do with herself, with her mother's fears for the future. *I worry about Anne. Who will take care of her if I'm not around? Who will keep her safe?*

In April, there was an abrupt shift in tone. Her mother began a series of letters, all addressed to the same person. *Dear Steven,* she'd written on the 6th. *You are my one shining ray of hope. When you told me today I have to fight with every breath, with every ounce of strength I have left, it was the best tonic in the world. With your help, I will get well.*

The letters continued, twice a week, through August. *Dear Steven, I got lost on my way to see you this afternoon. I was driving and all of a sudden I couldn't remember where I was or where I was supposed to be going. None of the streets looked familiar. I drove in circles, staring through the windshield, hoping to spot a store or sign I recognized. That's the real reason I was late. I know I should have told you, but I couldn't. I didn't want you to be disappointed in me.*

Once, in early June, her mother had written his full name on each line of the page, like a schoolgirl practicing her penmanship. *Steven Hillyard. Steven Hillyard. Steven*

Hillyard. Again and again. Up and down both sides of the page.

Dear Steven, You make me laugh so hard my stomach hurts. I'd forgotten what it feels like to laugh. Isn't that peculiar? Such a small thing, really. I tried to explain it to George, but he looked at me so strangely, I stopped in mid-sentence. Sometimes I think he hates me. The way he watches me, expecting something bad to happen. You never look at me that way. You are so patient, so good. I feel I can be myself around you, my crazy, mixed-up self. I can say anything, do anything, and you will understand. You are my rock. My salvation.

The last entry, dated August 21, was addressed to him, too. *Dear Steven, I can't go on this way. You seemed so troubled this afternoon. Why won't you tell me what you're thinking? I have a right to know. Am I slipping down the path to madness? You say no. But they tell me the things I do and it makes me afraid. My neighbor crossed the street to avoid me today. Even the minister's wife looks away. The episodes are taking over. What if I forget who you are, how to get to you? George took the car keys away again. He says it's not safe for me to drive. But I know where he's hidden them. Till Thursday, Steven. If Thursday ever comes. Without you, I'm nothing. Lost.*

The T in lost trailed off forlornly. After that, a few blank pages. Anne closed the diary. In August 1974, she'd been at sleepaway camp in upstate New York. Eight weeks on a sun-dappled lake, sailing and learning to play tennis. At least that's what her parents had thought. In reality, camp was all about trying to fit in with the eleven other 15-year-old girls in her bunk. It was about not being picked on or singled out, blending in with the group, whether she was called on to sneak a smoke from the counselor's pack of cigarettes or let some boy from the camp across the lake stick his tongue in her mouth. While she was struggling to be liked, her mother was mooning over some man. Did her father know about this guy? Who was he? Evelyn's friend? Her lover?

Evelyn Hardaway had been an attractive woman. Certainly, she was lonely. Anne had seen her father turning away, distancing himself from both of them long before he moved out. Had her mother sought comfort in another man's arms? And if she did, had it been a betrayal of her marriage or a matter of survival, a flicker of hope in the darkness that was Alzheimer's?

Taking the book with her, Anne turned off the light and left the attic. In the bedroom, Jack was lying on his side, his arm curled around a pillow. The cat was sleeping on Anne's side of the bed, as though protecting his turf. Harry wasn't overly fond of Jack. He didn't like change of any kind and when Jack came to visit, he sometimes expressed his displeasure by turning his back to them both for the duration of Jack's stay.

Anne glanced at the clock on the night stand. It was now 6:18 A.M. There was no point in trying to go back to sleep. She was too keyed up. She changed into sweats, a long-sleeve cotton shirt, and a nylon wind breaker, laced up her sneakers, and trotted downstairs.

She hadn't been able to do her customary three-mile run during the storm. And yesterday, the ground had been too wet. Maybe things had dried off overnight. Grabbing her Walkman, she stepped outside. Another cool October day. The sky over the ocean was dappled with pink, the water a deep charcoal gray. Sunrise was the best time to go running. She liked to watch the light tickle the waves, the empty expanse of sand broken only by the wooden lifeguard stands.

She did some perfunctory stretches on the porch, then jogged down the front steps, setting the Walkman to a jazz station. The wind lifted her hair. This was just what she needed. A relaxing run along a deserted stretch of beach. She felt a surge of energy as her body set the pace. The ocean smelled wonderful, salty and clean. She prepared to empty her mind. But as lilting piano music filled her ears, her mother's words drifted back to her.

Without you, I'm nothing. Lost.

Chapter 5

If your table wobbles, one of the legs is probably loose. Where the leg joins the table you'll see a bolt with a nut. (It looks like a square donut.) Use a wrench or a pair of pliers to tighten the nut by turning it clockwise.

When she got back home, she peeled off her running clothes and jumped into the shower. By the time Jack got up three hours later, she had nuked a plate of frozen waffles and was already on her third cup of coffee. She'd paged through the Bell Atlantic phone book for Monmouth County. There were no Hillyards listed in the residence section of the White Pages and only one S. Hillyard in the business listings, with an address on Route 35. She dialed, got no answer, and hung up.

Incredibly, she didn't feel tired at all. Maybe this meant she needed less sleep than she thought. Which would be fantastic. She could go to sleep later, wake up earlier, get more writing done at off hours, have more time for fun. She grabbed the pad by the phone and wrote the word *Resolutions* on the top line.

1. Have more fun.
2. Make more money.
3. Travel to exotic places that don't take American Express.

She was trying to decide between *Get a master's degree in creative writing* and *Lose ten pounds* for number four when Jack walked into the kitchen.

"Morning," she said, glancing up. "There's Lucky Charms, Cap'n Crunch, powdered donuts, cinnamon donuts, eggs, English muffins, three kinds of juice, frozen waffles, and lots more coffee."

Jack rolled his eyes.

"What can I say? Breakfast is the most important meal of the day."

"Did we take our manic pills this morning?" Jack said, with a grin. "You're talking a mile a minute."

"I didn't get much sleep."

"You should take vitamins. Seriously. You'll feel incredible."

She crumpled up the list and lobbed it toward the garbage pail. Swish.

"Nice shot, Annie."

She smiled. Jack was the only guy she'd ever known who didn't look rumpled when he woke up. His hair wasn't mussed, and he never seemed to get dried crud in the corners of his eyes. His breath wasn't even bad. How could she wake up every morning next to a man this annoyingly perfect?

From his perch on the kitchen window, where he was contentedly sunbathing, Harry glared at the intruder and licked his paws.

"You think that animal will ever learn to like me?"

"If you're very, very good," Anne teased.

She watched him take out a frying pan, pour some canola oil into it, and fix a pepper and mushroom egg-white omelet. He'd brought the oil, peppers, and mushrooms with him, along with walnut vinaigrette dressing, smoked salmon, sun-dried tomatoes, and dozens of other foods that would normally never get within a hundred feet of her refrigerator. Jack used to love junk food, same as she did. But lately, he'd been eating a lot more healthily. Taking echinacea and vitamin C. Counting calories. Watching his cholesterol.

She grabbed a donut and bit into it defiantly, waiting for him to comment. But he was talking about an upcoming project at work, a health club his company was constructing along the West Side Highway with an olympic-size swimming pool and a driving range. Once, he'd told her he would rather design houses than commercial buildings, new Victorians with gingerbread and wraparound porches and turrets. But it didn't pay as well as being in a large architectural firm. Besides, he'd miss the excitement of New York, the challenge of pleasing high-profile clients.

He set her omelet on the table and frowned when it wobbled. "I've got to fix this thing," he said. "Can't enjoy a meal when your food's bouncing around on your plate."

"I'll take care of it."

Jack made a face. "It's been like this for months." He returned to the stove and started making a second omelet. "So what's on the agenda?" he asked, sipping a cup of tea. He'd given up coffee three weeks ago. Bad for the kidneys, increases the heart rate. "I told my dad I'd drop by this morning. But afterward, the day's wide open. You want to come?"

"That's okay," Anne said quickly.

Actually, she'd rather have her stomach pumped than visit Troy Mills. He was a nasty old drunk with a foul mouth and a penchant for denigrating his son. Jack

couldn't stand his father either. After graduating from
college, Jack had spent years traveling the world, back-
packing through Tibet, Malaysia, Kenya, and Australia.
When he came back to the States, he'd settled in New
York City, returning to the Heights twice a year on
Thanksgiving and his mother's birthday. After his mother
died, he didn't come back at all. But now that he was
seeing Anne, each time he came down from New York
he paid his father a brief visit. It was as if Jack felt he
owed Troy something. What that was she didn't know.

"I don't blame you," Jack said wryly. "Pop's not exactly a laugh a minute. Can we meet up for lunch instead?"

"Sure. How about Quilters around twelve-thirty?"

Jack rolled his eyes. "Fried chicken, yams, creamed
spinach. Meat loaf and mashed potatoes. That place is a
heart attack waiting to happen."

"You used to love Quilters. And I happen to be in the
mood for meat loaf and mashed potatoes."

"Fine." He flipped the omelet over. "It's your funeral."

The office where S. Hillyard worked was located in a
nondescript two-story brick building on Route 35, sandwiched between a Friendly's and a Wawa. Anne parked
the Mustang in the lot behind the building. When she'd
called Hillyard a second time, she'd reached a receptionist who'd answered the phone with a cheery one-word
greeting: "Institute." The moment Anne started asking
questions about the Institute and Hillyard, the woman had
insisted she would have to speak to Dr. Hillyard in person. Anne had made an appointment for eleven o'clock.

Now, as she entered the seedy vestibule and climbed
a narrow, dusty staircase to the second floor, she wondered whether this man could have treated her mother.
Evelyn had seen so many doctors back then. Specialists,
psychologists, neurologists, you name it. At the top of
the stairs was a long corridor. Anne wandered down it,
looking at the doors on both sides. *Ace Travel Agency.*

Geico Direct. Barash Import Export Co. Tiny Tot Modeling Agency. At the far end of the corridor, she found the door she was looking for. *Institute for Clinical Hypnosis.* And underneath that, in red letters: *The Experts in Habit Change.*

Anne pushed the door open and found herself in a tiny reception area, opposite one of the largest women she'd ever seen. The receptionist must have weighed at least three hundred pounds. She was short, of indeterminate age, with flyaway hair and a series of chins that partially obscured her throat.

"Oh," the woman said, looking up from her computer screen. "You're his eleven o'clock. He'll be right with you. In the meantime, have a gander at these."

The receptionist opened a desk drawer and shoved a handful of pamphlets at Anne, each printed on pastel colored paper. *Smoking Cessation. Weight Loss. Anxiety and Stress Management. The Phobia Program.*

Anne sat down in a plastic bucket chair and leafed through them. The Institute for Clinical Hypnosis offered hypnotherapy, counseling, and psychotherapy. A private one-hour session with Dr. Hillyard would run you $100. Semiprivates were $50. And there was a $25 group rate.

Hypnosis, once regarded as little more than a primitive ritual, was formally recognized by the American Medical Association in 1957 as a potent weapon in the treatment of many of the problems once deemed "untreatable" by traditional psychotherapy. At no time during a hypnotic state are you unconscious, asleep, or out of control. You are able to hear, think, move, and even talk.

Maybe her mother had tried hypnosis. Could that be the link?

"The doctor will see you now," chirped the overweight receptionist, who obviously hadn't availed herself of Hillyard's services.

Anne walked in the direction the receptionist was pointing and entered a small windowless wood-paneled office, furnished with two black vinyl Barcaloungers and a gray metal desk.

Dr. Hillyard was in his middle to late forties, a large man with a brown fuzzy beard, aviator-style glasses, and big chocolate brown eyes that blinked every few seconds. He looked a little like a disheveled teddy bear. His tie was askew and ink had leaked from a pen in his breast pocket, forming a blotchy stain on his shirt.

"Come right in," he said, extending a large, warm hand for Anne to shake. "I'm Stuart Hillyard. Have a seat."

Stuart. Obviously not the man in her mother's diary. She felt a surge of disappointment, followed by embarrassment. Now what?

She sat down in one of the Barcaloungers, with her legs resting on an ottoman, wondering how she could talk her way out of this without being charged. The office was about the size of a large walk-in closet, bordering on claustrophobic. The doctor's desk overflowed with papers. There was a large microphone in the center and a two-foot-high statuette of a wizard in a blue gown and flowing white beard. Above the desk, a sign said *The Wizard Is In*.

"Have you ever been in hypnosis before . . . ?" He looked down at an index card, searching for something. ". . . Anne?"

She shook her head.

"What can I do for you?"

For half a second, she considered telling him the truth, but instantly thought better of it. Maybe this wasn't a complete waste of time after all. "I have a phobia I'd like to get rid of."

Dr. Hillyard leaned forward, causing two pieces of paper to swoop off his desk. "Fear of flying?"

"Fear of commitment." It was true, sort of. Did her reluctance to move forward with Jack have to do with him specifically or would she be just as gun shy with any other man?

Hillyard picked up a pencil and stuck it absentmindedly behind his ear. "You're seeing someone, I presume."

"Yes."

He tapped his fingers together, then picked up a snow dome on his desk and gave it a gentle shake. He said, "I believe I can help you figure this out, if you let me, that is. Using hypnosis, we can delve into your inner psyche, probe the workings of your innermost thoughts. I realize it's a somewhat daunting process. But the success rate is amazingly high. If there's anything you'd like to know about the process or the Institute or myself, for that matter, ask away. I'm entirely open to your questions and suggestions. Actually, I'm a bit of a chatterbox. You'll find that out, as we work together."

"How did you get involved with hypnosis?"

Was she really going to sit here and let this guy hypnotize her? What was she thinking?

"I'm a New Jerseyan, born and bred. Grew up in West Long Branch. Graduated from Rutgers with a degree in psychology. I think I've always been fascinated with the subconscious mind. Ever since I was a child. I remember trying to hypnotize my pet hamster and later, kids in the neighborhood." He smiled shyly. "Silly, no? But my interest in hypnosis never waned. I'm pleased to tell you I've helped thousands of people over the years, including members of my own family."

Family. Maybe he had a relative. It was a long shot. But what did she have to lose?

"Are they still in the area?" Anne said. "Your family, that is."

"My wife and I live over in Red Bank. Beautiful town. Have you been lately? Plenty of artists, antiques, lots of new stores. Anyhow, we have three wonderful children, one of whom I treated for bedwetting. My mother's an administrator over at the Sunnydale Nursing Home. My father was a psychologist. So I suppose I come by this naturally."

"Is he deceased?" Anne asked quickly.

"No. I mean . . . Well, quite honestly, I can't say as I know. I haven't seen him in nearly twenty years. He disappeared one day. Went out for a pack of cigarettes and forgot to come back." Hillyard chuckled a little too long and loudly at his joke.

"Really?" Anne said, trying to contain her excitement. "My father did, too. Disappeared from my life. Only it was because of my parents' divorce."

"I see," Dr. Hillyard said, scribbling something on the index card.

Could it be? She was almost afraid to find out.

"Was your father named Stuart, too?" It was an awkward question, but she didn't know how else to ask.

Dr. Hillyard looked up, his expression mildly curious. "No," he said. "Steven."

Chapter 6

> *Hairline cracks in concrete
> can be repaired with auto-
> body filler. Dip a rubber-
> gloved finger into the
> compound, then press
> it into the crack.*

"I can't believe it," Jack said, stirring a cup of pale chicken broth. "I can't believe you found him."

"Well, not exactly," Anne said. "It's Hillyard junior. Not senior."

They were sitting at a white table imprinted with tiny green flowers, in the back corner of Quilters. The oldest restaurant in town, Quilters served "hearty family fare" guaranteed to clog your arteries for life: slabs of roast beef, potatoes swimming in butter, baked ham, macaroni and cheese, franks and beans, caramel custard, six kinds of pie. On the walls hung quilts sewn by members of the Historic Preservation Committee. Above their table was a Double Wedding Ring quilt, with concentric, interlocking rings stitched in pale pastel hues.

Anne had brought Jack up to speed on the morning's activities, leaving out one small detail—what Stuart Hillyard would be treating her for. Today's visit had been a "consultation." Before she'd left his office, she'd made an official appointment for tomorrow morning at eleven. Although tomorrow was Sunday, Hillyard assured her he was seeing patients. "Here at the Institute, we work around the clock," he'd said solemnly.

She pictured Stuart Hillyard's face, his roly-poly feel-good countenance as he explained the benefits of hypnosis. Was this what his father had looked like? Was Steven Hillyard the dead man in the basement?

She'd told Jack that Hillyard was helping her deal with procrastination. She wanted to be able to meet her deadlines instead of habitually asking for extensions. Better that than the truth: Honey, I'm a commitment-phobe. Or not. She wasn't sure what the sessions would reveal. But it was a way of getting to know Stuart Hillyard, without making him suspicious.

She pushed pieces of pork tenderloin around on her plate. She didn't like pork all that much. She'd just ordered it to prove to Jack that eating roast pig wasn't fatal. He was having the fruit salad, definitely not a Quilters specialty: canned peaches arranged in a semicircle on a wilted lettuce leaf, next to an unappetizing lump of cottage cheese and a wobbly square of red Jell-O.

"By the way," Jack said, "I started doing some work on the house. Recaulking some of your windows so they'll be waterproof next time. Fixing those squeaky floorboards in the attic, which is leaking, by the way."

"Thanks. I appreciate it. But I told you that you didn't have to do that. I can take care of it myself."

She supposed she should be grateful. After all, how often does a person get treated to free home repair work? But it irked her that Jack was playing Mr. Fix-It without even bothering to consult her. She hated being reminded that she wasn't handy around the house. She intended to figure things out for herself, especially with this new book project.

"Look, it's no big deal," Jack said. "I enjoy doing it. Did you know the fourth stair on the staircase is loose?"

Of course she knew. It jiggled every time she went up and down. Just another repair she never got around to making. She'd meant to ask Jennifer Joan about it, in fact. Jennifer Joan probably knew exactly what to do.

"So what's our next move?" Jack asked, changing the subject. He'd picked at the Jell-O and was building a tower with the cottage cheese and peaches.

"Hillyard told me his mother works at the Sunnydale Nursing Home. I want to go over there, take a look around. I called Trasker and told him I think the bones might be the remains of Hillyard's father. He's working on matching the dental records."

"Doesn't he need to notify the family for that?"

"Yeah. But he's going to leave my name out of it. I'd like to nose around a little first. No one's going to tell me anything if they know I'm involved."

"Sounds like a plan. Do we need an appointment or can we walk right in?"

"They give tours every Saturday afternoon at two. They're always advertising them in the *Oceanside Heights Gazette*. With the number of elderly people in town, they've got a built-in market." She paused, spearing a chunk of canned pineapple. "We don't have to do this today, Jack. I mean, you're down here for the weekend. I bet the last thing you want to do is spend time with a bunch of old folks who can barely get around anymore. I could put this off until next Saturday. Or maybe I could arrange a tour during the week."

"Are you kidding? It's important to you. Which means it's important to me. So count me in."

He smiled and she smiled back. This was what was so great about Jack. He'd go to the moon with her, if she said the word. What was *wrong* with her? Jack was a great guy—kind, caring, fun to be around. She'd have to be nuts to screw this up.

The Sunnydale Nursing Home was on the outskirts of town, a yellow and orange, three-story brick building with a wide front porch and slender yellow columns. From the circular driveway, you could see the entrance to the Heights, a wrought-iron gate sandwiched between two stone portals. On top of the gate, the founding fathers had spelled out a greeting in large black letters: *Enter Into the Kingdom of Heaven on Earth.*

Anne hadn't set foot inside Sunnydale since her mother was a patient there. It was the second of four nursing homes Evelyn had been placed in. She'd lasted a grand total of nine months, before being kicked out for setting a chair in the rec room on fire, in the days before Alzheimer's was understood. She'd lived in the old wing, in the back, which was now under renovation. Three dumpsters and a crane signaled the fact that work had begun. But Anne couldn't see that much progress had been made. The back of the building was caked with dirt and many of the windows were boarded up. An elm tree, its trunk splintered by the storm, was tilting precariously toward the building.

But then the whole place was shabby looking, even the newer parts. There were cracks in the pavement, the bricks were filmy with dirt, and the sign was so faded it was barely legible. A couple of small trees were down in the front, and Anne saw cable and phone wires tangled in the branches of a sick-looking birch. Inside, the decor hadn't changed much since the late '70s. Orange cinderblock walls, fluorescent overhead lights, institutional furniture. Cardboard black cats, ghosts, and witches were strung along a wall in the lobby. Taped to the reception desk was a sign with a picture of a large beetle on it. The beetle held up one leg cautiously. A balloon over its mouth said, "Stop if you have influenza or other contagious diseases. Bring love, not bugs!"

The tour was led by the head nurse, a tall, broad-boned woman in her late fifties with a horsy-looking face, one long connecting eyebrow, and bad breath. She wore a navy blue skirt, a white blouse under a navy cardigan, and flat, lace-up white shoes. Pinned to the sweater was a nametag that said *G. Koch.* During the tour, she clutched a clipboard to her chest as if someone were threatening to snatch it away. Anne didn't remember her from the days when Evelyn had been a patient. But that wasn't surprising. Back then, Anne hadn't paid much attention to the staff in these nursing homes. She was consumed with her mother's suffering, with the lost, empty spaces that Evelyn could no longer bridge.

On the drive over, Anne had made up a cover story. She told Nurse Koch (whose first name was Greta) that she was thinking of placing Grandma Betty in Sunnydale, a lie that would have made Grandma hopping mad. As far as Grandma Betty was concerned, nursing homes were a pit stop on the road to the great beyond. But the staff of Sunnydale didn't need to know that just yet.

Greta Koch led them down a long hallway lined with black-and-white photos of patients. The patients had all been photographed from about fifteen feet away. There was a certain uniformity to the portraits. Whoever had taken them had stood off to one side, so the subjects were all viewed from an angle. The soft focus created a sense of distance. Expressions were slightly blurred. You couldn't tell what the patients were thinking or whether they knew they were being photographed at all. Each was engaged in a different activity, labeled on captions: *Charlotte, At the Sewing Circle*; *Herbert, Tossing Salad*; *Sarah, Making a Clay Mug;* and so on.

At the end of the hall, on the right-hand side, was a small, cheerful-looking solarium, a cluttered, sunny room crammed with assorted potted plants. "Each of our clients is assigned a plant," said Miss Koch, pointing to a long windowsill packed with ferns, geraniums, cacti, and a host of other plants Anne didn't recognize. Some of them were exotic looking, with long, trailing vines and black-hued berries and broad, palm-shaped leaves. They reminded her of the plants in the glass solarium she'd seen in Longwood Gardens, outside of Philly. "Studies have shown that one tends to live longer when one has something to care for," Greta intoned. "Personal responsibility, that's our motto."

The nurse took them upstairs to the second floor and showed them a typical room, about fifteen by twelve feet, with two single beds, two metal lockers, matching chests of drawers, and a mini refrigerator. There was a sink and a mirror in the corner, but the toilets were in out the hall, in bathrooms equipped with handicapped shower stalls and special tubs. Anne noticed that water leaked from the ceiling into a pail in one corner of the hall and that vinyl tiles in some of the bathrooms were coming loose.

Each floor had a Day Room, containing an eighteen-inch TV. When Anne peered in, she saw a half-dozen elderly men and women sitting in wheelchairs lined up against the wall, watching NASCAR auto racing. One man's limbs were shaking uncontrollably. Parkinson's disease, Anne said to herself.

Today's date is: Saturday, proclaimed a sign on the wall. *The season is: Fall.*

"When I'm old and gray, make sure I don't wind up in this place," Jack whispered, as they proceeded down the hall.

Anne gave him a gentle poke in the ribs and kept walking. Being here was making her jittery. She hated the concept of nursing homes, the way every aspect of the day became part of a routine, depersonalized. Infirmity was emphasized, expected almost, so that the littlest thing—spooning up oatmeal, tying your shoe—turned into an ordeal, something other people helped you do. But that wasn't the worst of it. When she used to visit her mother what struck her was how you could feel so alone without ever spending time by yourself. None of the homes encouraged solitude. Group activities were the norm. Eating, exercising, and arts and crafts were performed *en masse. Adult supervision*, they called it. At each facility, Anne had sensed a quiet, unspoken desperation. The elderly were inmates. Trapped in decaying bodies, abandoned by friends and relatives, betrayed by fate.

Her worst fear was ending up in one of these places, unconnected to anyone who cared. She could feel her heart skipping distractedly in her chest, beating much too fast. She'd had two cups of coffee with lunch to try and stave off a growing sense of weariness. Now she was wired, her nerve endings raw. She turned a corner, trailing the group, and came upon the Activity Room.

Someone had painted a huge Monopoly board on the floor, with all the appropriate squares: *Illinois Avenue, Park Place, Boardwalk*. On the *Jail* square, it said, *Just Visiting*.

Anne's attention was immediately drawn to a dark-haired woman standing by the window. The woman looked to be in her late fifties, with thinning dark hair and a long, aquiline nose. What struck Anne was the way the woman was contemplating the view, as though she weren't really seeing it. Anne glanced at the woman's wrist and saw the familiar identification bracelet that beeped if you ventured outdoors. Alzheimer's probably. The woman could live another twenty, thirty years. A living death sentence. Anne remembered the objects that had been placed in her mother's room in each nursing home she stayed in: a big daily calendar, a night light, a clock with large numbers, and a radio. All to help tether Evelyn to the here and now. It hadn't worked. Each week she drifted a little further away, like a sailboat that had slipped from its mooring. The nurses treated her like a wayward child.

Anne knew there was believed to be a strong genetic component to the disease. In twenty years or so she might start forgetting things. Little things, at first—her car keys, the weather report, the name of the neighbor down the block. And then one day she wouldn't be able to take care of herself, she'd have to spend her life in one of these places. Ailing and alone.

Pushing the thought from her mind, Anne tore her gaze away from the Alzheimer's patient. In the center of the room, wheelchairs were pulled up to a gray metal table laden with yarn, felt, colored markers, and bottles of Elmer's glue. Seven old women and one old man were gluing triangular shaped pieces of black felt onto paper pumpkins. The pumpkins were fat and orange and had big toothy grins.

"Here at Sunnydale," Greta Koch announced, "there's no sadness. You'll never see a wheelchair off in a corner. Every minute of the day there's something to do."

Anne smiled wanly. The lighting in the activity room was harsh. The air smelled faintly of disinfectant. She had the odd sensation that she was being watched. She looked over at the window, but the dark-haired woman didn't seem to notice her.

Nurse Koch surveyed the group at the table. "How are we doing today?" she asked loudly.

One old lady looked up, the rest remained hunched over their pumpkins. Miss Koch nodded approvingly. "Full of fun, Mrs. Z?"

"And mad for more," the woman shot back.

Anne looked her and felt a jolt of recognition. Maggie Zambini. Her mother's oldest, closest friend.

"Mrs. Zambini," she called out.

The woman met her gaze. "My stars. If it isn't Anne Hardaway. I haven't seen you in ages."

"I know. How are you?"

The question seemed redundant. Margaret Zambini had aged badly. The last time Anne had seen her, she'd been a robust middle-aged woman. But she'd suffered a stroke two years ago and now she was thin and frail, her cheeks sunken, her face a road map of wrinkles. White tufts of hair sprouted from her head, barely covering her scalp. The flesh under her arms hung in loose flaps. The only thing that hadn't changed were her eyes, which were pale blue, the color of Easter eggs.

"How am I?" Mrs. Zambini said wryly. "Alive and kicking."

Nurse Koch had moved over to the ceramics area and was ticking off a list of activities for later that day: Bingo, Bible Study, Current Events Discussion, Movement to Music, Cooking Hour.

Mrs. Zambini flipped a switch on her wheelchair and the motorized chair slid away from the table. She signaled for Anne to follow, gliding briskly over the Monopoly board floor toward the far end of the room where two armchairs were positioned in front of a tall bookcase. Anne sat down in one of them, a lumpy plaid chair that had seen better days. On the table between the two chairs was the September issue of *Modern Maturity* and a copy of the *Landsdown Park Press.*

"The library," Mrs. Zambini said, with a shrug. "It's not great, but they've got every Jacqueline Susann ever written. And I get a chance to see the newspaper every day."

Mrs. Zambini folded her hands and sat up straighter in her chair. She gazed at Anne, then looked away. Maggie Zambini and Evelyn Hardaway had known each other since grammar school. They'd roomed together at college, gotten married within months of one another, raised children together, and shared coffee in each other's kitchens every morning. But when Evelyn had gotten sick, when things started getting really bad, Maggie had drifted away and let the friendship fade. How ironic, Anne thought, that Mrs. Zambini had ended up in the very place where Evelyn had been treated some twenty years ago.

As if reading Anne's mind, Mrs. Zambini said, "I think about her often, you know. There's not much else to do around here but rehash the past." Anne stared at her, not speaking. "I'm sorry," Mrs. Zambini continued. "I just wanted to let you know that I'm terribly, terribly sorry."

"For what?" Anne's tone was sharper than she intended. What good were apologies now? Her mother had been dead for years. It was too late to change any of it. "Look," she said aloud. "It's not like you were the only one who turned your back on her. The whole town did that."

"I don't blame you for being angry," Mrs. Zambini said slowly. "I would too, if I were in your shoes. I only wish I could have made things easier in the end. I guess what I'm saying is I wish I had been there for her."

Anne looked into the older woman's eyes. Tears had formed in the corners and were threatening to spill down her wrinkled cheeks. "You know," Anne said, her voice softening, "the two of you shared a lot of good times. That's what you should focus on."

Mrs. Zambini wiped at her face. "Please forgive my foolishness." She waved her hand at the Activity Room, taking in the tour group and the old people working away on their pumpkins. "It's tough sometimes. To stay positive."

"How are you feeling?" Anne said.

"Better than I was. In the beginning, my whole right side was paralyzed. Now, it's only my right leg.

Across the room, Greta Koch was showing off the ceramics kiln and a host of clay vases with fat, bulbous necks. Jack had shoved his hands in his pockets and was staring longingly out the window.

"Do you see much of Teri?" Mrs. Zambini asked.

Anne shook her head. "Not really." Teri Curley, nee Zambini, was Mrs. Z's stuck-up, prima donna daughter who lived over by the marina.

"I wish I saw her more often," Mrs. Zambini said plaintively. "Her and the girls. My husband visits once a week. But most of my friends have passed, except for Andrew." Mrs. Zambini pointed to the gray-haired man at the table, who spotted her and waved. "He's one of the good guys. But the others? You know what they do all day long?" Anne waited expectantly. "Catalog their aches and pains. Arthritis, shingles, colitis, you name it. Good Lord, it gets boring."

Mrs. Zambini sighed. Her head drooped to her chest. Her eyelids fluttered. Anne wondered if the old lady wanted to take a nap. But just then she looked up.

"People keep dying here," she said suddenly. Anne made what she hoped was a sympathetic noise.

"Not like you think." Mrs. Zambini lowered her voice. "One minute they're fine," she whispered. "The next they're . . . dead."

Anne stared at her. What could she say? Nursing homes were a way station before the end of the line. Lots of people felt that the minute you entered you were signing your own death warrant. She thought about what Greta Koch had said about the plants. As if tending a geranium could prevent disease, as if love could extend your life.

"I think . . ." Anne began.

A blond nurse in a starched white uniform walked by, her white-soled shoes padding noiselessly over the floor.

Mrs. Zambini looked up. "I love Jacqueline Susann," she said brightly to Anne. "Have you ever read *Valley of the Dolls*? It's a classic."

"I read it years ago," Anne said. Maggie Zambini was smiling so broadly her lips curled back over her gums.

"Don't mind me. I'm rambling again. Oh, my. I think your tour is about to leave." Across the room, Greta Koch was ushering people out of the Activity Room and into the hall. "If you're ever in the neighborhood and feel like dropping by . . ." Anne shot the older woman a questioning look. "I don't get many visitors," Mrs. Zambini explained. "Teri's so busy. And my husband . . . He doesn't enjoy coming here." She sounded sad, resigned. "Of course, I can't get out much these days." She patted her leg, which was thrust stiffly out in front of her.

Then she reached into the pocket of her flowered housecoat and pulled out an eight-by-ten–inch square of paper. "This is how I keep busy."

Unfolding the paper, she handed it to Anne. It was a painting of crows in a wheat field, the brushstrokes slashing across the page, drenched with color.

"It's a Van Gogh," Mrs. Zambini said. "I copied it from a book on impressionism. I've done dozens of them. In Arts and Crafts. Degas, Manet, Monet, Van Gogh."

Anne thought of Van Gogh's *Starry Night*, the way the cypress trees raked the sky, the stars swirling like yellow suns. When her mother had been at Sunnydale, they'd done paint by number drawings. The place had obviously traded up.

Anne handed the painting back to Mrs. Zambini and said her good-byes. As she crossed the room, her shoes clicked against the Monopoly board floor. She passed Baltic Avenue, New York Avenue and the Pennsylvania Railroad.

When she reached the doorway, she turned and glanced back. The woman with Alzheimer's was gone. Margaret Zambini was holding the wheat field painting in her lap, gazing blankly into space.

Chapter 7

To wick away water from a leaky roof, divert the water temporarily by tacking a rag to the rafter in the water's path and placing a bucket underneath it. The cloth strip will help redirect the water until you can fix the leak.

Fifteen minutes later, while Jack waited in the lobby, Anne found herself sitting across from Claire Hillyard, R.N., Chief Administrator of the Sunnydale Nursing Home. Claire's office was on the third floor. It was the least institutional place she'd visited in Sunnydale. The decor was traditional, but homey—an imposing cherrywood desk, two burgundy leather wing chairs, a kilim rug, a corner cupboard filled with decorative glass cocktail shakers from the 1950s. On the windowsill, a cheerful-looking pumpkin was slowly decaying. Anne settled back in one of the wing chairs, sipping coffee from a Styrofoam cup. How much caffeine had she consumed today? She was starting to lose track. She put down the cup and looked out the plate glass window to the garden, which seemed to have escaped the storm unscathed. Leaves swirled to the ground, silent as snowflakes. A few wooden benches were grouped around a small bronze statue of a boy playing a flute.

"You do understand you can always call us if you have further questions," Claire Hillyard said kindly.

She must get this all the time, Anne thought. Anxious people with misgivings about putting their relatives in a nursing home. The guilt, the second guessing, the nagging fear that you were doing the wrong thing. Luckily, Anne had only been sixteen when her mother hopped onto the nursing home merry-go-round. The decision had been her father's to make.

"I understand," Anne said aloud. "But I do have some concerns about how Grandma will adjust."

Claire Hillyard smiled understandingly. "Of course."

Anne had been expecting to meet an impersonal, clinical sounding administrator, efficient in a brusque, by-the-book way. Claire didn't fit the bill. She appeared to be in her mid-sixties, broad and tall, with an attractive, placid face and a voice that was so youthful and soothing she probably could have gotten a job as a late night disc jockey or a narrator of audio books. Her eyes were slate gray. Her hair was also gray, short, blown straight, and parted in the middle with wispy bangs feathered across her forehead. She wore black slacks, a plum-colored turtleneck sweater, and a strand of pearls. The clothes looked expensive, better suited to the executive suite of a Fortune 100 company than a third-rate nursing home. But then Claire herself seemed too classy for Sunnydale, like a thoroughbred running with the trotters.

She reached into a manila folder, brought out some papers, and handed them across the desk to Anne. "Inside, you'll find the financials, a sample menu, a calendar of October's activities, and a copy of our newsletter, *Sunnyside Up*."

"Is there a waiting list to get in?"

"Not at all. But you'll need a form from your grand-mother's doctor. When a client is admitted, we do a thor-ough intake and evaluation."

"Do you offer any psychological counseling?"

"Certainly. Your grandmother will be assigned a social worker who will monitor her moods and act as her patient advocate. Occasionally, a client may feel depressed at the outset. But we quickly get them into the swing of things."

There were two photographs on a shelf above Claire's desk. One was of Stuart, posed on the beach, the ocean fanning out behind him. A second showed three children standing in front of a painted floral backdrop. The kids were smiling self-consciously, a Kodak moment captured at the local Sears. Her grandchildren, probably. Anne wondered which of them was the bedwetter.

No photos of a husband, boyfriend, or significant other. And Claire didn't wear a wedding band.

Just then, there was a sharp knock on the open door. Anne turned to see a broad-shouldered man with a shock of gray hair standing in the doorway.

"Oh, Philip," Claire said. "Were you looking for me?"

"I was. But it can wait."

"This is Anne Hardaway," Claire said. "Anne, I'd like you to meet Philip Reynolds. He owns Sunnydale."

Philip Reynolds pumped Anne's hand once and let it drop. Handsome in a craggy, B-movie actor way, he was in his middle to late sixties, with a tanning salon tan and enough cologne to drown out the diesel fumes on the Jersey Turnpike.

He flashed his teeth at Anne. "You're in good hands with Claire. If you have any questions . . ." He waved his hand in Claire's direction and continued down the hall with a parting look that said, "Don't bother me with your petty problems."

"Philip is working around the clock these days," Claire said, picking up a paper clip and bending the metal until it formed a straight line. "What with the storm and the renovation work."

"When will the new wing be finished?"

"Next April."

Anne nodded politely. She was no expert in construction work, but it seemed highly unlikely the building would be renovated in just six months.

"Will there be room for more patients at that point?"

"Nearly seventy-five more. But the staff will increase, of course. As I was saying, we provide van service to town and to the doctor. There are also special trips to concerts, Atlantic City, the occasional Broadway show."

Anne nodded. She pictured Grandma Betty in an orchestra seat at *Cats*, surrounded by other little old ladies, their walkers and wheelchairs bunched together at the end of the front aisles.

"Is there anything else I can help you with?" Claire Hillyard asked. Her tone was pleasant, almost consoling.

Yes, Anne wanted to say. Tell me about your husband. What kind of man was he? Dynamic? Caring? Manipulative? Was he having an affair?

"Not right now. I think that about covers it."

She called Trasker from a pay phone in the lobby while Jack brought the car around front. The detective had a few things to report. He'd placed a call to Claire Hillyard earlier in the day and she'd referred him to her husband's former dentist, a Dr. Morton Katz, in West Long Branch. Katz had put him in touch with Hillyard's periodontist, an Anthony Scaduto, in Little Silver.

"We caught a break on that one," Trasker said. "Katz only had wing bites. But Scaduto had x-rayed Hillyard's whole mouth."

"Can you make a positive I.D.?"

"Absolutely. An x-ray is as good as a fingerprint. And teeth don't deteriorate that much over time. We're x-raying the skeleton's mouth this afternoon. It'll show crowns, roots, pulp chambers, missing teeth. We should be able to see if they match."

"How did Mrs. Hillyard sound?" Anne asked.

"You mean was she upset? Curious? Grief stricken?"

"Yeah."

She heard the sound of papers rustling, phones ringing in the background. "None of the above. Fact is, I thought she took it pretty well, considering. Said her husband had been missing for years. Far as she was concerned, he was history. End of story."

"Did she ask about the skeleton? About where it was found?"

"Nope. I thought I'd have to fudge a little. To leave your name out of it. But she didn't want to know the particulars. She told me to notify her if it turned out to be her husband." She heard some more rustling. Trasker cleared his throat. "Anne?"

"Uh huh."

"What are you up to?"

"Meaning?"

"Did you talk to Mrs. Hillyard?"

Anne tightened her grip on the receiver. "I might have."

Trasker chewed that over a moment. "What's on your mind?" he said, his voice betraying a note of concern.

"Nothing."

"Are you telling me this has nothing to do with you? Personally, I mean. You're just following up because it's your civic duty?" This time, his tone was sharper.

Two honks sounded outside. She looked toward the entrance and saw Jack parked in front of the building.

"Listen, I gotta go. Call me if the x-rays match. Or if they don't."

She hung up before Trasker could respond and hurried to the entry way. The disinfectant smell was stronger in the lobby and she wanted to be rid of it.

As the glass doors swung open electronically, she nearly collided with Chester Higgins. He was dressed in his coveralls and cap and carried a silver saw.

"Got that problem straightened out?" he said.

He sounded nonchalant. As if he were referring to a faulty circuit or a squeaky porch step.

"Not yet. I didn't know you worked here."

"A couple things happened on account of the storm. Leaks. Damaged drywall." Chester tugged on the brim of his cap. "You let me know when I can get back to work on that basement of yours." Then he was gone.

Anne stepped outside and inhaled deeply, letting the scent of autumn fill her lungs. Earth, dead leaves, a slight chill in the air. It had turned a little colder and the wind had picked up. Clouds scudded overhead in a pale silver sky. At the fringes of the parking lot, the trees were ablaze with color, postcard perfect. She climbed into Jack's red Corvette and rolled down the passenger side window.

"Remind me never to get old," she said, as the car swung out of the parking lot.

"Hey, it's better than the alternative."

"Just barely."

"Where to now?"

"Well, I've spent the whole afternoon talking about my grandmother. Want to drop by and see her?"

"Sure. If you don't mind a quick side trip first."

Jack made a right and the car sped back toward the Heights.

"My turn," Anne said. "Where to?"

"It's a surprise."

She leaned her head back against the seat and felt a wave of tiredness wash over her. What she wanted most in the world right now was a nap. "Okay," she said, fighting to keep her eyes from closing.

They drove through town. On Main Street, the cleanup crews were still out in force—patching, plastering, painting. Most of the streets had been cleared of major debris, with downed trees on the side of the road instead of blocking it entirely. The Boy Scouts were collecting small twigs and branches and putting them in large plastic sacks. The plate glass window of the doll shop had shattered and a display of porcelain dolls was sitting on the sidewalk. Nagle's was closed. Outside the Strange Brew, a sign said, *Storm Got You Down? Try a Cup of Our Delicious Worry-Free Coffee*. It looked like the storm had left its mark on nearly every house. Anne wondered how much the northeaster was going to cost the town. A million? More?

When they got to Ocean Avenue, Jack turned left, toward Landsdown Park. She rolled the window down all the way. Her head was foggy with exhaustion. But she could feel something tugging at the corners of her mind, a thought she couldn't shake loose.

"Jack," she said.

"Uh huh."

"Why the basement?"

"What do you mean?"

"If I shot someone and wanted to hide the body, I'd wait till it got dark and bury it outside. That way, there'd be less chance of someone finding it. The basement seems too risky. Not to mention the odor. I mean, wouldn't a corpse start to smell?"

"I dunno."

"And what about the clothes?"

"Clothes?" Jack repeated.

"Yeah. Again, assuming I shot somebody, he or she would be dressed, right? Shirt, socks, shoes. So why weren't they on the skeleton?"

"Maybe so many years have gone by that they've deteriorated."

"Shoes don't deteriorate."

"Sounds like you think your mother was involved."

Anne turned toward him. "He was probably treating her. That's all. But what if she knew how he wound up in the cellar?"

"You don't know for sure Hillyard was buried down there."

"I hope it's not him. I hope the bones are a hundred years old and there's some logical explanation for all this."

The Corvette rolled to a stop at the end of what used to be the boardwalk. To the south, she could see the dilapidated buildings on the fringes of Landsdown Park. Soot and grime caked the crumbling brickwork. Ahead, the ocean was a hard, metallic shade of gray. "Come on," Jack said, scrambling out of the car.

She got out and followed him, stepping over splintered pieces of wood, navigating around sand dunes that seemed to have mushroomed in size overnight. The beach had shifted here, too, spilling out onto the road, altering the familiarity of the landscape. Dune grass had disappeared. The only thing remaining of Fisherman's Pier were the pilings, jutting up out of the sea like a minimalist sculpture. They plodded toward the water, their shoes sinking into the sand. Halfway there, Jack stopped.

"Kind of like being on a boat, isn't it?" he asked, looking over his shoulder.

She turned in the direction of Ocean Avenue. The Victorian houses lining the road were partially screened from view, their lower floors swallowed by the dunes.

Further down the beach, an elderly man was training a metal detector on the sand, sweeping the machine over the ground like he was vacuuming. Ed Klemperer. He came out nearly every day to hunt for buried treasure.

"Think he'll find anything?" Jack asked.

"Not today. Any loose coins are probably buried too deep under all this sand."

"I was out here this morning. It's enough to make you stop and think. The power of nature and all."

He fumbled in his pocket and took something out.

"This belonged to my mother," he said, offering it to her. "I want you to have it."

She stared at the ring in stunned disbelief, as if someone were playing a not very original practical joke. It was a small, oval-shaped diamond, with a baguette on either side and a platinum band. She'd been considering living with Jack; marriage had never crossed her mind.

"This is the reason I went to visit Pop this morning," Jack said. "He told me Mom would have wanted you to have it."

Anne looked up, startled. Troy Mills wasn't especially fond of her. But she tried not to take it personally. He didn't like anyone.

"Okay," Jack amended. "So Pop didn't exactly say that. But *I* know she would have been behind us one hundred percent."

Anne felt numb. She stared at the ring. It was pretty, dainty almost. Simple. Not what she would have chosen if she'd picked it out herself. Too old-fashioned. Too precious looking.

Jack held the ring up, twisting it so the diamond caught the light. "I know I said no pressure. And there is none. Really. It's just . . ." His eyes bore into her, his jaw was set. "I think it's time. And I don't see how waiting is going to change how we feel about each other. I mean, either we get married or . . ."

"Or . . . ," Anne prompted. Where was the excitement? Where were the fireworks? Jack was proposing and she didn't feel anything except a vague sense that the whole thing was unreal. The changed beach. The houses swallowed by drifting sand. The prospect of happily ever after. It was as though she was seeing him through a sheet of filmy gauze.

Jack said, "If you're not ready, maybe we should think about, you know, what it means if we don't get married. Where we go from here."

His eyes fastened on her, waiting. His expression was earnest, the ring extended in his outstretched hand. She knew the way Jack's mind worked. Once he'd decided to do something, there was no turning back. No shades of gray. No waffling, no waiting.

In other words, she had to decide right this minute. Her mouth was dry. It felt like bugs were fluttering in her stomach. What if Jack walked out of her life forever? How would that feel? She thought of him lying in bed beside her, his tenderness, how supportive he was, how caring, the way he stroked her hair, the time they'd picnicked on the beach by moonlight.

Anne held out her hand and he eased the ring onto her finger. It was a little too big for her, so the diamond wobbled to one side.

"I want to hear you say it out loud," he said.

A wave crashed against the beach, sending up a plume of spray. His eyes were the color the sky would be if it weren't already cloudy.

"Yes," she said, as he bent down to kiss her. Was she crazy about him or just plain crazy? "Yes, I'll marry you."

Chapter 8

A temporary fix for a storm-damaged roof is to cover the hole with plastic sheeting. Fold over the edges of the plastic and staple them to sound roofing shingles surrounding the opening.

The thing about Grandma Betty was you never quite knew what to expect. She'd invite you over for Thanksgiving dinner and serve canned ham. She'd borrow ten dollars and give you back twenty. She dyed her hair bright red, swore she was decades younger than what it said on her birth certificate, but chewed out the clerk at the Cineplex if he didn't give her the senior discount. She had a dog named Boop whom she dressed in striped knit sweaters and treated better than she had her three husbands. But she couldn't stand other people's dogs and threatened to call the cops when her neighbor's chow peed on her forsythia bushes. She had a quick temper, an easy laugh, and she never hesitated to let you know exactly what she was thinking.

Which is why Anne wasn't looking forward to telling her about the engagement. Grandma Betty might throw her arms around Jack and welcome him to the family. (After all, she'd met Jack on several occasions, and had made it clear she liked him.) But it was also entirely possible she'd turn to Anne and say, "What the blazes are you doing? Since when do you want to be saddled with a husband?"

When they rang the bell of Grandma Betty's two-story white cottage and no one came to the door, Anne felt a twinge of relief.

"Doesn't look like anyone's home," Jack said.

"Guess we should have called first. She probably has a bridge game. Or she got a ride to the Freehold Mall. I read in the paper there's a white sale at Macy's."

Anne looked up at the house and noticed the storm had knocked a small hole in the roof, near the chimney. *What you don't know can't hurt you.* Maybe. Maybe not.

"Well, we have to tell somebody," Jack announced, "to make it official. I wish my brother was here." His blue eyes clouded over for a moment. His hands inadvertently clenched, but then he relaxed and said, "Let's see if Helen's around."

Helen lived three blocks away, on Crestwood, and Anne knew that telling her best friend would make it real. They left the car in front of Grandma Betty's house and walked over. Helen was home. When Jack broke the news, grinning from ear to ear, Helen let out a whoop.

"Congratulations," she said, hugging Anne and Jack at the same time. "When's the wedding? Where's it going to be? I want to hear everything right this minute."

"We haven't worked out all the details yet," Anne said. She was still in a haze, like her whole body had been injected with novocain.

"But we're not going to wait too long," Jack chimed in. "Six months, at the latest."

"Six months!" Anne exclaimed, feeling a surge of panic. "That's way too soon. I thought we'd wait at least a year."

"Long engagements are the pits," said Helen, as she ushered them inside. "It only gives you more time to worry about the big day."

She led them through the living room to a cozy study lined with books.

"Have a seat," Helen said. "This calls for a toast. I'm out of champagne, but I can whip up a couple of Bloody Marys."

Anne sat down in an armchair slipcovered in green chenille. Jack sat next to her in a bentwood rocker.

"I'll have tomato juice on the rocks," Anne said. "I hardly got any sleep last night. If I have alcohol now, I'll collapse."

"Make that two tomato juices," Jack added.

"Coming right up." Helen said, going over to the wet bar in the corner and fixing the drinks. She was a big fan of Jack's and a big supporter of marriage. Her own was entering its tenth year, and with no plans to have kids, she'd confided to Anne that she still felt like a newlywed.

"So where's the honeymoon?" Helen asked.

"I was thinking about Peru," Jack answered. "There's this company that runs these amazing camping trips to the outback. You hike fifteen miles a day. Mountain climb. See some amazing ruins."

"I don't know how well I'd do in the outback," Anne said. "The last time I went camping, I was eight. The first night, it rained and the tent collapsed. I woke up completely drenched."

"This tour is completely different from Girl Scouts or whatever," he said to her. "They have these wonderful guides who really know the countryside."

"Hey," Helen broke in. "If you guys get married next summer, you could have the ceremony right on the beach," she said.

"Too hippy dippy," Jack said, making a face. "I want

this done right. I called my friend at the Water Club and everything's set. It's going to be black tie, with a twenty-piece orchestra, a video—the whole nine yards. The food's great. The view's to die for. And it helps to know the owner. He can free up the first Saturday night in March for us."

"March!" Anne yelped. "That's less than five months away. I couldn't possibly . . ."

"Hey, I could help you look for the dress and shop for flowers and stuff," Helen enthused.

"Actually," Jack said. "A friend of my cousin hired a wedding planner, and this woman took care of everything. I think we should use her. That way Anne doesn't have to worry about every little detail. I'd rather she spend the time redecorating our apartment."

"I don't need a wedding planner and we still haven't decided where we're going to live," Anne said testily. She was wondering when he'd had time to call the Water Club; he'd barely proposed an hour ago. Then it hit her. He'd called before he asked her. That's how sure he was that she was going to say yes.

Jack said, "Don't you think it makes sense to use the cottage as a summer place?"

"No, I don't."

She jumped up to assist Helen with the drinks and flashed her friend a look that said, "Help me out here."

"You know, it might be nice to wait till May or June," Helen said, studying Anne. "Better weather. I've been to the Water Club. They have a great deck. It'd be warm enough outside in late spring." She raised her Bloody Mary in a toast. "Meantime, to the happy couple. I wish you health, happiness, and years of love."

They drank.

"I don't want to get married in the city," Anne said, putting her glass down. "I can't believe you've already planned the whole wedding." This wasn't the way it was supposed to be. She had a headache. What she wanted most was to lie down and take a nap.

"I checked out Windows on the World. And the Rainbow Room. The Water Club is better, believe me."

"Hold on!" Anne exclaimed. "We haven't even talked about this yet. Besides, all those places are really pricey."

"Considering that I'm paying, who cares?" Jack said. He had that superior tone in his voice, the one he used on construction sites to remind the hired help who was in charge.

"Like hell you're paying," Anne shot back. She hated it when he belittled her finances. So she didn't make a lot of money. She was doing okay, thank you very much. "The bride's family is supposed to pay for the wedding," she reminded him. "And marriage is a partnership. Meaning you don't get to make big decisions all by yourself."

Jack's eyes blazed. "If I left it up to you, we'd have meat loaf at Quilters."

"Sounds good to me," Anne said angrily. The numbness was wearing off. Now she felt irritated with him. Was this the way it was going to be? Jack planning every facet of their lives, taking over?

"Guys, calm down," Helen said. "You don't have to decide right this minute. Annie, anything new on the skeleton?"

Anne took a deep breath and switched gears by bringing Helen up to speed on the Hillyards and Trasker and the bones.

"So you got the grand tour of Sunnydale," Helen said, when Anne had finished. "I've never been inside. What's it like?"

"Depressing as hell. It doesn't help that the place is a wreck."

"That's odd," Helen said.

"What?"

"Sunnydale should be in tiptop shape, seeing how the owner has so much money."

"It's a dump," Jack said. "I wouldn't leave my father there overnight."

"How do you know Philip Reynolds has money?" Anne said to Helen.

"He's one of our biggest customers at the bank. In fact, he's opening a chain of nursing homes up and down the east coast. Apparently, he's got pretty deep pockets."

"It doesn't look like he puts much money back into the business."

"He's got a bunch of investors backing him. I've seen the floor plans for some of the new buildings. They look pretty nice." Helen took another sip of her drink. "It's sad, when you think about it. Seems like every other week there's a funeral at Sunnydale. I don't ever want to end up in one of those places."

"Life's a bitch and then you die," Jack said curtly. "At least that's what the T-shirts say."

He was staring down at the carpet, his arms crossed tightly over his chest. Anne knew he was still stewing about the Water Club. Well, he could sulk all he wanted. It was great that he wanted to get so involved in the wedding plans. But she wasn't getting married in March and she wasn't moving to New York. No way, no how.

She turned to Helen. "How do you know about the deaths at Sunnydale?"

"The obituary column is the first thing I read in the paper," Helen said, with a rueful smile. "Crazy, right? But I got in the habit of looking at it, and to tell you the truth, some mornings it's the only thing I read."

Anne looked out the window. The sugar maple in Helen's yard was half-bare, its golden leaves drifting across the lawn. What was it Mrs. Zambini had said? *People keep dying here.*

Chapter 9

Mildew usually looks like clusters of black dots, but it can be green, brown, or yellow as well. To remove it, use a solution of one part bleach to three parts water.

Mark Trasker was leaning against his car, in front of Anne's house, when Jack's Corvette pulled up to the curb. A cigarette dangled from the detective's lips. Underneath his tan raincoat was another of the smartly tailored suits he favored. It was a quarter to six. The wind was blowing hard off the ocean, and the sky was the color of spoiled milk.

Anne got out of the car and introduced Trasker and Jack. The two men shook hands, and Anne thought she saw Trasker give Jack the once over, sizing him up.

"I've got some information for you," Trasker said to Anne, stubbing out his cigarette. "How about we take a walk?"

"Why don't you two go ahead," Jack said, although he

hadn't been included in the detective's invitation. "I have to make a few phone calls."

Without waiting for a reply, he bounded up the steps and let himself into the house. They hadn't talked much on the ride home. Anne was too tired and Jack appeared to have shut down. She didn't fight with him often. She supposed it was because they mainly saw each other on weekends, and neither of them wanted to spoil what little time they had together. The problem was she was flying blind. She didn't know how this was supposed to go. Who would be the first to smooth things over? Would they discuss what had happened? Ignore it? Which one of them would break the ice first?

"He your boyfriend?" Trasker said, as he and Anne ambled down Ocean Avenue.

"Fiancé." The word tasted strange, like an exotic fruit.

Trasker gave her a long, hard look. "Congratulations."

Something in his voice made Anne stop walking.

"What?" she said.

"Nothing."

"If you have something to say, go ahead and say it."

"It's just . . ." Trasker frowned. "I never took you to be the marrying sort."

"Why is that?" she challenged him.

Trasker's gaze slid away from her, toward the ocean. Whitecaps flecked the water, the surf smacking the shoreline hard and sending up bursts of spray. Clouds threaded the horizon, purple-hued, wispy, like distant bruises. "I know we haven't known each other all that long. But I thought I recognized a kindred spirit."

He started walking again and Anne fell into step beside him.

"Meaning?" she said.

"You seem like you can take care of yourself. A lot of women get to a certain age and all of a sudden, they need a man around the house. They're lonely. Or they're scared. The clock's ticking too loud. That doesn't sound like you."

"What about love?"

"What about it? You can love somebody without giving away your independence. Some women don't get the concept though. After you've had a few dates, they're all over you like flies on molasses."

"Guess you're not in a hurry to walk down the aisle."

"Nope. I do just fine on my own."

Anne threw him a sideways glance. This was the most personal he'd ever gotten with her. She wondered if he was disappointed to learn she was getting married. What would dating Mark Trasker be like? In some ways, she had more in common with him than she had with Jack. They skirted a pile of driftwood that had once been part of the boardwalk. A telephone pole swayed unsteadily above them, buffeted by the wind.

"So what did you want to tell me?" Anne said, getting back to business.

"The dental x-rays. They're a perfect match."

Anne felt her stomach lurch. In the back of her mind, she was hoping that the skeleton had no connection to her family—that it was unrelated to any of their lives.

"You were right," Trasker continued. "Steven Hillyard's remains were buried in your basement. Forensics is analyzing the wound in the skull. Preliminary report indicates the bullet entered the back of the skull, ricocheted around the head, passed through the occipital lobe, and exited out the side. They figure he was killed twenty to thirty years ago. I did some checking. Hillyard disappeared on August 23, 1974."

Anne's mind was racing. Her mother's diary had ended August 21. She had still been away at summer camp. The season had run until the very end of August. And her father. Where had her father been living then? Still at home. He didn't move out until later that fall. Could her father have been involved in the murder?

"Looks like he was shot from behind," Trasker continued. "We'd like to send someone over tomorrow to examine the basement walls. Could be a fragment will turn up."

"Do you know anything about the gun?"

"Probably a small handgun, a Smith and Wesson, a Colt—something of that nature." They'd reached Fletcher Lake, which separated the Heights from the neighboring town of Bradley Beach. Trasker picked up a stone and threw it in the water, neatly skimming the surface. "Now it's your turn. You going to tell me how you had such an incredible hunch?"

Anne turned up the collar of her jacket. The light was fading from the sky. It was getting colder. She smelled the sharp scent of a wood-burning fire. Her neighbors would be using some of the splintered wood for kindling, salvaging small pieces of the storm. It wouldn't surprise her if somebody got the bright idea of selling them as souvenirs. Own a piece of the northeaster. Reinvent the past for profit.

She took a deep breath and told him about Evelyn. The Alzheimer's. The diary. All of it. When she finished it was dark, which helped a little. She couldn't see his eyes that clearly, couldn't tell what he was thinking.

"I'll run a check on Hillyard," he said. "And another on the wife. See what we turn up."

"So it could be unrelated? I mean, the fact that he happened to be in the house could be a coincidence, right? It doesn't mean . . . it doesn't mean he was killed there."

"Doesn't mean anything yet. All we've got is circumstantial evidence."

They started walking back. The curved, old-fashioned streetlights on Ocean Avenue still weren't working, another casualty of the storm. The only illumination came from the Victorian houses, their fanciful balustrades and gingerbread porches creating a false sense of coziness and warmth amid the rampant destruction.

"Anne?"

"Yeah."

She felt Trasker's hand on her arm. His touch felt reassuring. "I'm sorry about your mother. It must have been tough on you."

She paused, not knowing exactly how to answer. When faced with other people's sympathy, her standard response was to brush off their concern, to be stoic, strong, to reveal nothing.

"It was hell," she said softly, surprised by her own admission. She felt his hand squeeze her arm, then drop away. They continued on in silence.

When she got home, the light in her office was on. Her fax machine was whirring, her printer was printing, and Jack was sitting at her desk, her cordless phone pressed to his ear. Harry was sprawled on the radiator keeping his one eye on the intruder.

"I don't care about the blueprints," Jack was saying into the phone. "The whole damn floor is going to have to be redone."

He looked up and saw her standing in the doorway.

"Just a sec," he said into the phone, then covered the mouthpiece with his hand. "Turns out I have to work late tonight," he told her, his tone distant but polite. "I'll fix myself a sandwich."

She nodded and backed out of the room. Jack returned to his conversation. "The heating ducts are exposed," she heard him saying. "It's a real mess."

So this was how it was going to be. Scratch one kiss and make up session. Instead of cuddling with Jack in front of the fireplace, she had a long, solitary evening ahead of her. Good. She could turn in early and get some much-needed sleep. She went into the kitchen and wolfed down a plate of cold chicken and rice from the night before. She'd take leftovers over the original any night of the week. They always tasted better. After she'd cleaned her plate and, against all reason, downed a cup of coffee, she felt herself getting a second wind.

She wandered toward her office, heard Jack burning

up the phone wires, and walked back to the living room. She didn't need her computer to start sorting through Jennifer Joan's extensive, disorganized notes. Let's see. Where to begin? Leaky chimneys, leaky gutters, basement cracks, draft-proofing, squeaky floors? All of the above applied to her house—except for the gutters. They no longer leaked since they'd been ripped from the facade during the storm. Okay, chimneys.

Anne began reading about flashing and mortar, but it was tough to stay focused. Had Hillyard been treating her mother? It was a safe assumption, but she wasn't one hundred percent sure. Did records still exist? Who would know? Her mother's old friends, maybe. But she wasn't sure how much her mother had confided in any of them.

She put aside Jennifer Joan's scrawled instructions and looked around the room. The furniture was pretty much the same as when her parents had been alive. Anne hadn't the time or inclination or funds to fix the place up much. The chintz sofa could stand to be recovered, the oak coffee table wobbled, and the quilt draped over the floral wing chair was threadbare.

Her eyes fell on the blue plastic newspaper recycling bin, stacked with back issues of the *Landsdown Park Press*. She pulled out one of the papers and flipped to the obituary page. Her eyes scanned the death notices. Nothing there. She tossed the paper aside and pulled another one from the pile. This time, she found what she was looking for:

MYRA D. STANTON

Myra D. Stanton, a secretary for the Harry Fabey Insurance Co., Neptune, before retiring, died September 28 at the Sunnydale Nursing Home, in Oceanside Heights. She was 83 and is survived by a cousin. Francis L. Tomberlin Funeral Home, Landsdown Park, is in charge of arrangements.

Anne tore the notice out, set the paper down, and continued to search through the pile. It contained about three months' worth of issues, some of which she hadn't gotten around to reading and others she hadn't bothered to throw away.

Several minutes later, she had torn out the obituaries of twelve other people. The most recent deaths were Beatrice Weissman and Ernest P. Kamber, who had also lived at Sunnydale. Weissman was 78, Kamber was 81. The memorial services for both had been held at the Tomberlin Funeral Home.

Thirteen deaths in three months. Not an especially comforting statistic, but then these people had been old. And old people died. There wasn't anything suspicious about that. Was there?

Anne rummaged through her bag and took out the manila envelope that Claire Hillyard had given her. She tossed aside the monthly menu and the schedule of activities and read the Complete Admissions Guide cover to cover. The private payment costs were staggering: $8,100 a month for a semiprivate room and $9,145 for private accommodations. That worked out to $295 a day; for the same money, you could go to New York and stay at the Plaza.

At Sunnydale, if you had Medicare, you were covered for one hundred days, but only if you had recently been discharged from a hospital and met the "required medical criteria," which meant you had to have suffered a hip fracture, a stroke, or a serious illness. You could also be admitted if you needed physical therapy, tube feeding, or injections of insulin, heparin, or antibiotics.

If you had something called "nursing home Medicaid," your social security and pension checks had to be turned over to Sunnydale for as long as you stayed in the nursing home. On the admissions application, you had to list your brokerage accounts, bank accounts, stocks, bonds, real estate investments, and any and all benefits you received. You also had to put down the cemetery you wished to be buried in, the owner of the lot, the lot number, the holder of the deed, the person responsible for the burial arrangements, and the undertaker's address.

Death and money. For your trouble, you got a boxy antiseptic-smelling room and all the gelatin you could eat. Sounded like a lousy deal. At least it had been for her mother.

She tossed the nursing home packet on the coffee table, clicked on the TV, and did some quick channel surfing: Sitcom reruns. A made-for-TV movie about a serial killer. A nature program on pythons. Infomercials selling Zirconium earrings and Stairmasters.

When her mother had been in nursing homes, she'd always had the television on. Evelyn didn't watch the shows; it was more like background music, a mindless melody that helped while away the hours. Anne supposed the boob tube was comforting in a way. Familiar characters, regularly scheduled programs, a parallel universe where most people's problems were neatly resolved at the end of half an hour. It helped offset the loneliness of life in an institution, made Evelyn forget that she couldn't remember.

Anne clicked the set off and glanced at the clock. Eight P.M. Sunnydale allowed visitors up until nine. She wondered if Mrs. Z might like some company.

Chapter 10

If a leak has stained the ceiling, dab the spots with equal parts of water and chlorine bleach. Dab the stains with a moistened sponge. If the ceiling still isn't clean, seal the spots with a primer, then apply a coat of ceiling paint.

The fluorescent bulbs in the ceiling lit the lobby of the nursing home with a harsh, cold glare, accentuating the dinginess of the place. The lobby itself was deserted. The paint on the walls was cracked; the white linoleum floor had a grayish cast. Cheesy Halloween decorations lent the place a sad, almost maudlin air. Anne checked in with the bored-looking guard at the front desk and asked for Mrs. Zambini's room number, which she promptly received.

While waiting for the elevator, she read the posted schedule of activities for the week: Choir Practice, Spa Night, Cooking Hour, Bible Study, Arts and Crafts, Social Teas (off-site!), Book Club, Bingo, and Create a Pizza. The elevator came and Anne pressed the button for the third floor. The metal box creaked as it slowly ascended, discharging her with a groan. The hallway was quiet. In fact, the whole building was still as a tomb. Walking down the corridor, Anne caught glimpses of the beds in each room. Men and women lay wrapped inside white cotton blankets, like thin ghostly mummies. Occasionally, she heard the hum of a television set, a sudden, low moan, then silence. She quickened her steps. Sunnydale was bad enough in the daytime. At night, it gave her the creeps. Once when she was about sixteen, visiting her mother in a nursing home—not here, the one in Red Bank—Anne had heard a sudden high-pitched shriek. Her mother had claimed it was a patient who clawed at her skin every night and had to be wrapped in bandages for her own protection. The image had given Anne nightmares for weeks.

When she reached the room assigned to Mrs. Zambini, she saw it was a carbon copy of the others she'd seen on the tour. Two beds. Two dressers. A mini refrigerator. Mrs. Zambini was seated in a chair, talking to the elderly man Anne had seen earlier in the Activity Room. He was a large, heavyset fellow, with thinning, white hair and small, close-set eyes. Over his pajamas, he wore a vest and cardigan sweater. His feet, planted firmly on the metal stand below his wheelchair, were encased in expensive-looking leather slippers.

"Hi," Anne said, knocking on the open door. They both craned their necks at the sound, peering at her like herons who'd been startled from their nest. "I hope I'm not disturbing you."

Mrs. Zambini blinked and stared at the doorway.

"It's Anne. Anne Hardaway. We talked this afternoon."

"Oh, yes. Anne." Mrs. Zambini waved her hand. "How are you, hon? Come in. I'd like you to meet a friend of mine."

Anne entered the room and looked around her. Copies of impressionist paintings in Plexiglas frames adorned the wall: landscapes, ballet dancers, still lifes, portraits. On Mrs. Zambini's dresser were pictures of Teri, Teri's husband, and their three precocious daughters, whose first names Anne could never remember, though she was fairly sure they all began with the letter T. The other side of the room looked unoccupied.

"This is Mr. Andrew Deretchin."

"Nice to meet you," Anne said, moving toward him.

"The pleasure is mine." His voice had a vaguely southern lilt. She was taken by surprise when he reached for her hand and brought it to his lips to kiss. His mouth felt papery, dry. She instinctively pulled her hand away. "I was just on my way out," he said. "Maggie." He turned to Mrs. Zambini and saluted. "Until the morrow."

Placing his hands on either side of the chair, he swiveled expertly around Anne and rolled out of the room.

"I hope I didn't chase him off," Anne said.

"Not to worry. Drew and I could gab all night. He has some kind of rare nerve disease, so he's confined to a wheelchair all the time, like I am. When you can't walk, you talk. And it's nice to have someone new to talk to. Please," she indicated the bed. "Sit. Would you like a Snapple? There's iced tea or lemonade."

Anne sat. The mattress was surprisingly lumpy and the blanket had a slight pear-shaped stain. "No thanks," she said, declining the drink offer. "You're probably surprised to see me again so soon."

"For a moment, I thought you were Teri. She hasn't come by this week."

"When does she usually visit?"

"There's no set time. You know how busy Teri is. What with the PTA, her aerobics class, the historic preservation society. She's redoing her kitchen, too. Her decorator found countertops that look like real marble."

Anne nodded. It was just like Teri to spend thousands on a new kitchen, and not give a damn that her mother was living in a nursing home that was falling apart at the seams.

"I actually stopped by to ask you something," Anne said. "I know it was a long time ago, but do you happen to remember if my mother was ever treated by a hypnotherapist?"

A nervous look came over Mrs. Zambini's face. Her eyes darted back and forth. Anne saw that her hands were trembling. "I can't say. We lost touch after a while, as you know. Why do you ask?"

"I was going through some of her things and it got me curious about her treatment," Anne lied.

Mrs. Zambini let out a small sigh. "Alzheimer's. Yes. There's a woman here who has it. Susannah. Perhaps you've seen her."

"Dark hair? Long nose? She wears an I.D. bracelet?"

"Yes. It's quite sad. But then, so much at Sunnydale is sad. Thank heaven for my paintings. They take my mind off living here."

"They're quite beautiful," Anne said. "I especially like the dancers." She pointed to the far wall, where two ballerinas in identical powder blue tutus stretched their legs at a barre.

"Degas. He studied law before he took up art. Did you know that? I wish I'd taken art classes. Then maybe I'd be doing original work instead of making copies. I have so many regrets." Her eyes welled up as her voice shook. "Could of, should of, would of. That's what it'll say on my tombstone—*Regrets Only*."

Embarrassed, Anne studied the Degas again. The dancers faced away from one another, each absorbed in her own body. Their faces were indistinct, their limbs elongated, a portrait of concentration, of solitude. After a few moments, she turned back to Mrs. Zambini, who appeared to have composed herself.

"I've been thinking about what you said earlier. About how people keep dying here."

"Teri doesn't want to hear it. She thinks I'm being morbid."

"I don't. I went back and looked at the obits in the paper. Thirteen deaths in the last three months. Most recently, Beatrice Weissman, Ernest Kamber, and Myra Stanton."

Mrs. Zambini flapped a hand at the door. "Could you close that?"

"Sure."

Anne got up and shut the door, which let out a sharp squeak when she closed it. Then she sat down again on the bed.

"Myra was my roommate," Mrs. Zambini said sadly. "A bit of a fussbudget, but we got along. They're supposed to stick somebody new in here next week."

"What did she die of?"

"Congestive heart failure, they said. But I don't believe it." Mrs. Zambini reached up and stroked her chin. Her hand was streaked with thick green veins. "Myra was a diabetic. She had osteoarthritis. And she'd been operated on twice for carpal tunnel syndrome. Her hands bothered her a lot. She had trouble picking things up. But there was nothing wrong with her heart. She never complained of chest pains. Never appeared short of breath. To my knowledge, she wasn't taking any heart medication."

"Could Myra have had a heart condition without any obvious symptoms?"

Mrs. Zambini frowned, the wrinkles in her forehead deepening. "I suppose. But it was all so peculiar."

"What was?"

"The way it happened. It was a Thursday. I remember because we had a pottery class that morning and Myra didn't want to go because she wasn't feeling well."

"What was wrong?"

"She thought it was something she ate. She was nauseous. She had some diarrhea. And her stomach hurt. I almost stayed here with her, but I was out of sorts myself and sometimes it's better to pretend you're interested in

things, instead of sitting around feeling blue. Anyhow, I
went. I stayed for about fifteen minutes staring at an ashtray I was supposed to glaze, until I thought, 'Who am I
kidding? No one smokes anymore.' So I came back."

Mrs. Zambini paused and took a breath.

"Myra was sprawled in her bed," she continued,
"which was unlike her. Once she'd made up her bed in
the morning, she never got in it again until it was time
to go to sleep. She could walk pretty well. Wouldn't
dream of using a wheelchair. When I left for the class,
she was sitting in that chair watching *Matlock* on TV."
Mrs. Zambini pointed to an ugly wooden armchair across
the room, upholstered in saffron-colored vinyl. "Fifteen
minutes later, she was dead. If she'd had a heart attack
or heart failure or whatever, wouldn't it have happened
in the chair? The program had just started."

"When you got back to the room, Ms. Stanton was in
bed? Under the covers?"

"Yes. I tried to revive her." Mrs. Zambini's voice
cracked. "When I couldn't, I called for help. But it was
too late. She was gone."

Anne sat quietly for a few moments, looking around
the room. She noticed a series of spots on the ceilings—
an unmistakable sign of leaks. This place needed a thor-
ough inspection by the Buildings Department, not to
mention the Board of Health.

"Do you know how the others died? Mr. Kamber and
Miss Weissman?"

"Heart trouble, I think. Heart attack. Congestive heart
failure. The staff won't talk about death. I asked once,
about a friend of mine, a cranky old bird, tough as steel.
You know what they told me? 'She's gone to a better
place.' Hell, yes, I wanted to shout. Anyplace is better
than here. Even the great beyond."

There was a sudden rap on the door and it swung open
with a loud squeak.

A frightened expression crossed the elderly woman's
face. She looked like a deer that had wandered onto a

dark highway at night and suddenly sensed the presence of danger.

A nurse in a white uniform poked her head in, the same one who'd walked by when Anne and Mrs. Zambini were talking in the Activity Room. "Ten to nine," the nurse announced brightly. She was a bottle blonde with faintly pockmarked skin and the alert, wary expression of a rabbit expecting to be snapped up by an unexpected trap. On her blue nametag it said *K. Crowley.* "Let's wrap things up, shall we? Visiting hours are almost over."

"I was just getting ready to leave," Anne said.

The nurse smiled and ducked out of the room, leaving the door ajar.

"I'll be back tomorrow," Anne told Mrs. Zambini. "Would you like me to bring you anything? Magazines? Food?"

"Actually, I have a birthday present. For Teri. Could you get it for me?" She pointed to the bureau. "It's in the bottom drawer."

Anne went over to the bureau and removed a small package wrapped in flowered paper and tied with a floppy pink ribbon.

"Her birthday was three weeks ago," Mrs. Zambini said. "But she hasn't been by to visit. I do hate to be late with my gift."

Her expression was so wistful, so full of suppressed longing it made Anne sad. She thought of her mother, shunted from one nursing home to the next, living out her last years among strangers.

"Sure," Anne said, though the last person she wanted to see was Teri Curley. "I'll drop it off. No problem."

"There's one more thing," Mrs. Zambini said. "If you wouldn't mind, that is. I've asked Teri to get me some new paintbrushes. Could you see if she has them yet? The ones here are worn and stiff."

"Okay. You have a good night." Anne headed for the door, then stopped and turned back. "Can I ask you something? You seem wary of the nursing staff. Why?"

Mrs. Zambini fixed Anne with her clear blue eyes. "They're a nasty bunch, the whole lot of them. Greta Koch pretends to care, but she's got a real mean streak. Anna—the night nurse—she makes fun of people behind their backs. Sue Strunk would love for every last one of us to meet our maker so she wouldn't have to change another bedpan or hook up another feeding tube. And Katie, the one who was just in here, she pinches something fierce."

"Pinches?" Anne repeated.

"When you won't take your meds. Oh, they put on a good show for outsiders. But you have to be careful. The worst one is Hillyard. She's a cold bit of goods. Runs this place with an iron fist. I keep my nose clean, try not to attract attention."

Mrs. Zambini paused. Her expression was watchful. She gazed at the door, as if she expected the nurse to return any moment. Her voice was a cracked whisper. "So many have died. Better safe than sorry."

Chapter 11

*The best position for
sitting on a roof is with
your lower leg flat and the
upper one bent up with
the sole of your shoe on
the shingles. This position
helps center you and
prevents you from leaning
dangerously in either
direction.*

When Anne got back to the house, Jack was still in her office, talking on the phone. She was just heading upstairs when the doorbell rang. She went back down, opened the front door, and was met by a blinding white light. She blinked, startled. Colored spots danced through the air. She stepped back, throwing her hand up in front of her face.

"Anne Hardaway?" said an unfamiliar male voice.

"What?" she stammered. "Who are you?"

The man lowered his camera, looking pleased with himself. Standing on her porch was the skinny photographer from the *Landsdown Park Press* who she'd seen on the street the day before.

"I'm from the *Press*. I want to talk to you. About your skeleton."

"It's late," she said.

The photographer shrugged. Up close, he didn't look a day over twenty-one. Small brown eyes, bad teeth, all elbows and knees. He appeared to be trying to grow a beard and failing.

"I'm a photojournalist. And this is a big story. You going to talk to me or what?" he said, his tone hopeful, but cautious.

Anne pointed past him, at the beach that wasn't. The tide had risen. White sprays of foam licked the asphalt on Ocean Avenue. "There's your story. The storm and its aftermath. Look at my lawn."

He turned around and looked, taking in the bench, the broken driftwood, the tawny waist-high sand piles.

"Everybody's covering the storm," he said, pausing to study the lawn. A loose piece of siding flapped against the roof. "Besides," he added eagerly, trying to win her over, "no one else at the paper knows about this yet. It's kind of a scoop."

Anne sighed. The Heights was a small town. You couldn't keep a buried skeleton quiet forever. But she didn't have to speed the process along.

"Sorry," she said, shutting the door.

He stuck his dirty sneaker out and wedged it in the frame. "Wait. How'd the skeleton end up in your basement?"

"If you don't remove your shoe," Anne said evenly, putting all her weight against the door, "you're going to need foot surgery."

He yanked his sneaker out of the way and stepped back just in time. The door slammed so loud it scared the cat, who crouched in a corner, looking peeved. Anne crossed the hall and entered her office.

Jack was sitting in front of his laptop, with his feet propped up on her desk.

"Is somebody here?" he asked.

"A reporter, asking about the skeleton. But he's gone. Did you get your work done?"

He swung his feet off the desk hurriedly, a guilty expression on his face, like she'd caught him doing something illegal. She glanced at the screen. It was blank.

"Not all of it," he said. "You got a fax from Jennifer Joan. It's about a mile long. I left it in the machine."

"Jennifer Joan can wait," she said. "I think we should talk about what's going on between us."

"Okay." He leaned back in the chair and waited for her to begin. He'd changed into gray sweats and a navy blue T-shirt that said *JMG Architects*. His hair was wet from the shower, slicked back from his face. He looked like a football player unwinding after the big game.

"I don't want a big fancy wedding," she said slowly. "I don't want to get married in New York. In fact, when you get right down to it, I don't want to live there either. This is my home. This house. In Oceanside Heights."

"I thought you were the one who said marriage was about compromise."

"What would that be exactly? A condo in Ft. Lee? An expanded split in Montclair?" She wished she sounded less defensive. But Jack seemed so sure of himself, so sure of what was best for her.

Jack cleared his throat. "Anne, I like my work, I'm good at what I do, and I'm not leaving the firm. It's just not an option. You, on the other hand, could work anywhere, write from anyplace. What's the big deal? It's not like you've got tons of friends and family here."

His words stung her. That was the problem with revealing things about yourself; what you said could easily be turned against you. She twisted a strand of hair between her fingers, a nervous habit. "I might not win any popularity contests," she said carefully, "but that doesn't mean I want to uproot my whole world. This house means a lot to me. You know that. It's all I have left of my mother. She asked me not to sell it. I made her a promise."

Jack switched off his laptop.

"Then we'll use it as a summer house," he said. "A weekend getaway."

She found a split end and snapped it off. What could she say? He made a good case. So why wasn't she sold on it?

He seemed to sense her confusion and misread it. "I don't want us to have a long distance marriage," he said emphatically. "It won't work."

"Look, we don't have to settle anything right this minute," Anne said. When in doubt, procrastinate. Not the best way to solve a problem, but it would do for now.

"Fine," Jack said. But he didn't look fine. His eyes had a flinty cast and his expression was tense.

"I'm really exhausted," she said. "I can barely keep my eyes open."

He nodded and reached for the phone.

She was so tired she stumbled on her way up the stairs and almost fell. No sexy nightgown tonight. Without bothering to change clothes, she got into bed, flopped onto her stomach, and immediately went to sleep.

She woke with a start, her heart pounding. In the dream, her mother was still alive, baking banana bread. The kitchen smelled heavenly, the air thick with the bread's hot doughy scent. Evelyn was at the sink, the sleeves of her flowered dress pushed up past her elbows, patting the bread into neat, perfect loaves. Her red hair spilled down her back. Water was running in the sink. Sunlight streamed in through the open window. A summer afternoon, hot, delectable. Anne heard the faraway pounding of the ocean and the screech of gulls.

She could almost taste the bread. *Not yet*, Evelyn told her gaily. *Not till it's ready*. Heat broke from the oven in waves. Anne crept closer to the sink, closer to her mother who was kneading the bread, standing on tiptoe to plunge her fingers into the dough. *Not yet.* Anne peered into the silver baking tin and drew back, horrified. The dough was mushy, tinged with pink. A stew of flesh, bone, and flour. The odor was sickly sweet, putrid. Her mother stirred it with the big wooden spoon, smiling as she worked, an icy, self-satisfied smile that made Anne scream and scream.

When she woke up she was sweating, tangled in a nest of sheets. She could feel the blood pulsing in her temples, the dream as real as the clock on the night table that flashed 2:50 A.M. She rolled over and tried to push the nightmare away. But she couldn't stop seeing it—her mother, the sunlit kitchen, that awful stew. Beside her, Jack was snoring. The sleeping cat was stretched out on top of the armoire.

She went into the bathroom and splashed cold water on her face. Then, without returning to the bedroom, she padded downstairs, flicking lights on as she went. In her office, she flung the window open and let the cool ocean air into the room. It had a sharp, salty tang. She took deep breaths, trying to clear her brain. The dream had upset her and she wanted to shake it loose, or bury it so deep she'd forget she'd ever conjured it up. She turned on the computer, reassured by its steady hum, by the whirring of the phone wires that summoned up the Internet.

She hadn't checked her e-mail in a couple of days. There was lots of junk: companies hawking scanners and adult videos and assorted get rich quick schemes. She deleted them all, then logged onto the World Wide Web. Using a search engine, she entered the words "congestive heart failure." Over a thousand entries were listed. She whittled it down to 750, then 300, then 100, taking her time, trying to find the clearest, most comprehensive sites. She printed out the information from the best ones, and settled on the loveseat to read through them.

Congestive heart failure, known as CHF, was the inability of the heart to keep the blood moving, which in turn, caused congestion in the lungs and later, in other tissues of the body. There was a big link between heart attacks and CHF. Twenty percent of people who'd suffered a heart attack developed CHF within six years. Three million people had the disease; over 400,000 new cases were diagnosed each year. It accounted for more hospital visits by people over the age of sixty-five than any other ailment. Only half of the patients lived more than five years. Of those, only fifteen percent of women survived longer than eight to twelve years.

Anne leafed through the material detailing causes of the disease (hypertension, anemia, coronary artery disease, alcohol or drug abuse, inflammation of the heart muscle). She studied the symptoms and the treatments (Cedilanid-D, Crystodigin, Digoxin), beta-blockers, ACE inhibitors, the effectiveness of herbal medicines, how to combat CHF with a healthy, low-fat diet. *Death by deception*, one doctor called it. *A hidden killer because the body hides the disease until it's too late.*

As she read, a faint blue light seeped into the room. Although she'd only had four hours of sleep, she felt alert, centered. She turned off the lamp and went over to the window. Outside, a faint glow illuminated the horizon. She watched as a pink wash appeared in the sky, quickening to streaks of scarlet orange. It was still dark out. She could hear the ocean pelting the beach. She was about to turn away when she saw a car parked across the street. Someone was hunched down in the driver's seat, but she couldn't make out the face. Pulling the curtain back, she watched the driver watch her house. What was the person doing out there? Anne glanced at her watch. Six-thirty A.M. She walked out into the hall and opened the front door. As soon as she stepped outside, the car gunned its engine and sped down Ocean Avenue, heading south. A rusty white Ford, from the looks of it. Before she could make out the license plate, the car turned the corner and disappeared from view.

There was no way to tell how long the driver had been sitting there or why he or she was casing her house. Her thoughts flew to the skeleton. What if the person who'd killed Steven Hillyard was still around? What did that mean for her?

Her appointment with Stuart Hillyard was at eleven. The overweight nurse wasn't at her usual post. In fact, the waiting room was deserted, and the door to Dr. Hillyard's office was closed. She heard the low murmur of his voice from behind it. She sat down on the couch in the waiting room. She was twenty minutes early. She would have arrived even earlier except she'd stopped off at Dunkin' Donuts for a toasted coconut and a cup of the world's best coffee.

Jack had been up on the roof when she'd left, repairing the shingles and tacking down the torn aluminum siding. It annoyed her that he'd begun working on the house, even after she'd repeatedly told him not to. She was beginning to feel like the whole thing was a mistake. The engagement. His visit. Everything. Why couldn't they leave things the way they were? Seeing each other a few times a month, talking on the phone. It seemed like a more sensible arrangement than spending twenty-four hours a day together, every single day.

She twisted his ring over her knuckle, then pushed it back. When you came right down to it, she wasn't good at compromise. But it wasn't just the house. Or whether she'd have to move to New York. Ever since Friday night, when Jack had arrived, she'd been feeling antsy, claustrophobic almost. She was aware of his presence, his stuff, in ways she hadn't been before. His shaving kit in the bathroom, his clothes hanging in the closet, the drawer she'd cleared for him to use, the food he'd brought neatly stacked in Tupperware containers in the refrigerator. Little things, except it felt like he was taking over, invading her life. His cologne seemed to overpower the house, lingering in the air long after he'd left the room.

They'd never really fought much before. How could you fight with someone who lived sixty miles away? But it was clear that the more time they spent together, the more they were going to argue. The thing about Jack was he liked being in control, taking charge of a situation, fiddling with the details until they formed a perfect whole. It made sense, his being an architect. What were buildings really? Structured bits of stone and brick, each element carefully planned out, with nothing left to chance. And let's face it, she wasn't exactly a pushover. She wanted what she wanted when she wanted it, period—with no delays, no backseat driving, no unasked-for second opinions.

She sat down on the couch in the waiting room. On the table next to some magazines was a black looseleaf folder. She picked it up and opened it. Inside were a bunch of press clippings, mostly from small newspapers, free weeklies that survived on advertising and the summer tourist trade. Anne leafed through the articles. "Hypno Doc Helps You Shed Pounds." "Stop Smoking, Start Living." "Hypnosis Boosts Self Confidence."

She couldn't believe she was doing this, spending a hundred bucks to discuss Jack with a hypnotherapist. He'd freak if he found out. Privacy was important to Jack. She guessed that came with the territory when you were the son of an alcoholic. There'd be family secrets you'd never reveal, stories you'd never tell out loud.

She was about to put the book down when she noticed a yellowed article stuck to the back of the next to last page. "Doctors Found Clinic to Combat Anxiety." Her eyes shifted to the photo at the right, then to the date: September 12, 1973. In the picture, a younger Philip Reynolds was standing next to another man. Both men wore white lab coats and were probably in their midforties. So this was Hillyard. Dark hair, beard, thin face. Not drop-dead gorgeous, but attractive in an understated way. He looked like a folk singer or a Save the Planet type. He gazed straight ahead at the camera, his lips parted in a half smile, his eyes suggesting a certain raw intelligence. His expression was serious, but kindly, his lips parted every so slightly, faint lines crinkling the corners of his eyes. He looked like a guy you'd want to know better, a guy you'd trust to hypnotize you. He didn't look like he was going to wind up with a bullet hole through his skull.

Anne began reading:

Dr. Steven Hillyard and Dr. Philip Reynolds, both local psychiatrists, have founded the Stress Reduction Clinic in Neptune. The clinic, which opened its doors to the public last Monday, will treat physical and emotional responses to stress and help patients live a healthier, stress-free life.

"When you're stressed, your body goes through a series of changes," explained Dr. Hillyard. "You may experience heart palpitations, dizziness, dry mouth, shortness of breath, insomnia, panic attacks, and a host of other related symptoms. Our job at the clinic is to get to the root of what's bothering you and help you address the problem in a calm, straightforward manner."

Techniques for destressing include psychotherapy, biofeedback, meditation, and hypnosis. The clinic accepts referrals from physicians, but you need not be under a doctor's care to enter the Stress Reduction program.

"Sometimes, people are aware that something's wrong, that they're constantly anxious and tense, but they dismiss it because it's not a clearly defined illness like influenza or pneumonia," Dr. Reynolds said. "We want to improve the quality of your life by deconstructing the symptoms and attacking the underlying issues. Stress is a disease. If left untreated, it can have far-reaching consequences on your health and well-being."

Anne closed the book and set it back on the table. So Reynolds and Hillyard were partners. Interesting. Had her mother gone to the Stress Reduction Clinic? Was that how she'd met Hillyard Senior? Anne tried to picture it: her mother, sitting straight and tall, twisting a handkerchief in her hands, and telling Dr. Steven Hillyard about the embarrassing, hateful things she'd done. Not knowing it was beyond her control. Trying to make sense of behavior she herself called insane.

The door to Stuart Hillyard's office swung open and Hillyard walked out. "Anne, hello," he said heartily. "Good to see you."

As she stood up and followed Hillyard into his office, she got a weird sense of deja vu, the link between father and son echoing the link between her and Evelyn. The papers on Hillyard's desk had been arranged into piles, but otherwise, the room appeared the same as it had yesterday—claustrophobic and dingy. The microphone rested on a stack of books.

"How have you been?" Hillyard asked, when Anne was seated in the Barcalounger with her feet resting on the ottoman.

"Okay," she lied, not wanting to tell him about her insomnia or what was causing it.

"How are things going with Jack?"

"We got engaged and we had . . . um . . . a fight. A disagreement," she amended, "about the date of our wedding."

Stuart Hillyard laced his fingers together and smiled. He wore a polkadot bowtie over a striped shirt. The tie was tilted to the left. It made him look like an absentminded professor. "Then you're moving forward. That's wonderful."

"I guess." Anne shifted her weight in the chair, wishing the office had a window. The room felt airless and dry, and she sensed a tickle forming in her throat. "Actually, I'm not one hundred percent sure."

Hillyard opened a desk drawer and took out a rectangular cardboard lid with a circular bulls-eye painted on it. Each ring of the bulls-eye was painted a different color: red, yellow, and green. Anne noticed there was a shallow hole cut into the middle of each colored band. At the bottom of the lid was a small silver ball on a silver chain.

"Here," Hillyard said, handing the lid and the chain across the desk to Anne. "Rest it on your lap."

She did so, feeling foolish.

"Now pick up the chain with both hands and hold it above the red part, over the little hole."

Again, Anne did as she was instructed. The ball hung straight down from the chain, an inch above the hole cut into the lid.

"Make sure the ball is perfectly still," Hillyard said.

Anne looked down. The ball was suspended in the air. She could feel the tickle in her throat getting worse.

"Now," Hillyard said, "I want you to move the ball. But not with your hands. With your mind."

"Huh?"

"Concentrate very hard. Will the ball to move. But don't use your hands. That's cheating."

Feeling ridiculous, Anne stared at the little silver ball she was holding and silently commanded it to swing back and forth. Thirty seconds passed, then a minute. The ball remained motionless.

"All right," Hillyard announced. "Time's up. What have we learned?"

Anne looked at him blankly. Then the tickle got the best of her and she started to cough. "That hypnosis is a crock?" she gasped.

Hillyard threw back his head and laughed. His brown beard bobbed merrily up and down. "We've learned that there are no magic tricks here. Nobody can will inanimate objects to move, just like nobody can put you in some kind of trance and make you cluck like a chicken."

"That's good to know," Anne said dryly. "I'd make a lousy chicken."

"See, most people have the wrong conception about how hypnosis works," Hillyard explained. "You never lose control. Never."

Anne wondered if he went through this spiel with everybody who walked into his office. Probably. It'd be a real hit at parties. She sneaked a glance at her watch. Ten minutes had elapsed. Sixteen dollars down the drain.

"So are you game for the real thing?"

Anne hesitated. He seemed on the level, but in the back of her mind she envisioned a possible TV expose: "What Hypno Doc Made Me Do, Next Geraldo."

"If you don't respond to the hypnosis," Hillyard said, "there's no charge for the session."

"Great," Anne said, unsure how he'd be able to tell if she was faking or not.

"I'd like to record the session and give you a tape to take home."

A tape. Now there was a concept. Jack working away on the exterior of the house, while inside, she listened to a recording saying, "You must commit . . . you must commit . . . you must commit . . ."

"Now then." Hillyard moved the microphone closer to his face and flicked several buttons on a black stereo near his desk. "Close your eyes and take several deep cleansing breaths."

She leaned her head back against the chair, shut her eyes, and breathed in through her nose and out through her mouth. She was incredibly tired, jet-lagged almost. Her body felt heavy, weighed down with stones.

Hillyard cleared his throat. "Trust," he intoned, "is a precious gift, not to be taken lightly. During the course of your life, you may encounter someone about whom you have strong feelings, someone you love very deeply."

She wondered if he was making this up as he went

along or reading from a prepared script. But it required too much effort to open her eyes and peek.

"Sometimes loving this person can be easier than trusting them. Love is long walks in the rain, romantic candlelit dinners, two hands reaching out, two hearts connecting."

Great, Anne thought sleepily. A talking Hallmark card.

"When you love, you do so unconsciously and the feeling is as natural and as easy as breathing. But trust. Trust is different. Trust is harder."

Hillyard's voice was bland and modulated, the aural equivalent of vanilla ice cream.

She tried to pay attention, to take in what he was saying. But she was so tired, so physically and emotionally exhausted, that his words slid together, like the innocuous tapping of rain on a roof.

After a few minutes, her head listed to one side and she promptly fell asleep.

Chapter 12

If you live in an area prone to storms, consider this: according to the U.S. Forest Service, the sturdiest tree specimens are live oak, bald cypress, black gum, sweet gum, Southern red oak, magnolia, white oak, beech, sugar maple, and sycamore.

She woke with a start and opened her eyes. Stuart Hillyard was studying her intently.

"How are you feeling?" he inquired gently, as if she'd just run a marathon or stepped off the mammoth roller coaster at Great Adventure.

"I . . ." Anne glanced at her watch. It was five of twelve. She'd slept through the whole thing. "I'm fine."

She actually did feel better after the nap. Clear-headed, alert. Maybe she should play a tape of Hillyard's voice before she went to bed each night. It was more effective than a glass of warm milk. But at these prices, she couldn't afford to nod off.

"Hypnosis is always difficult the first time," Hillyard said, his tone reassuring. "People don't know what to expect. And of course, they're apprehensive."

Was it possible he hadn't noticed she'd been snoozing? Had he mistaken her somnolence for a hypnotic trance?

"You know, I might have missed some of what you were saying," Anne told him.

"Not to worry. Sometimes the power of hypnosis is so strong it's hard to take everything in. That's why I'm giving you the tape."

Anne watched him rummage through his desk. In 1974, when his father disappeared, Stuart Hillyard would have been in his mid to late twenties, just starting out, probably not living at home anymore. She wondered what kind of an impact his father's disappearance had had on him. You couldn't experience something that traumatic and not have it affect you, not have it change your life. Had he searched for Hillyard Senior himself, hired a detective, identified unknown bodies at the morgue, turning away with relief at the very last moment? Had he eventually decided that his father was never coming back, so that some days he didn't think about it at all, or did the mystery eat away at him still?

Stuart Hillyard looked contented, exempt from pain or disappointment. Odd how both he and Claire seemed untouched by the vanishing. But then what had she expected? Twenty-three years had gone by. The anguish had to have faded.

Only how would they feel when they found out Steven Hillyard had been killed and left to rot in a cramped, dusty basement? For they would find out, of that Anne was certain. She wondered if the news would come as a relief.

"Aahh," Hillyard said, smiling. "Here we are."

He'd finally located what he was looking for: a small

manila envelope. Sliding the tape inside, he came around his desk and handed it to Anne.

"I hope you found the session helpful," he said cheerfully. "I recommend playing the tape once a day."

As she took the envelope, his fingers brushed against hers. His eyes were warm and kindly behind his gold-rimmed glasses.

He beamed down at her and for a moment she half expected him to recite some sort of blessing. "Will that be cash or check?"

Margaret Zambini's daughter lived in a rambling Queen Anne–style "cottage" that was traditionally the last stop on the Historic Preservation Society's annual house and garden tour. Lord only knew why anyone ever bothered to call Teri's house a cottage. It was the largest, most elaborate house in town, built at the turn of the century and loaded with fancy ornaments—balconies, turrets, projecting bay windows, brackets, fancy molding, enough lacy looking gingerbread to fill up a children's storybook, and a massive stone chimney. The outside had an asymmetrical front, and a steeply gabled roof. It had been constructed from a melange of brick, clapboard, and shingles, as if the architect couldn't make up his mind which material he preferred. All of these elements made the house stand out. But the real reason you couldn't miss Teri's "cottage" was its color—four shades of pink ranging from pale dusty rose to a deep, burnished salmon.

The storm had not bypassed Teri's pride and joy. A pine tree had crashed onto the sidewalk, narrowly missing the house. The pink picket fence was down, and some of the shingles had come off the facade.

As Anne climbed the steep front steps, a little girl in a white tutu and tights opened the front door and stared out at her. The girl had Teri's kewpie-doll lips and dark straight hair. Was it Tara? Tess?

"Mommy," one of the three T's yelled. "Somebody's here!"

The girl ducked back inside the house, leaving Anne on the doorstep. This was a spur of the moment visit. She'd planned on having lunch with Jack, at Jean's Sandwich Shack or Gingerbreads, but when she'd called to arrange it, he'd said he had too much work. Something about a botched elevator installation in the Tribeca hotel project, which meant Anne had the entire afternoon to herself. She was both disappointed and relieved. Jack would be going home later the same day and there was still so much that needed to be resolved between them.

Still, who'd have thought she'd be spending a perfectly good Sunday afternoon dropping in on Teri Curley? Back in the fourth grade, Anne and Teri had been inseparable—the "Bobbsey Twins" Mrs. Zambini had called them. Teri became the sister Anne never had. Not a day went by without one of them ensconced in the other's house. They did homework together, got crushes on the same boys, experimented with lipstick, talked for hours on the phone. But that changed a few years later when Anne's mother started acting crazy, and Teri turned from best friend to chief tormentor. It had been Anne's first lesson in betrayal. She could still remember the vile names Teri had called her mother, the way Teri used to pick on her, then ignore her in school, as if she were invisible. She remembered crying herself to sleep, wishing she'd never met Teri Zambini, trying unsuccessfully to erase from her memory all the fun they'd had together, all the secrets they'd shared.

Just then, Teri came to the door smiling the smile you'd flash at a tax collector or a salesman peddling Fuller brushes. Over the years, she'd refined her hostility toward Anne, adopting a phony cordiality when they met by accident at the Mini-Mart or Moby's Hardware. Acting as though she were the beneficent grand dame and Anne was the little match girl. It drove Anne nuts.

"Annie," Teri exclaimed, surveying Anne like an aphid that had landed on her prize rosebushes. "Good to see you."

Teri's long black hair was pulled back in a pony tail, and she wore tight black stretch pants and an emerald green cable knit sweater. She had beautiful skin—pale, flawless, like a porcelain doll—and she accentuated it expertly with carefully placed hints of blush and powder. In all the years Anne had known her, she'd never seen Teri look disheveled or tired or just plain stressed out. Marriage to Bobby Curley, who owned Curley Construction Co., meant she had plenty of money to spend on herself and her house. And though people claimed money couldn't buy happiness, Teri seemed determined to prove them wrong.

"I probably should have called first," Anne said carefully. If she'd phoned, she knew Teri would have made up an excuse not to see her.

"That's okay," Teri said. She was blocking the doorway and didn't seem inclined to invite Anne in. "But now's not the best time. I'm in the middle of lunch and . . ." She hesitated ever so slightly. "My dad dropped by."

Uh oh, Anne thought to herself. *A visit from Daddy. For Teri, this was worse than a bad hair day.* Teri Zambini Curley was ashamed of her father. Anne knew she'd always been ashamed of him ever since they were kids. Teri had grown up across town from where she lived now, in a campground cottage that reflected its name, a small-scale, narrow house with a double-leafed door like an opening in a tent. She'd worn hand-me-downs from thrift shops, watched her mother collect plaid stamps, and from the time she learned to talk, had started planning for a better life.

"Peasant stock" was how Teri referred to both of her parents. She'd probably lifted the phrase from a book, and it had stuck with her. "They're good people, but extremely simple," Teri liked saying, making *simple* sound like the worst kind of ignorant. When Teri talked about her childhood, which wasn't often, she cast herself in the role of a princess who'd been unceremoniously deposited with the court stable hands.

"Actually," Anne said. "I came by to give you something. From your mother."

"My mother," Teri echoed. Surprise had made her voice rise an octave.

You know, Anne wanted to say. *The woman you never visit. But then. Who am I to judge? I hated visiting my mother, too.*

"When did you see Margaret?" Teri asked. She looked both stunned and annoyed.

"Yesterday." Anne couldn't help feeling heartened by Teri's discomfort. It was rare for the Ice Princess to lose her composure. "I was taking a tour of the nursing home. Kind of checking it out for my grandmother. Anyway, your mom asked me to drop off your birthday present. And she mentioned something about paintbrushes you have for her. Could I come in?"

Teri hesitated, deciding. "Sure," she said finally. "*Entrez.*"

She ushered Anne into the hallway decorated with massive gilt-edged mirrors and hanging botanical tapestries. Not the usual Heights decor. But then there was a reason why Teri's home was always selected to cap off the house and garden tour. Decorated to a fare-thee-well, it had enough swags, flounces, stenciling, and chintz to outdo Martha Stewart. The dining room was toward the rear, a large salon with a crystal teardrop chandelier, a huge mahogany table and twelve uncomfortable looking ramrod straight chairs that were Louis XIV or XV. Anne could never keep her Louies straight.

Dominick Zambini sat awkwardly at one end of the large table. He was in his late sixties, with ears that stuck out prominently from his head and a broad, beak nose that looked as if it had been broken when he was younger and had never healed properly. His left leg was stretched stiffly out in front of him, next to a wooden cane. (Anne knew his leg had bothered him for years, but she couldn't remember exactly what was wrong with it.) His nose and cheeks were red, splashed with broken capillaries that left him perpetually flushed. His thick gray hair was covered by a Phillies baseball cap that matched his Phillies jacket. He was staring down at the table, where a can of Budweiser rested on a tortoiseshell coaster next to a fluffy looking salad that had barely been touched and a piece of focacia bread. At the other end, a place was set for Teri, with salad and a glass of white wine.

"Daddy," Teri announced brightly. "Look who's here."

Dominick glanced up, nodded to Anne, and resumed studying his beer can. He looked distinctly out of place amid the burgundy velvet drapes and the polished mahogany furniture. A plumber by trade, he could never manage to hold a job for very long without mouthing off to the boss or arguing with a client. Teri used to hate that about him when they were kids. She was embarrassed to have a father who sat around the house in his undershirt all day, watching the soaps. He'd always struck Anne as a man who was itching for a fight. Mad if it rained, mad if it didn't. Woe to the driver who cut him off at a stop sign or the neighbor whose dog took a dump on his lawn. As Dominick Zambini would be the first to tell you, he "didn't take nothing from nobody."

"Could I get you something, Anne?" Teri asked, unenthusiastically.

"No, thanks." She slipped into a chair, reached into her tote bag, and pulled out Teri's birthday present, which she placed on the table.

"I can't imagine why Mother asked you to be her delivery girl," Teri said, gazing at the flowered wrapping and the cheerful pink bow. "My father could have picked this up for me later today. Right, Daddy?"

Dominick Zambini grunted his assent.

Teri picked the present up and tore the paper off. She held the small painting in its Plexiglas frame out in front of her and squinted at it. Poplar trees reflected in a river at dawn. "Oh," Teri exclaimed. "Mother's copied another masterpiece. What do you think, Daddy? Is it Renoir this time?" She tossed the painting on the mahogany side-board and turned back to Anne. "You mentioned something about paintbrushes."

Anne repeated what Mrs. Zambini had told her.

"Just a minute," Teri said. "I'll go get them."

As soon as she disappeared through the swinging door, Dominick Zambini picked up his beer can and took a long, slow swig.

"How you been?" he said to Anne.

"Good. Fine." Then, almost as an afterthought, "I'm engaged." The word still tasted funny on her tongue. *Oh, boy, Dr. Stu. Do you have your work cut out for you.*

The news of her engagement appeared to have absolutely no impact on Dominick Zambini. "S'nice. All the best." He waved his hand at the room. "Fancy spread she's got here, no?" He sounded scornful. "How much money you think it cost, to outfit a house like this?"

"I don't know."

"Twenty grand? Fifty?" He leaned forward, his eyes boring into Anne. "Some folks work their whole lives and never see that kind of money." He took off his cap, looked at it, mashed it back on his head. "So how much you think it's worth?"

"I don't know," Anne said again. "It's not my taste." She found herself wondering who was footing the bill for Maggie Zambini's care. Teri and Bobby, most likely.

Teri came back into the room, holding three thin paint-brushes. "Here we go," she announced. "I picked these up last week when I was getting watercolors for Taylor. Daddy, would you give these to Mother when you see her?" She placed the brushes on the table.

Ignoring them, Mr. Zambini picked up his cane, scraped his chair back, and got to his feet. Most of his weight rested on his right leg. The left one was slightly bent at the knee. "I got to be going," he said gruffly.

"Of course you do," Teri replied, with forced gaiety.

"Say hello to Mother for me. Tell her I might stop by a week from Wednesday, if I get a chance."

Dominick Zambini looked hard at Teri. He leaned on his cane, but made no move to leave.

For a long moment, father and daughter stared at one another, like two gunslingers in a Western movie. Teri blinked first. She went over to the sideboard and opened one of its slender drawers. Reaching inside, she took out a pale pink check. "Well," she said reluctantly. "Here you are."

Her father stuck out his hand and grabbed the check. His expression was both ashamed and angry. He muttered something under his breath, stuck the check in his pocket, and limped to the door, without looking back.

Teri examined her French manicure. Her bottom lip stuck out in a pout. "Thanks for stopping by," she said to Anne. "We should really do lunch one of these days."

"Sure," Anne said, matching Teri's insincere tone. "I'll call you." She spotted the brushes on the table and picked them up. "Your dad forgot these. I'll give them to him."

She walked back through the house, let herself out, and caught up to Teri's father on the front lawn. It was a gorgeous fall afternoon. A boy on a bicycle rode by and threw a newspaper wrapped in plastic on the Curleys's front steps. "If you're heading over to Sunnydale now, I could give you a ride," Anne offered. She brandished the brushes. "I'd like to deliver these in person." And have another crack at Claire Hillyard while I'm at it, she added silently.

"Thanks. My car's in the shop."

Even with the limp, he moved at a brisk pace. Why wasn't he the one taking care of his wife? For most people, a nursing home was the absolute last resort. Why dump your wife with strangers if you didn't have to? Anne watched him climb into the Mustang, favoring his left leg. Another one of Teri's dark-haired daughters was jumping in a pile of leaves on the lawn. She waved at her grandfather, but he didn't seem to notice.

As the car sped toward Sunnydale, Anne found herself thinking about the check Teri had given her father. Was it a one-time thing? A regular allowance? The exchange had been conducted with resentment on both sides. Dominick Zambini still looked furious. He sat rigidly in the passenger seat, his hands balled up into fists, his jaw muscles clenched. She tried making small talk with him, but gave up halfway there. Instead, she flicked on the radio to a station playing hits from the 1970s.

The songs were upbeat and safe—boppy bubble gum music for the Me Generation. In the '70s, her mother had gone crazy and her father had walked out of their lives for good. So much for smiley face buttons and "have a nice day." In retrospect, Evelyn Hardaway had picked the wrong decade to check out. It would have been easier in the '90s, when experiencing mental illness—not to mention talking about it on *Oprah*—was almost chic.

Anne braked at a storm-damaged stop sign that spun crazily in the wind, and stared through the windshield at the road ahead. On the radio, Gloria Gaynor was belting out "I Will Survive." Anne was quick to blame Dominick Zambini and Teri for abandoning Mrs. Zambini. But really, she herself had been no better. She'd couldn't stand seeing Evelyn in nursing homes—she'd dreaded every minute of those visits. Half the time, her mother didn't know who Anne was and acted like she didn't much care. She could picture Evelyn now, the confused eyes, the trembling hands, talking dirty, fouling her clothes. She felt ashamed for them both. Beneath the Alzheimer's, who had Evelyn Hardaway been? A woman who'd betrayed her husband with a lover? A woman desperate and troubled enough to commit murder? Or a woman whose strength and courage was overlooked by her own daughter? Anne wanted to peel away the layers of Evelyn's life and find a bright, hard kernel of truth that was bigger than the illness, that made her mother whole again.

"Hey," Dominick Zambini said. "We just gonna sit here all day?"

"Nope."

Anne stepped on the gas and the car slid forward.

Chapter 13

> *To test if paint is sound,
> use a utility knife to cut a
> small X in the paint film.
> Apply the tape part of a
> Band-Aid to the X and pull
> it off sharply. If the paint
> comes off, it means it has
> to be removed.*

When they got to Sunnydale, it was one-thirty. As soon as they walked through the sliding doors, Dominick Zambini's eyes glazed over and his body tensed up even more. Anne recognized the symptoms: Nursing Home Aversion. She'd experienced it herself on numerous occasions. In Mr. Zambini's case, it got more pronounced the longer it took to find his wife. She wasn't in her room, or the Day Room (where the TV was switched to a program on romantic inns of America) or the Activity Room (where finished decorated pumpkins were lined up along the windowsill, and another project was beginning: adorning Styrofoam turkeys with feathers and pipe cleaners).

She wasn't in the physical therapy area or the dining room either, although Anne did see Chester Higgins up on a ladder, examining the peeling paint along one of the corridors. She was about to ask a nurse for assistance when they came upon Maggie and her friend, Andrew Deretchin, sipping tea in a small room lined with candy, snack, and drink machines on the first floor. Their two wheelchairs were pulled up to a table. They had their heads together and were speaking in low, hushed tones.

"Dominick," Maggie said, glancing up. A thin smiled played on her lips. She wore a powder blue sweater that was two sizes too big over what looked like a baggy white housedress. "I wasn't expecting you till three. You remember Drew."

Anne saw Dominick Zambini's face as he looked at them. It seemed to darken, turning a deeper shade of red. His teeth were clenched and his eyes blazed. He started to speak, stopped, then jammed his hands into the pockets of his jacket and glared at his wife.

"I take it Teri's not with you," Maggie Zambini said, after Anne had given her the brushes and said hello to Andrew Deretchin.

"She might come a week from Wednesday," Dominick Zambini rasped. Anger had thickened his voice. But Anne saw it was directed at his wife, not the absent Teri.

"A week from Wednesday," Maggie echoed. She didn't bother trying to mask her disappointment. It played upon her face like an old, familiar song. As for her husband's anger, she seemed oblivious to it, although Andrew Deretchin was staring at Mr. Zambini with curiosity. Anne had sat down, but Dominick Zambini still stood, his weight resting on his good leg. He looked almost like a cartoon character standing there. Anne could picture steam coming out of his ears. The knuckles that grasped his cane were white.

"Quite a storm, wasn't it?" Andrew Deretchin said conversationally. "I'm surprised this old place wasn't blown clear off the map." Deretchin had a courtly, old-world charm that didn't quite match his features. There was a cruel, almost greedy quality to his mouth. His eyes bored into you, as if he were figuring out what made you tick and how he could tamper with the machinery.

Everyone agreed that the northeaster was powerful, and then the group lapsed into an uncomfortable silence.

"Dom, please sit down," Maggie said. "Tell me about Teri. Did you get a look at the new kitchen?"

Dominick Zambini drew in his breath and exhaled loudly through his teeth. Turning to his wife, he hissed, "You can't keep away from the men, even in this place."

"What?" Maggie said weakly. Her face had turned a shade paler. Her hands plucked nervously at her sweater. "Sit down, Dominick. Have a cup of hot chocolate. It's delicious, from the machine."

"How long has it been going on?" Mr. Zambini shouted. "You and this one?"

Andrew Deretchin surveyed him with bemusement. "What on earth are you suggesting, sir? Have you lost your mind? There's nothing untoward between myself and your wife."

"Why dredge this up?" Maggie said to her husband. "Are you deliberately trying to upset me?"

The look Dominick Zambini gave her could have turned salt to stone. "You won't make a fool of me again," he spat out, nearly choking on his wrath. "Not again."

He looked flushed, invigorated, ten years younger than he had twenty minutes ago. It occurred to Anne that his rage was fueling him, keeping him going.

"Dominick," Maggie pleaded. "That's enough."

Anne felt a flash of sympathy for her. It couldn't have been easy to be married to this man, to be on the receiving end of his fiery temper.

"Do what you want," Zambini yelled. He scowled at Deretchin. "Just leave me out of it."

With that, he wheeled around and limped from the room.

"I'm so sorry," Maggie said quietly, when he had gone. "Please excuse him. He hasn't been himself lately."

"The man visits once a week, for a measly forty-five minutes," Deretchin mused, "and this is how he behaves. It's disgraceful, Margaret. Simply disgraceful."

"I'm sorry," Mrs. Zambini repeated. "Please, let's not speak of it." Then, in an effort to change the subject, she turned to Anne and said, "Did you give Teri her birthday present? I was hoping she'd hang it in the guest room."

"Teri loved the picture," Anne lied. "She was so pleased."

A smile broke through the worry clouding Maggie Zambini's face. For the next few minutes, the three of them made small talk, and then Anne excused herself. Mrs. Zambini seemed distracted. She could barely focus on the conversation. Well, who could blame her? Dominick Zambini had practically accused her of adultery. Anne wondered what that had been all about. Maggie was pushing seventy, with a host of ailments. She seemed barely strong enough to drink her tea, let alone carry out an affair in the unromantic confines of Sunnydale.

Anne wandered back out into the hall. A schedule of the day's events was posted on a cork bulletin board on the wall. There were three different religious services, a book club meeting, a cooking class on how to make bread pudding, and a line dancing lesson. They certainly did keep you hopping at Sunnydale. Never a dull moment. She heard classical music coming from the solarium across the hall and poked her head inside.

Two frail elderly ladies in wheelchairs were sitting by the window, surveying the rows of plants as if they were alien life forms they'd never laid eyes on before. Greta Koch was standing over them, her back to the door, holding a small green vial.

"Here we are, ladies," Nurse Koch announced cheerily. "Your plant food has arrived."

She gave the vial to one of the women, who held it out uncertainly. "Now, now," said Greta, "musn't keep our friends waiting." She guided the old woman's pale thin wrist over to the nearest fern and waited until the liquid contents of the vial had dutifully been dispatched. The procedure was then repeated with the second old lady, whose eyes were clouded by cataracts. The women looked tired. They barely seemed to notice what they were doing.

Plant therapy, Anne thought disdainfully. They might as well be practicing voodoo or saying novenas, for all the good it appeared to be doing. But she could see Greta Koch was adamant. Her plain, rather horsy looking face was lit with the flame of zealotry, like a minister guiding her wayward flock. Anne knew Greta's type. She was probably a lonely old maid who took in stray cats and treated herself to a glass of schnapps once a week. Many women like her entered the "helping" professions. Taking care of others was a good way to avoid noticing the small rips and tears in the fabric of one's own life. Anne had encountered similar nurses at other homes her mother had been in. They had a kind of savior complex, performing each task as if they were the only thing that stood between their patients and the great beyond. Anne had resented it at first—resented the way they'd pretended to know her mother better than she herself ever could.

Greta turned around. When she saw Anne standing in the doorway, she gave a startled gasp. "Oh," she exclaimed, looking at Anne strangely. "It's you."

"I wanted to talk to somebody about volunteering here," Anne said. "I read about the Sunshine Helpers program in *Sunnyside Up.*"

Actually, the last thing Anne wanted to do was spend more time at Sunnydale. Even now, she longed to run out the glass doors in the lobby and breathe in great draughts of fresh air, not the sanitized, disinfectant smell of the home, which was so strong it felt like it was piped in through vents. But how else was she supposed to get to know Claire Hillyard? How else could she find out if all those deaths were on the level?

And where was she ever going to get another chance to make it up to Evelyn? Each time Anne visited Maggie Zambini, Maggie seemed genuinely glad to see her. Maybe she could get to know some of the other patients, too. Like the women with Alzheimer's. It was late in the game. But if she could connect with these people, talk to them a little, make them feel they weren't alone, it'd be worth the effort.

"Come to the Activity Room at ten o'clock tomorrow morning," Greta Koch said slowly. "There'll be an orientation."

For some unexplained reason, the nurse was staring at Anne as if she'd suddenly grown two heads. Didn't people ask to volunteer here?

"Okay."

"Remember. A smile is our umbrella," the nurse said grimly. "No sad faces, no sitting in corners."

"Right," Anne said ruefully, wondering if she'd ever be able to spend five minutes in Sunnydale without wishing she were anyplace else on earth.

Anne found Claire Hillyard behind her desk, reading the newspaper. A sheaf of applications was piled in front of her, next to a coffee mug. Afternoon light streamed through the window.

"Hi," Anne said, knocking on Claire's office door.

Claire looked up and saw Anne. Her expression hardened and she noticeably stiffened.

"Remember me, from the other day?" Anne entered the office and slipped into one of the burgundy leather wing chairs.

"I remember," Claire said evenly.

What was going on? Was it Shun the Visitors Day?

"I had some more questions. About my grandmother."

Claire leaned back in her chair. She was dressed in another fabulously chic outfit: black silk blouse, gray slacks, a strand of black pearls. How much money could you make as a nursing home administrator? It wasn't exactly the fast track.

"First," Claire said coldly, shoving the *Landsdown Park Press* across the desk, "I have a few questions for you."

The headline jumped out at Anne: SKELETON SPOOKS HOMEOWNER IN HEIGHTS *by Bart Mendinger*. Right on the front page, below the fold. Next to the story was her picture, her eyes reduced to two dots, her startled expression captured mid-flash. *The Press* was an afternoon paper. By now, the whole town would know. No wonder Greta had looked at her strangely. Turning to the article, she hurriedly began to read.

A homeowner in Oceanside Heights got the fright of her life Friday afternoon when a skeleton was discovered buried in her basement. Anne Hardaway, a 37-year-old writer who resides at 11 Ocean Avenue, in a Victorian "painted lady," refused to discuss how the skeleton got there. But this paper has learned that it was buried under mounds of dirt in Hardaway's basement with a bullet in its skull. No one knows how long its bony remains were sequestered in Hardaway's house. But old Mr. Bones was quickly carted off to the state Medical Examiner's office in Newark, where tests determined it to be the remains of Dr. Steven Hillyard, a noted Neptune psychologist who disappeared in 1974.

Anne turned to the jump page and kept reading, aware that Claire Hillyard's eyes were boring into her. The rest of the piece consisted of Anne's bio, interspersed with your basic no-comment from a cop at the sheriff's office she didn't know. Bart Mendinger had gotten his scoop. And it had landed him on page one.

"Is this why you came to see me?" Claire said. Her tone was icy. "I hardly think it can be a coincidence."

"Partly, yes. When I found out your husband's remains

were buried in my house, I was naturally curious."

"I believe this is a police matter."

Two spots of color had appeared on Claire's cheeks. She picked up her mug and brought it to her lips. Anne noticed that Claire's hand was trembling, but couldn't tell whether it was from anger or fear.

"I realize how hard this must be on you," Anne said. "After all these years, for your husband to turn up this way. It must have come as a shock."

Claire's laugh was brittle. "You know nothing about my husband."

"I was hoping you could help me there. I'd like to know more about him. His interests, his friends. His character."

Claire slammed the mug down on the desk. Coffee sloshed over the rim, staining some of the applications. "Why? He's dead."

Exasperated, Anne tried another approach. "Aren't you the least bit curious how your husband ended up buried in my basement with a bullet in his head?"

"I really don't have time for this," Claire interrupted. She'd gotten some tissues from her desk and was hastily wiping up the spill. "I'm very busy."

Too busy to question Hillyard's connection with the Hardaway family? Too blasé to react when Trasker had first phoned with the news? How very strange.

"Okay," Anne said, changing course. "Is Mr. Reynolds available?"

"Philip." Claire raised a perfectly shaped eyebrow. "Why?"

"I really do have an elderly grandmother. If she ends up in Sunnydale, I'd like to meet everyone who'll be involved in her care. Mr. Reynolds . . ."

". . . is unavailable," Claire interrupted. She'd regained some of her composure, but her cheeks were still flushed. "If you're serious about Sunnydale, which I highly doubt, send in an application. Otherwise, our business is at an end."

"When will Mr. Reynolds be free?"

"I'm not sure," Claire said, glancing pointedly at her watch. "He's extremely busy. As am I. If you'll excuse me."

"Certainly."

Anne got up and walked to the door. What was the deal with Claire Hillyard? How could she be that uninterested in her husband's disappearance and death? Maybe she was masking her true feelings beneath a wall of indifference. Or maybe she was simply cold and unfeeling. Or intensely private. No, Anne thought. There's something more. Something she's not telling me.

Chapter 14

Silence a squeaky hinge by lubricating it with a drop or two of light household oil. Raise the hinge pin slightly so you can drip oil onto the shaft above the hinge's upper barrel. Swing the door back and forth a few times to distribute the lubrication along the entire length of the hinge pin.

In the lobby, Anne saw Maggie Zambini's wheelchair parked at the sliding glass doors, like a sentry on patrol. In her lap was a copy of the *Landsdown Park Press*.

"I was hoping to catch you," Maggie exclaimed breathlessly. "Thank God you haven't left."

"What's wrong?"

"I need to talk to you. About Steven Hillyard. Could you come back to my room?"

Anne was so surprised you could have knocked her

over with a feather. In a million years, she would never have guessed at a connection between the two of them. "Sure," she said aloud. As she followed Mrs. Zambini to the elevator, she was aware that people were casting curious glances her way. Now that the article had come out, she was finding out what it felt like to be famous for fifteen minutes. It was something she could have lived without.

On the way upstairs, Maggie Zambini was silent. But once they were safely inside her room, and the door had shut with a squeaky groan, the old lady began to cry.

"I can't believe he's dead," she sobbed, clutching the arms of her wheelchair. "But you know what it means, don't you? It means he didn't abandon me. I never believed he did. Not really. I had fantasies of him coming back for me, taking me out of this wretched place."

"You and Dr. Hillyard . . ." Anne began, incredulous. It was the last thing she'd expected.

"We were in love." Tears spilled down the elderly woman's cheeks. She took a pale blue handkerchief from the pocket of her house dress and noisily blew her nose. "I was going to give up everything for him. Dom. Teri."

"This was when?"

Mrs. Zambini squeezed the handkerchief into a ball and mopped her face. "The summer of '74. The last time I saw him was the day he disappeared. August 23. He left the clinic at six o'clock. And he didn't come to work the next day."

"The police must have talked to all his patients."

"Yes, they interviewed everyone he was treating."

"Did that include my mother?"

Maggie Zambini stared down at her hands. "Yes."

"But when I asked you yesterday, you told me you didn't know if she was seeing a hypnotherapist."

"She asked me never to mention it. She didn't want anyone to know. Not even your father."

This last struck Anne as peculiar. What difference did it make if the entire world knew Evelyn Hardaway was trying hypnosis? Just one more cure in the laundry list of drugs, talk therapy, self-blame, self-help, acupuncture, and scores of other medical and psychological treatments she'd subjected herself to. But what did Maggie Zambini have to gain by lying?

"Did Dr. Hillyard have an appointment with my mother that evening?"

"Not that I knew of. If he did, it wasn't written down in his appointment book. His last appointment was at five and he left right afterward."

"You never heard from him after that? No phone calls or letters?"

"No."

"Did you ever try to find him?"

Maggie moistened her lips. She looked exhausted, worn out. "I thought he'd changed his mind. About running off with me. His marriage was unhappy. He wanted to go away from here." Her voice wavered, broke. "I figured he took off and left me behind."

"How did you and Hillyard know each other?"

"I was the receptionist at his clinic. Oh, it was strictly business at first. But after a while, we fell for each other. He was so dynamic, so brilliant, so completely unlike any man I'd ever known. Wait." She pointed to the copy of Degas's ballerinas hanging on the wall in its Plexiglas frame. "Bring me my painting. I'll show you."

Anne lifted the copy of the Degas off the wall and brought it over. Mrs. Zambini turned the frame on its side and touched a small latch on the back. The plastic appeared to loosen slightly. Hooking a fingernail under the edge of the frame, she slid a photograph out from under it, handling the picture gingerly, as if it might break. "This is Steven," she said proudly, her eyes shining.

Anne studied the black and white photo. It was an arty shot, the play of light and shadow imbuing the subject with an air of mystery. In it, Hillyard was standing with his back to the ocean, wearing a short-sleeve shirt and shorts. He looked more relaxed than in the newspaper clipping, less the pioneering young doctor than a regular Joe out for a stroll along the beach. But his face reflected a certain intensity and sense of purpose that made Anne wonder how easy life with him would be. Even in repose, Hillyard looked like a type A personality.

"What was he like?" Anne said.

"Oh, he was a remarkable man. A brilliant clinician. A great thinker."

"But what made you fall in love with him?"

Maggie paused and her face was suddenly radiant, as though the years were rolling back in her mind. "It's hard to put into words," she said slowly. "But he made me feel . . . important. I was more than just a secretary or a wife or a mother to him. He really talked to me. And he listened, too. He valued my opinions, my advice. We used to have long talks about practically everything. I still miss our talks, even after all this time."

But there was more to it, of course. Maggie Zambini had been having an affair with Hillyard. Could he have charmed Anne's mother, too? Or was he merely a capable, understanding doctor who'd befriended a sick woman? Who had buried him in the cellar? Flesh dissolving from bone.

Anne handed the picture back. "Did you tell anyone about the two of you? Like my mother, for instance?"

"God, no. Steven was treating Evelyn at the clinic. But I guess you already know that. I told her about the work he was doing. It was because of me that she started treatment."

Anne could feel herself tensing up. She leaned forward, trying to think how to phrase her next question. "Do you think it's possible," she said slowly, "that my mother was also romantically involved with Dr. Hillyard?"

Maggie Zambini drew back. She looked as though she'd been slapped. "No. Of course not."

Anne felt a surge of relief.

"But he did sometimes go to your house to treat Evelyn. She was so forgetful that summer. Once she missed her regular appointment because she couldn't remember how to get to the office."

Anne's stomach did a quick flip-flop.

"That's what I can't figure out," Maggie continued, her face streaked with tears. "How Steven was killed and why. He was such a good man. So generous and kind."

"Did Claire Hillyard know?"

"She may have suspected he was having an affair. I don't think she knew it was with me. But I made the mistake of telling Dom about us. I had to let him know I was leaving. I wanted to take Teri with us. But he forbade it. He said he'd never give me a divorce and he'd never let me have custody of her. If I wanted to live with Steven, he said, we'd have to live in sin."

"Is that why your husband's not taking care of you at home? Why he put you in this place?"

Mrs. Zambini shook her head. "It was my decision to come to Sunnydale. My cross to bear."

"I don't understand."

Maggie Zambini moaned softly. Her face was wet with tears. "I betrayed Dominick with Steven, then I begged Dom to take me back. Don't you see? I deserve to be here. It's only right."

Rage and retribution. It explained a lot. Dominick Zambini's fury. Maggie's helpless passivity. Teri's withdrawal from both of them.

"Do you think your husband could have killed Dr. Hillyard?"

Maggie Zambini paused. Her face was suffused with pain. "I don't know. Dom was so furious when I told him about us. He went on and on about justice. I think he would have liked to hurt Steven. I think it would have made him glad."

Anne felt a sudden chill and glanced around the room. She'd had the same feeling the other day when she'd come here, the feeling she was being watched.

"Your husband's leg. How did he injure it? Did it have anything to do with Dr. Hillyard?"

Mrs. Zambini shook her head. "No. Dom has gout, in his big toe. It's funny. Gout's a rich man's disease. The only thing Dom has in common with rich folks." She laughed harshly and accidentally dropped the photograph.

Anne bent down to get it and as she did, she caught a glimpse of something white in the doorway. The door was slightly ajar. Anne gave the picture back to Mrs. Zambini and quickly walked across the room. As she threw the door open and it let out its customary squeak, she startled the woman standing to one side of the threshold. It was the blond nurse who had poked her head into Mrs. Zambini's room the previous evening. K. Crowley.

"Hi," Anne said loudly.

"Oh," the nurse said, giving a rabbitty little jump. "You startled me."

That's what you get for eavesdropping, Anne thought. She wondered how much the nurse had overheard. Did the staff make a practice of spying on patients? The thought filled her with a sudden dread.

Aloud, she said, "Mrs. Zambini was just about to take a nap. Is it okay if I close her door all the way?"

"Certainly," the nurse said crisply, giving her clipboard a reassuring pat. Her face was washed-out looking, wan. But her eyes remained watchful, as though she intended to sidestep trouble by spotting it well in advance.

"Thanks."

Anne stood there a moment, waiting, until the nurse turned on her heel and scurried down the hallway, as if there were a pressing medical emergency that needed her immediate attention. Closing the door firmly behind her, Anne stepped back inside. Mrs. Zambini was gazing at the photo, her mouth trembling slightly.

"That nurse I was talking to. Nurse Crowley. What do you know about her?"

"She's mean. And nosy. When people die, she paws

through their things. I think she even took a garnet ring that belonged to my friend Myra. I saw Katie Crowley wearing it once. It has a gold band and two small diamonds inset on either side."

"Did you tell anyone?"

Mrs. Zambini pursed her lips. "She'd only deny it if I did. It's better, safer, to hold your tongue." She took one last look at the photo, devouring it with her eyes, and slid it inside the Plexiglas frame. Then she motioned for Anne to hang it back on the wall. "Please try and find out what happened to Steven," she said. Her fingers gripped the handles of her wheelchair. "I'll never rest easy until I know."

Chapter 15

*When hiring a contractor,
remember it's going to
cost twice the amount of
money and triple the
amount of time it should
take to complete the job.*

Driving home, Anne kept replaying what Maggie
Zambini had told her. She felt tired and vaguely
sick. Her head swirled with questions. Had Claire
Hillyard known about the two of them? Had her mother
known? If Hillyard had treated Evelyn at the house, it
explained what he was doing there. Clearly, Evelyn had
had feelings for him. The diary revealed that much. If
Evelyn learned about her friend's affair, would those
feelings have led to murder? How would she get a gun?
Where would she hide it afterward?

She wished with all her heart that Chester had never
dug the skeleton up. Let the past be. Let old bones rest
in peace.

When she pulled up in front of her house, she stared
at it in amazement. All of the sand had miraculously been

removed from the lawn. The bench was gone, too. Plastic sheeting covered the roof. The torn shutter had been repaired, and new gutters had been attached. Jack must have worked straight through the afternoon.

As she turned her key in the lock, she heard laughter coming from the living room. All the lamps were on. The coffee table was laden with hors d'oeuvres: carrot and celery sticks, pâté Jack had brought from the city, a plate of brie and crackers, and macadamia and pistachio nuts.

Grandma Betty sat in the flowered wing chair, sipping a glass of sherry. She wore a pale gray velour running suit and her bright red hair was cut short and curled at the sides, like a flapper. Around her neck were two long silver chains and several heart-shaped glass pendants. Her bulldog Boop rested his floppy chins against her black hightop sneakers. From across the room, Harry arched his back and hissed at the dog. Jack sat opposite Grandma Betty on the sofa, holding a glass of club soda.

"Thank God you're back," Jack called out. "Delia and Helen both called. Plus three local news stations, two radio stations, someone from the Jersey bureau of the *Philadelphia Inquirer* and that reporter from the *Press*, the one who wrote the story. Everybody's asking about the skeleton."

Before Anne could reply, Grandma started in. "Forget the damn bones. What's this I hear about you locking me up in Sunnyhell? I may be old, but I'm not loony tunes!"

Anne shot Jack a questioning look that Grandma's sharp eyes picked up on.

"Your fiancé didn't spill the beans, Annie. It's all over town how you want to commit me. I had to put off going to Atlantic City and come over here to straighten you out."

"Grandma—" Anne began.

"Don't you Grandma me," her grandmother said angrily, shaking her finger. "The very idea! That place is for *old* people."

Jack chuckled softly. Grandma Betty was eighty-nine, rail thin, with a penchant for costume jewelry. She had a touch of arthritis in her left wrist, and her bridge game wasn't what it used to be, but other than that she was doing just fine, thank you very much.

Anne poured herself a glass of sherry—extra dry Fino from Domecq, Grandma's favorite—and quickly gave her the *Reader's Digest* version of what had happened since the skeleton was unearthed.

"So you're not going to put me in that horrid place after all," Grandma said, reaching down to scratch Boop's head.

"Of course not," Anne said. "You're my front, my cover."

"Well, then," Grandma Betty said. "Congratulations on your engagement to this charming young man." She bestowed a big smile on Jack, put two fingers to her mouth, and blew him a kiss.

"Your grandmother has graciously offered to throw us an engagement party," Jack said, smearing pâté on a cracker. "And I have more good news. As of right now, I'm officially on vacation in the Heights. For a week."

"That's great," Anne said, trying to inject some enthusiasm into her voice.

Part of her was genuinely glad. She and Jack would have more time together, be able to work things out. But another part of her was anxious, suddenly put upon. Like finding out you had to go to school all weekend. Or have company stay a whole lot longer than they'd originally planned. Christ, what was wrong with her anyway? Why couldn't she be happy he was staying longer without wanting her privacy, her own personal space, back?

"What happened to the sandbox out front?" she said, changing the subject.

"I borrowed your neighbor's snow blower," Jack said. "Blew the stuff clear across to the beach."

"Thanks."

Only she didn't feel grateful. She felt annoyed. She

would have taken care of it, handled her own home repairs. Eventually. Besides, what part of *no* did Jack not
understand?

"This fella here is one in a million, Annie," said
Grandma Betty. Her clear blue eyes were positively twin-
kling. "I want us to double date. Tomorrow night."

"Anne, you didn't tell me your grandmother has a
beau," Jack interjected.

He was probably only trying to be nice, but Anne
thought he sounded a tad too condescending. "I told you
about Carl," she said. "He used to be my grandmother's
eye doctor."

"Carl drives at night," Grandma chimed in. "You don't
find too many fellas who do, at his age."

Grandma sipped her sherry and beamed at them. Well,
this was a surprise. Her grandmother was pleased about
the engagement. In fact, she seemed positively ecstatic,
despite the fact that Anne had sat in Grandma Betty's
small, cluttered kitchen on more than one occasion and
confided her doubts about Jack, her fear of moving forward with him, of making a bigger commitment.

Grandma raised her glass and tapped a bright red fingernail against it, like a woodpecker tapping on the trunk
of a cedar tree. "I'd like to make a toast," she announced.
"To my wonderful granddaughter and her Jack. May you
cherish and protect each other. And may you be friends
and lovers for the rest of time."

Jack put down his glass and applauded heartily. Anne
felt tears form at the corners of her eyes, but couldn't
say whether she felt happy or sad. Boop the dog
scratched his ear and let out a long, low belch.

Jack reheated their dinner in the microwave. He'd gone
to a gourmet shop in Red Bank and picked up braised
salmon with dill sauce, new potatoes, a tomato and cu-
cumber salad, and nonfat cranberry biscotti. At this rate,
Anne would never have to cook franks and beans again.
She'd taken a hot bath and changed into a pair of black

slacks and a white cable knit sweater. In honor of the fancy food, she'd gotten out her mother's good china. The table was covered with a snowy white cloth, the overhead lights were off, and two beeswax candles illuminated their meal. Anne almost felt like she was dining in a three-star restaurant, instead of her waterlogged dining room.

After she'd brought Jack up to speed on Hillyard, he spelled out what had to be done to the house: Replace the chimney flashing, the chimney caps, and about half the shingles on the roof, patch the masonry joints, weather-strip the doors, buy new shutters, fill in the cracks in the walkway, replace three of the windows, replaster the walls and ceilings, and last but not least, regrade the foundation wall so the next time a northeaster hit, there'd be some kind of drainage system in place.

She listened in a partial state of shock, doing the math on her fingers. Where was she ever going to find the money for repairs?

As if reading her mind, Jack said, "I was thinking about how much this is going to cost. Twenty, twenty-five grand, at least. The way I figure it, this is an opportunity for us. We could renovate the whole house from top to bottom. And still come out ahead of the game."

"Renovate?"

"The house needs work. No doubt about it. But while we're at it, we could do the floors, install a new kitchen, redo the bathrooms, even build a small addition out back. A new office for you."

"Wait," Anne said, throwing up her hand. "Wait a second. I don't have the money for that. And besides, it's hell living through a home renovation. Jennifer Joan is planning a whole chapter on how to cope."

"Look," Jack said, pushing away his plate and breaking out the biscotti. "We're a team now. What's mine is yours and vice versa. Don't worry so much about how much it'll cost. I've got it covered. And if we build that addition, it's tax deductible."

Anne was beginning to see where this was headed. "So what do we do in the meantime, while it's raining plaster dust, and workmen are knocking out walls and drilling and making a colossal mess?"

"That's the beauty of it."

He got up from the table, walked around behind Anne and started massaging her shoulder blades. It felt wonderful, soothing. She didn't want him to stop.

"We live in New York until the work is done."

"Then what?" she said, tilting her head from side to side, feeling her muscles relax, a tingly warmth spreading from her neck down her back.

"We cross that bridge when we come to it."

She shook herself loose reluctantly, looked up at him. "You don't play fair."

"Hell, no," he agreed. "But my methods can be most enticing."

He took her hand, pulled her to her feet, and started waltzing her around the room. Out of the corner of her eye she saw the soggy wallpaper, the water stains on the ceiling, and the jagged cracks in the plaster. Then she shut her eyes, felt the room spin beneath her feet, whirling around and around in Jack's arms.

Later, in bed, Jack traced the edges of her body with his fingers and she thought of the skeleton—the hollow sockets where its eyes had been, its grinning ivory teeth. The drapes in the bedroom were open. Outside, Anne could see a thin sliver of moon suspended high above the ocean, like a distant kite. The wind whipped against the side of the house, a sharp tearing sound. She could almost feel the foundation groan. That skeleton, rotting away all these years, like a jinx. And now the house was rotting, too. Her old, broken-down house.

"What?" Jack said, tracing the line of her jaw. "What's wrong?"

"Bones," she whispered back. The wind rattled the windowpanes and whipped the plastic sheeting on the roof.

His thumb brushed beneath her chin. "Inferior maxil-lary." Running his fingers over her throat, he pressed lightly against her vocal chords. "Cervical vertebrae. Clavicle." His hands continued their downward sweep. "Scapula. Sternum. First rib. Fifth rib," he recited. He'd reached her thigh. "Femur." Her knee. "Patella. Fibula." He lifted her foot off the bed, indicating the various bones. "Tarsals. Metatarsals. Phalanges. Heel bone."

"How do you know this stuff?" she said.

"I was premed at Princeton, before I switched to ar-chitecture."

"Why'd you change?"

He put her foot down and lay back on the bed. "I can't stand being sick, can't stand it when people around me are sick. I never even take the subway because everyone coughs and sneezes all over you. And blood, forget about it! I couldn't even dissect my frog in tenth-grade biology. Guess I wasn't cut out to be a doctor."

"Guess not." Anne stared up at the ceiling. She should do it now. Talk to him about the renovation. About mov-ing to New York.

But he chose that moment to take her in his arms again and kiss her hard on the mouth. She felt his fingertips stroke the side of her face and forgot about the renovation and living in New York, forgot everything but this.

In the dream, her mother was at the beach, sitting un-der a large striped umbrella. It was one of those perfect summer afternoons, where the sun made you feel healthy and happy. Waves lapped the shoreline, the water a gen-tle swatch of blue velvet stretching toward the horizon. Evelyn was wearing a black velvet evening gown with a deep, plunging neckline. A diamond tiara sparkled in her long red hair. Except for her and Anne, the beach was deserted.

Anne felt the sand beneath her toes, smelled the salty sea air. She was nine years old again, gawky, tall for her age, self-conscious about her body. The wind blew hot dry air into her face. She pulled the strap of her bathing suit higher. The navy blue suit with the white anchor. Above them, the gulls shrieked and keened, flying in frantic circles.

Ma, she said. *Can I go in the water?*

Wait, Evelyn admonished. She rose and glided toward the ocean, her skin as pale as a porcelain doll, her gown trailing after like a bridal train.

Anne watched from her blanket. *Not fair.* It was hot, too hot, and all she wanted was to dive into the water and cool off. She scrambled to her feet and ran after her mother. The sand burned the soles of her feet. Evelyn had reached the water's edge and was wading into the ocean.

Wait, Anne cried out. *Wait for me.* But the wind swallowed her words whole. She saw her mother's waist, back, and shoulders disappear, her hair fanning out like a mermaid.

Anne splashed into the icy cold water, arms flailing. The ocean was as smooth as polished glass, the sun glinting so brightly it hurt. One moment Evelyn was there, the next she'd disappeared. Anne dove under, swimming out and down. *Where are you?* Salt water flooded her mouth and eyes. Seaweed clung to her hair. Bloated fish with enormous shaggy heads swam by, barking out a song. Her knees scraped against a rock, and she watched the blood float up to the surface, a strand of red pearls.

Ahead, she spotted her mother's billowy dark gown. She swam toward it, aware that her lungs were aching, that she couldn't keep holding her breath. Her ears were ringing. She lunged for the dress, which was lighter than silk, lighter than the downy feathers of a gull. She saw the sockets where the eyes had been, the long bony wrists, prehistoric, primitive, that unearthly grin. The ringing in her ears was louder now. She couldn't breathe, couldn't scream until she let go, and the skeleton broke free of the dress, vertebrae, sternum, ribs floating silently to the bottom of the deep velvety sea.

Her eyes snapped open, her heart pounding, and she heard it again. A sharp trill. The phone. Next to her, Jack slept face down, his arm flung out across the bed. *Ring! ring!* She reached over and grabbed the receiver.

"Hello."

On the other end, she heard someone breathing.

"Hello," she said louder. She checked the clock on the night stand—4:25 A.M. She'd been sleeping for a grand total of three hours and twenty minutes.

"Anne?" The voice was faint, almost indistinct.

"Yes. Who's this?"

"I thought you should know," the voice whispered. Sexless, toneless, devoid of emotion.

"What? Who is this?"

"Margaret Zambini is dead."

Click.

Chapter 16

*Tighten a loose newel post
by screwing small angle
brackets to the base of the
post on both sides and
attaching them to the
staircase. To make the
repair less conspicuous,
chisel out a ⅛-inch recess
for the bracket, then cover
it with a wood filler, sand
it, and paint or stain.*

Anne threw on her clothes. Her heart was hammering so loudly it seemed to echo in her ears. But at the same time, she was keyed up, running on pure adrenaline. Jack slept on, oblivious to the turmoil she was feeling. But the phone had woken Harry, and the cat, sensing Anne's anxiety, paced the floor nervously.

She went downstairs and tried calling Sunnydale. But all she got was a flat computerized voice stating visiting hours and directions. This was insane. It had to be a cruel practical joke. Someone trying to scare her, that was all. Maggie Zambini was probably safe in bed, dreaming of lost love. Still . . . no harm in making sure. She grabbed her car keys and her purse and hurried out the front door.

The moment she stepped outside, the car parked across the street sped away. It was the same one from yesterday—the white Ford. Though the streetlights were on, she couldn't see the driver's face. A dark blur above the steering wheel, then it was gone. She ran to the Mustang, gunned the engine, and took off in pursuit down Ocean Avenue. It was still dark out. Birds sang tunelessly in the trees. In the chill morning air, the beach loomed black and shapeless.

The Ford had a four-block head start. But she had no trouble keeping it in sight. The road was empty except for the two of them. The other car was doing eighty-five. Anne careened after it past the silent, picturesque Victorian homes of the Heights, silhouetted against the night sky. Nothing stirred. The antique-style turn-of-the-century lampposts threw golden beams of light onto the road. Anne pressed down hard on the gas pedal, as she followed the Ford around Wesley Lake and into Landsdown. Here, the buildings were dilapidated, bleak—tumble down, deserted storefronts with letters missing from their signs. Two-story houses scarred with graffiti, their windows smashed, their yards strewn with garbage. It wasn't just the effects of the storm. Landsdown was always a pit. In the early dawn, the town looked like it had been bombed and abandoned.

The Ford darted through two red lights and Anne did the same. Who was driving the beat-up car? The same person who'd placed the crank call? The Ford swung onto Route 35, heading north. She was starting to gain on it. The license plate was crusted with mud. There were letters on the rear window, but Anne couldn't make them out. The name of a college, maybe? She was only about two blocks behind the Ford, but now there were a few other cars on the road. Anne passed a Corolla and a

Mazda, keeping the Ford in sight. It was heading for the Jersey Turnpike.

Neon signs lit up both sides of Route 35, though the stores below were dark and the car felt like a pinball shot from an arcade machine. She tightened her grip on the steering wheel and hugged the road. The speed limit was forty-five miles per hour. She was doing seventy. *Come on, come on*, she urged the Mustang.

Two more weeks till Halloween. Was that what inspired whoever placed the call? A cruel trick or treat? What was she supposed to make of it?

Up ahead loomed the railroad tracks. She heard, rather than saw, the train, saw the black and white crossing gate going down. The Ford ignored the warning and sped across the tracks, a few seconds before the oncoming locomotive. The train's whistle shrieked its disapproval. Anne slowed and braked, fuming at her bad luck. A freight train. She watched the cars hurtle noisily by, one after another. It seemed to take forever. When the train had finally passed and the gate lifted, she peered ahead, down Route 35. She could see for about a mile.

The Ford was gone.

She pulled into the Sunnydale parking lot at a quarter to six. The day had dawned gray and damp. It had rained in the night, with strong gale force winds—the trees were half bare. The foliage looked duller than it did a few days ago, as if the remaining leaves were already preparing to fall.

The front doors of the nursing home were locked. Anne peered through the glass into the lobby. The lights were all on, but there was no guard at the desk, no one in sight. *Damn.* She skirted the building, trying the side doors and the door at the rear. All locked. The old wing was shut tight as a drum. She went back to the parking lot and sat in her car, her eyes trained on the building. Maybe the nurses changed shifts soon and somebody would show up to let her in. She'd just stay a few minutes, long enough to make sure Mrs. Zambini was all right. Then she'd go home, eat breakfast, and drive back here in time for her ten o'clock orientation. A sigh escaped her lips. These days, it felt like she lived at Sunnydale.

Fifteen minutes passed. Anne leaned her head back against the seat. God, she was tired. What she wouldn't give for a good night's sleep. It was cold in the car. She got out, ran a couple of laps around the parking lot to wake up, climbed back in the Mustang. Another fifteen minutes went by. At twenty after six, a black BMW pulled into the lot. Philip Reynolds emerged from the car and strode toward the nursing home. He wore a double-breasted gray suit and black loafers and carried a black leather briefcase. Anne got out, locked her car, and fell into step beside him.

"Mr. Reynolds," she began.

"Visiting hours start at eight-thirty," he informed her curtly.

"I know. But this can't wait. I got a call a few hours ago that one of your patients had died."

Philip Reynolds stopped walking. He looked her up and down, frowning. "A call," he repeated.

"From someone at Sunnydale. They said she was dead."

"And you are . . . ?" Something in his tone told her he knew exactly who she was, but she decided to play along.

"I'm Anne Hardaway. We met the other day in Claire Hillyard's office. My aunt lives at Sunnydale. Mrs. Margaret Zambini." Anne was amazed at how quickly the lie came.

Philip Reynolds was studying her closely, as if trying to decide what to make of her. "This is highly irregular," he said finally, with the faintest hint of annoyance. "I am the first one notified when a patient passes on. I contact the families personally."

She couldn't help noticing that he was more concerned about policy and appearances than the news that a patient may have expired. Besides, how much contact could he have with the families if he bought her concerned "niece" story?

"I'd like to see my aunt," she said firmly.

He pursed his lips and shifted his briefcase from one hand to the other. "Certainly. Right this way."

Producing a key from his suit pocket, he opened the sliding glass doors, and she followed him through the deserted lobby to the elevator. The string of cardboard cats and witches sagged forlornly from the ceiling. "Your aunt has been with us a while?" he asked, as they waited for the elevator.

"About a year and a half."

He nodded gravely. "I trust she's been happy here."

It's been peachy, Anne felt like saying. *"Aunt" Margaret's afraid of the staff. She's lonely. And she's bored to tears.*

Instead, Anne said, "What's the protocol when a patient dies? Who would be made aware of the death, apart from the nurses who happened to be on duty?"

Hillyard frowned. "Myself, for one. And Claire Hillyard, of course. You've met Claire."

The elevator arrived and they stepped inside. The door clanked shut and the gears groaned as they ascended. Anne was trying to figure out how to talk her way out of this mess after they got to Mrs. Zambini's room and found the old lady brushing her teeth or working on a miniature Renoir. The purpose of the phone call had been to scare her, no doubt. Well, it worked. She was plenty scared. Why else would she be going through with this charade? she thought, as they walked down the third-floor corridor. There was no one else in the hall. But Anne kept craning her head from side to side, peering at each room as they passed, alert to each shadow, to the slightest noise or movement. It was eerie, this feeling she had practically every time she set foot in Sunnydale, that someone was watching her. *Tracking* her, like a predator tracks its prey.

The door to room 306 was closed. Philip Reynolds knocked once, twice, then tentatively swung it open. Anne let out a gasp. Maggie Zambini's things were gone. No photos on the dresser. No impressionist paintings on the wall. Both beds were made up. But the space was entirely devoid of personal effects, like a hospital room awaiting the next set of patients.

"Where is she?" Anne demanded.

"I'll find out for you," Reynolds said. "Please wait here a moment."

Anne went to the dresser and opened each drawer. Empty. Same as the metal locker, the medicine cabinet, the nightstand, and the wastebasket. She stood by the window and gazed out, aware that she was trembling, that her pulse was throbbing in her neck. She took a deep breath. *Please don't let it be true.* The room overlooked the road. In the distance, she saw gables and turrets rising from the sherbet-colored houses of the Heights. In the gray morning light, the town looked dreamy and still, like an ancient fresco. She heard a noise and whirled around.

Philip Reynolds was standing in the doorway. "I'm very sorry, Miss Hardaway," he said. His face was somber, his tone measured, practiced in doling out unpleasant news. "There's nothing more you can do here. Your aunt's body has already been taken to the funeral parlor."

The cause of death was heart failure. The time of death was around 3:30 A.M. Anne learned both these facts from a petite, sympathetic nurse named Marie, who'd happened to be on call when Mrs. Zambini passed away. Marie was new at Sunnydale. Only two weeks on the job. Marie had been the one who'd found the body. She was doing the nightly bed check and noticed how still Mrs. Z looked, how ghostly pale. It was too late for emergency medical procedures. So Marie had covered the body with a sheet, said a quick prayer, and immediately called Mr. Reynolds. There was no answer at his home, so Marie had contacted Claire Hillyard. Claire had instructed her to wait until morning before notifying the family.

Mrs. Z had seemed out of sorts earlier in the evening, Marie said. She appeared in the dining room but didn't touch her supper tray and wasn't her usual gregarious self. After the meal, she'd sat with Andrew Deretchin in her room for a little while, before retiring, as was her custom. When Marie popped her head in to say good-night—it must have been oh, around ten o'clock—Mrs. Z said she was feeling poorly. Sick to her stomach was how she put it. But then that's what happens to some of these old dears when they miss a meal. Their insides get weak, they need nourishment to keep up their strength. Marie was so very, very sorry for Anne's loss. Mrs. Z had been a charmer, a real lady. Yes, Katie Crowley was on duty last night. Did Anne want to speak to her? Katie had gone home a little while ago, but here was her address and phone number. No, she didn't know where Mrs. Z's things were. At the nurses' station, maybe? That's where the aides were supposed to leave personal effects.

Anne digested all of this information slowly. Trailing after the perky Marie, she felt like she was walking through a thick, dense cloud. Each step required effort and her thoughts were all jumbled up.

The nurses' station was a small room furnished with a green vinyl couch and four weather-beaten chairs. Coffee percolated on a counter, next to a half-eaten box of raspberry danish. Mrs. Zambini's "effects" were in a corner, in a small cardboard box. Anne picked through the contents, unsure of exactly what she was looking for. Maggie hadn't had much: some toiletries, pictures of her family, a few clothes, her impressionist paintings.

Anne reached into the box and pulled out the copy of the Degas. The ballerinas looked sadder than Anne remembered, lonely, isolated, unaware of one another. Anne imagined Mrs. Zambini imitating Degas's work, painstakingly recreating each stroke of the tutus, the dancers' expressions, the background colors. The old woman had unfairly belittled her own abilities. It took talent to miniaturize the world of the impressionists— talent, patience, and artistry. Anne felt a sudden pang of sadness. Mrs. Zambini had been so alone in the world. Unfastening the catch, Anne separated the front and back parts of the Plexiglas frame. Slipping her hand inside the frame, she felt around for the photograph. Nothing, except the painting. She looked inside the frame. Empty. Steven Hillyard's picture was gone.

Anne put the frame back in the cardboard box. Who would want to steal an old photograph of a dead man? Who would even know the picture was there? After thanking Marie, Anne left the nurse's station and went back downstairs.

In the lobby, she passed Dominick Zambini on his way in. She tried to offer him her condolences. But he pushed right past her. His eyes blazed. His face was flushed. He looked more angry than grieved. Now that his wife was dead, Anne wondered if he would finally be able to muster up some forgiveness. Somehow, she doubted it.

The sheriff's office of Neptune Township was located in a nondescript tan brick building off the highway. Anne gave her name to the officer on duty and paced back and forth while the cop phoned Mark Trasker and got her cleared to go back to the inner sanctum. It didn't look like much: a long corridor done in institutional grays, with tiny offices branching off on both sides. The whole place smelled like stale cigarettes and burnt coffee.

"Hardaway," Trasker said, looking up from his desk. He was sitting with his feet propped up, dressed in a navy blue suit and tie, sorting through a bunch of manila folders. "Somehow I figured you'd show up. You here to chew me out for how little progress we've made on your skeleton?"

"No."

She sat down heavily in a chair opposite his desk. She

looked like hell and she knew it. Flyaway hair. Bloodshot eyes. Pale, sleep-deprived, overwrought. When the phone had woken her up, she'd thrown on the first thing her eyes lit upon, which happened to be an old pair of sweats, her striped nylon running jacket, and a plaid shirt of Jack's that was three sizes too big.

"What's wrong?" Trasker asked, giving her the once over.

She took a deep breath and told him everything she knew about Sunnydale, starting with the obituaries she'd found in the newspaper and ending with Mrs. Zambini's death.

"Heart failure, huh?" Trasker said, when she'd finished. "With fourteen deaths in three months, maybe it was and maybe it wasn't. We'd need to do an autopsy to be sure."

"How long would that take?"

"A day. Maybe two. We have to get the family's permission first."

"Could you do me a favor?"

"If I can."

"Could you run some names through your computer, see what comes up?

"What are you looking for?"

"Anything suspicious, I guess. Crimes, misdemeanors, the usual stuff."

"Okay, shoot," he said, grabbing a pad and pen.

"Katherine Crowley. Philip Reynolds. And Andrew Deretchin."

"Why Reynolds?"

"He's the head man over there. Plus, he was Hillyard's former partner. I think there's a connection between the nursing home and the bones."

Trasker rested his elbows on his desk. His deep brown eyes had a serious cast. "The phone call?"

"Partly. But there's something else. It's a feeling I get when I walk around Sunnydale. Like someone's watching me."

Trasker raised an eyebrow. "You want me to arrange for a tap on your phone?"

"Yeah. That'd be great. In case whoever called me decides to check back in." Anne stood up. "I've got to get going."

"Could I buy you a cup of coffee and a stack of pancakes at Quilters?"

She smiled. "Rain check, okay?"

He returned the smile. "You got it. Hey, Hardaway?"

"Yeah?"

"Be careful, okay?"

"Aren't I always?"

His smile was exasperated. "Nope."

She turned and trotted back down the corridor, half regretting not taking Trasker up on his offer. She could do with a pot of coffee right about now. Black, lots of sugar. A cup of coffee and about twelve hours of uninterrupted sleep.

Outside, it had started to rain. A cold, light rain. The sky was gunmetal gray. The wind had picked up, gusting from the east. She ran over to the Mustang and headed home. Halfway there, she realized she'd been scanning the roads at every intersection, keeping an eye out for the white Ford. How could she track down the driver? Conduct her own private stakeout from inside the house? She figured the Ford would be back to spy on her, though for the life of her, she couldn't figure out why anyone would bother. Unless . . . She peered out the windshield as her car swung through the wrought-iron gates that marked the entrance to the Heights. Unless the skeleton wasn't the only thing buried in the house. Unless there was more.

The car cruised down Main Street. She drove carefully, swerving to avoid the broken tree branches that were piled by the side of the road. No one had come to collect them yet and with the weather so grim, it reminded Anne of the storm. It had come on suddenly, without much advance warning. The weather experts hadn't foreseen a northeaster and were caught unawares when the down-pour hit and the wind tore along the beach, forging a pattern of destruction.

When she pulled up in front of the house, the rain was coming down heavier. She lifted her jacket over her head, dashed from the car, and ran up the porch steps.

Jack met her at the front door, wearing a scowl.

"Where've you been?" he demanded.

"It's a long story." She went inside, threw off her jacket, and headed to the kitchen. Great. He'd made coffee. She was practically salivating at the smell.

"I woke up at six-thirty and you were gone. No note. No nothing."

"It's a long story." She poured herself a cup of the coffee, another care package he'd brought from the city, some designer blend from Starbucks, and gulped half of it down.

Setting the cup on the table, she opened the refrigerator and took out the orange juice and two powdered donuts. A quick sugar fix would help her feel human again. That and a shower.

"I didn't know what else to do," Jack said, "so I started working on the house. I fixed the loose newel post on the staircase."

"What?" Anne was only half listening. She had a splitting headache, and she was so tired she felt lightheaded. The sense of sadness that clung to her was almost palpable. She hadn't expected Maggie Zambini's death to hit her so hard. After all, she hardly knew the woman anymore. She drank the rest of the coffee quickly, feeling the warmth course through her body. "You fixed the post? Great. Thanks."

"The post was hollow. You might not thank me when you see what was hidden inside it."

Something in his voice made her look up. "What?" she said again, sharper this time.

Jack reached into his pocket and tossed a black wallet onto the table. "Take a look inside."

She put down the donut, wiped the powdered sugar from her fingers, and picked up the wallet. The leather had faded, it felt worn and soft. There was money in the billfold. Two twenties and a five. She opened the wallet wider, suddenly afraid of what she might find, and shook the contents onto the table: Credit cards. Business cards. Driver's license. Photo. She sifted through them, willing herself to remain calm, fighting the panic that was welling up inside her.

He looked younger than in the other pictures she'd seen. His hair was a little different. He had the blank, surprised stare of someone who'd blinked just as the flash went off. Anne stared at him for nearly a minute, weighing the implications, feeling her heart flip-flop in her chest. Finally, she put the license down.

"Anne?" Jack said.

Her gaze flew to Jack, then returned to Steven Hillyard's face.

It was as though Hillyard had become a part of her, a part of this house, haunting her from beyond the grave. Even though his bones had been removed, even though she could refinish the cellar, obliterate the crime, and pretend it didn't concern her, she would never really be rid of him.

Chapter 17

Place strips of double-sided adhesive tape on tables and other surfaces that are off-limits to cats. They hate the feel of adhesive on their paws and will soon learn to keep off.

"Where exactly did you find the wallet?" she said to Jack.

"Inside the post with a couple more of his things."

Anne gazed at him incredulously. "You mean there's *more?*"

Jack placed a simple gold tie clip and a silver Seiko watch on the table. Though the watch no longer told time, it looked almost like new. Anne stared at each object in stunned disbelief. Was this what the person in the car was after? No. There had to be something more.

"There's no wedding band," she said.

"Maybe he didn't wear one."

"Maybe," Anne said. But she wasn't convinced. Hillyard seemed like the type of man who would. "So who do you think hid this stuff in the post?" she asked Jack.

"I have no idea."

She rubbed the back of her neck. She was starting to feel lightheaded from lack of sleep. "What do you think of this scenario? Hillyard comes here on August 23, to treat my mother. She's in love with him. But she's found out he's having an affair with her best friend. In a fit of jealous rage, she takes out a gun, kills him, buries his body in the cellar, and hides this stuff inside the loose post."

"I don't like it," he said flatly.

"But do you buy it?"

Jack looked at her quizzically. "What are you getting at?"

"Do you believe that's the way it could have happened? Because I don't."

Anne got up and dumped her breakfast dishes in the sink. She turned on the tap and splashed cold water on her face. Yes, her mother had been behaving strangely. Forgetting where she parked the car. Forgetting familiar faces. Acting paranoid. Starting fires with cigarettes she'd forgotten to put out. But even during the worst of the Alzheimer's, she couldn't see Evelyn getting hold of a gun and shooting her precious doctor in the back of the head. Anne tried to imagine it. She still remembered her mother's tumultuous bouts of rage and fear. She tried to picture Steven Hillyard walking in the house and telling her mother he couldn't treat her anymore, that he was running off with another woman. If he would even reveal such a thing. Anne suspected he wouldn't. Too unprofessional, for one thing. Too much information imparted to patients who worshipped him as a man who loved and sought out not female companionship, but higher learning.

She dried her face with the dishtowel. She could feel

Jack's eyes trained on her neck. She was ashamed of herself, ashamed she'd thought her mother could ever commit such an act. But then it was always easy to let the Alzheimer's take over, to forget that underneath the confusion and pain and rage there was simply Evelyn Hardaway—the mother who loved her, the woman who had been handed a terrible, life-altering disease that was not of her making.

When Anne turned back around, she caught sight of Hillyard's things. She didn't want to touch them again, didn't even want to see them anymore, for that matter. "Could you put these in an envelope for me? I have to call the cops and ask them to come and collect the evidence."

"Sure." He was staring at her, his blue eyes filled with concern. "Anne, look. I know how much of a strain this has been for you. But I'm going to help you figure this out. Just like you helped me find out who killed my brother."

Tigger again. Jack acted like he owed her something. A truth for a truth. One good deed deserves another. Isn't that how their relationship had begun? Because she'd helped him discover who'd killed Tigger? She'd dredged up family secrets, torn the scabs off old wounds. Maybe it wasn't the best way to start out.

Aloud, she said, "Did you know Alzheimer's is inherited? They've done studies."

Jack looked startled. "I'd heard that. Yeah."

"Do you ever worry about it? Ever wonder if I'll get it someday?"

"No," he said quickly.

"Why not? I would, if I were you."

"You're not me. Besides, biology isn't destiny. If it were, I'd be a drunk like my old man."

"You're right. But you can't discount biology either. Our parents helped shape the people we've become. Their values and their choices affect us, don't you think? Look at my family. My father walked out on my mother at a critical time in her life. He walked out on both of us. Don't you think that affects the way I feel about trust and love?"

"I guess."

Jack was looking at her like he wanted her to stop talking, as if he were afraid of what she'd say next. But she couldn't stop. She felt breathless, keyed up.

"And my mother. She was sick, Jack. She was so sick she couldn't tell you what day of the week it was or even what my name was sometimes." Anne was talking fast, the words tumbling over each other. "But through the worst of it, she was still my mom. There was something, some connection between us, that never went away. Not even when they pumped her with drugs. Or when she got bounced from one institution to the next. You didn't know her, Jack. She wasn't a killer."

Anne got a glass from the cupboard, filled it with tap water, took out two Extra-Strength Tylenol, and washed them down. "I can't believe I ever thought she was capable of shooting Hillyard. That's what the killer wanted people to believe. And they would have, Jack. If the body had been discovered in 1974, this whole town would have believed she killed him. The Crazy Lady strikes again. But that's not the way it happened. Somebody knew Hillyard was coming here to see her. And whoever it was set her up."

"You think your mother knew who killed him?"

Anne thought for a moment, then shook her head. "She loved him. If she'd known, she would have turned the killer in. She would have become dangerous to that person."

Jack raised an eyebrow. "So you're saying that while your mother was making tea or gardening or whatever, somebody walked in here, shot him, and buried the body."

"She never locked the door, Jack. There was no reason to. You know what I think happened? She was starting to get lost on her way to see Hillyard. She couldn't find his office anymore. So they made an appointment to meet here. Only she forgot. She wandered off or something. Hillyard got here, let himself in, and the killer followed."

"What about the stuff in the post?"

"I doubt whoever killed him had time for carpentry. So my mother must have found those things and hidden them away. Maybe the killer purposefully left them lying around, as circumstantial evidence."

Jack didn't look convinced. "I guess it could have happened that way," he said slowly. "But you have to admit it sounds pretty farfetched."

"Not at all. Besides, there's something hidden in this house that will prove every word of it."

"What's that?"

"The bullet."

The orientation session at Sunnydale took exactly five minutes. Greta Koch rattled off the do's and don'ts of volunteering as though she were giving a speech to a room full of preschoolers: Do engage the patients in lively conversation. Do help out in the Activity Room. Do read to patients. Don't administer medication. Don't assist patients in and out of wheelchairs. Don't encourage negative or sad thoughts.

Anne was surprised to find she was the only one who'd shown up. She and Greta Koch sat in a corner of the Activity Room, at a table filled with supplies for the next art project—yarn, balloons, popsicle sticks, Elmer's glue, crayons. Anne couldn't figure out what the patients were going to be making. Balloon animals? Thanksgiving pilgrims? Why did nursing homes insist on treating the elderly as if they were celebrating a four-year-old's birthday party?

Although the Activity Room was nearly empty, Anne still had the feeling that she was being observed. Her eyes darted around the room, searching, searching. But the handful of old people in wheelchairs appeared not to notice or care about her presence. She'd caught a brief glimpse of Chester Higgins, toolbelt hitched to his pants, striding down the third-floor hallway, but when she raised her hand in a greeting, he rounded a corner and sped away.

"Are there usually so few volunteers?" Anne asked.

"Most folks have no patience for their elders," said Greta Koch, tapping her clipboard for emphasis. "They think old people are depressing. You know what I think?" Nurse Koch smiled, showing a mouth full of large, crooked teeth. "They're scared is all. Of getting old. Dying. Well, we'll all face that day eventually. In the meantime, it is our duty to protect those who cannot protect themselves—the weak, the helpless, the aged, the infirm. The elderly are not to be shunted aside in corners. They have rights. They have hopes. They need to be respected, revered for their wisdom and experience. Here, we treat the elderly with dignity. Without it, life isn't worth living. Loneliness and idleness have no place at Sunnydale. Our goal is to integrate each patient into the Sunnydale family, so each one feels a sense of belonging."

Anne barely listened as Greta Koch continued her sermon. The nurse could prattle on all day, but it wouldn't change the facts, which were that a nursing home was the last place in the world you wanted to spend your final years. Period. With all Greta's talk of family and wisdom, Sunnydale was no different from a half-dozen homes Anne had visited in the course of her life. As for respect, there was precious little of it. Line dancing and arts and crafts were no substitute for living in your own home, surrounded by friends and family.

"How well did you know Maggie Zambini?" Anne asked, changing the subject.

"Well enough," the nurse said. "She was a tough old bird, that one. Added a little zest to this place, if you ask me."

"Do you know who packed up her things?"

Greta Koch shot Anne a puzzled look. "Kate Crowley, I suppose. She was the nurse on floor duty. Why?"

"After a patient dies, is it customary for one of the nurses to pack that person's belongings? I would have thought a family member would take care of it."

Nurse Koch shook her head vehemently. "It's too distressing for the children and grandchildren. Too much of an ordeal. The nursing staff gets the job done quickly and easily."

"I see," Anne said. Though she didn't, really. It seemed like an intimate task that would normally be performed by members of the immediate family.

She glanced at the other side of the activity room, where the dark-haired woman with Alzheimer's was gliding over the Monopoly board floor. The woman's arms were stretched out in front of her like a sleepwalker. She was moving without seeing, the way a blind person would—tentatively, carefully, as if she expected the floor to open up and swallow her whole.

Greta Koch followed Anne's gaze and scribbled something down on her clipboard. "You sure you have time for this?" she said to Anne. "I read the story in the paper. About those bones of yours. Sounds like your plate is full."

"Not at all. The police are handling the investigation. I work from home, set my own schedule. My hours are pretty flexible."

"I see."

"Is there some paperwork I have to fill out?"

Anne hoped there wasn't. It occurred to her that Claire Hillyard might not want her hanging around.

"You're all set," Nurse Koch announced. "In fact, if you're free this afternoon, a group of us are going for a short walk to the library, followed by afternoon tea. We're meeting in the lobby at half past one."

"Fine. I'll be there." Anne pushed her chair back from the table and got up.

"Oh, there is one more thing. You haven't told me why you want to be a volunteer."

Anne watched as the dark-haired woman swayed back

and forth, then spun around slowly in a circle. It looked almost like dancing. "Why do I want to volunteer?" Anne repeated. "My mother was in and out of nursing homes for many years. I was a lot younger then. I didn't visit her as much as I should have. So I guess I'm making up for it now."

Oceanside Heights didn't have a gourmet shop. Or any fancy restaurants. Or stores that sold upscale linen napkins, flatware with colorful handles, cute woven hampers, and other picnic-type stuff. A trendy coffee bar had opened two summers ago, but it went out of business when the tourist season ended. Which meant Anne had to drive all the way to Red Bank to get lunch and a fancy fruit salad—an apology of sorts for Jack—for which she paid an obscenely high price. It was just as well, she told herself, on the ride back. If Starbucks opened a store in the Heights, the Gap, Banana Republic, and Barnes & Noble wouldn't be far behind. In no time at all, the Victorian storefronts on Main Street would come to resemble the Monmouth Mall. As things stood now, the town didn't have a bookstore. You had to drive to Bradley Beach to get a magazine. And when Moby's Hardware started stocking Martha Stewart paint, it caused a contretemps because some people bemoaned the shelf space lost by Benjamin Moore.

All in all, Anne thought, as she noticed how much repair work had already been completed on the familiar shops lining Main Street, it took more than a northeaster to change the face of her home town. The Heights looked the same today as it had fifty years ago, and there was something supremely comforting in that. Many of the shops and restaurants in town—including The Enchanted Florist, Baby Face, Advance Pharmacy, the Main Street Launderette, Moby's Hardware, Quilters, Gingerbreads, and Nagle's—had been around since she was a little girl. They were family-owned businesses, who still let you buy on credit and knew that you were a pushover for rice pudding or your that favorite flowers were pink roses or that back in the fifth grade you kept your UNICEF money after going trick-or-treating, instead of turning it in at school.

With strip malls sprouting up all over America, with the landscape becoming so homogenized it was hard to tell what part of the country you were in, the quirky, down-home stability of the Heights appealed to her. The off-season was part of that appeal. She felt like with the summer people gone, the town was hers again, and she could walk along the beach or wander past the Victorian homes she had come to love without bumping headlong into camera-toting tourists.

When she pulled up in front of her house, she parked behind a black Camry with a license plate that said HYPNO-DOC. *Well, what do you know. A doctor who makes house calls.* She got the shopping bags containing the food out of the trunk, unlocked the door, and found Stuart Hillyard standing in the living room. The cat was stretched out on the antique cedar blanket chest, idly scratching at the wood, even though Anne had tried to make it clear time and again that the furniture was off-limits. Through her closed office door, she heard the distant hum of Jack's voice, talking on the phone.

"You lied to me," Stuart Hillyard said the moment she walked in.

She set the bags down in the hall. "I can explain."

"I don't see how." Stuart looked in more disarray than usual. His shirttail was out. His bowtie was barely knotted. Even his beard seemed rumpled. "I take my work seriously. If I'd known that you merely wanted to pump me for information, I never would have agreed to treat you."

"You read the article in the newspaper," Anne said, restating the obvious.

"Yes. You might have mentioned the fact that the police dug up my father's remains on these premises." He looked around him warily, taking in the sofa, the rug, the oak coffee table, the oil paintings, as if they were some-how tainted.

"You're right. It was a lousy thing to do. But I wanted to get to know you and I thought if I told you the truth, you might not want to talk to me."

Stuart Hillyard cast his suspicious gaze on her as if seeing her for the first time. She felt a twinge of remorse at tricking him. The thing of it was she liked Stuart Hill-yard. He seemed like a stand-up guy, a little on the touchy-feely side, but someone whose heart was basically in the right place. Now she could sense his mind working overtime, trying to connect the dots.

"Did you know my father?" he demanded.

"No. Apparently, he'd come here to treat my mother. She had Alzheimer's."

"Was she involved in his death?"

"No," Anne said quickly. "She was very fond of him. She would never have hurt him."

"Then who did?"

"That's what I'm trying to find out. Look, now that things are out in the open, would you mind if I ask you a few questions?" She walked past him, into the living room. "Please come in and sit down. Can I get you any-thing? Coffee? Soda?"

"No, thank you." He hesitated, then followed her into the room and sat stiffly in the flowered wing chair.

"This whole thing has come as quite a shock, as you can imagine," Anne said, seating herself on the sofa, with her legs tucked underneath her. "This is the house I grew up in. I can't believe that I've lived here all these years without knowing . . ." She searched for a nice way to put it. "Without dreaming that . . ."

". . . his bones were in the cellar," Stuart finished.

"I can only imagine how upset you must be."

"Yes, but not for the reason you suppose," Stuart said. He took his glasses off, polished them on his shirt, and put them back on the bridge of his nose. "My father and I were not especially close. He was remote, self-involved.

Even when he was here, he was never around. When he disappeared, it actually came as a relief. Good riddance to a man who was never cut out to marry or have children. Now that he's surfaced again—literally—it's only served to dredge up all the old pain."

Anne waited for Stuart to continue, but he sat rigidly in his chair without speaking, his expression tense and unyielding.

"What do you mean?" she said sympathetically.

Stuart allowed himself a small tight smile. "Do you know where I thought he's been all these years? In Brazil or Fiji, sharing a villa with his latest conquest. I half expected to get a postcard saying, 'Having a swell time. Glad you're not here.' "

"So you knew he was having an affair."

Stuart laughed harshly. "Everyone knew, including my mother. My parents fought constantly. There were many nights when my father didn't come home. He never bothered to explain what he was doing or who he was with. And then there were the phone calls." Anne waited expectantly, while Stuart fiddled with his loosened bowtie. "The phone would ring and when you answered it, the person on the other end would hang up. It drove my mother nuts. Once, I overheard him talking to his lover on the phone. He was telling her to stop crying, to calm down." Stuart made a sound of disgust. "He was whispering 'Baby, I love you,' while my mother was in the kitchen, whipping up chicken à la king for his dinner."

"Sounds like a difficult situation."

"To put it mildly," he muttered. Stuart shifted in his chair and stared out the window. Anne could practically feel him trying to put a lid on his emotions. It didn't appear to be working. "I was living at home then," he continued. "I couldn't afford a place of my own, though I dearly wanted to get out of the great man's way. Oh, my father's patients worshipped him," Stuart said bitterly. "They thought he was brilliant, caring, trustworthy.

He treated them well. But he wasn't quite as solicitous of my mother and me."

"Yet you entered his profession."

"I could hardly blame his failings on hypnotherapy. Quite the opposite, in fact. As I delved deeper into hypnotherapy, I began to learn more about my father, about what made him tick."

"What did you find out?"

"That hypnotherapy suited him. It gave him a degree of power. To most, he was a great healer. A man of science, yet not so scholarly, so above the fray, that he failed to feel his patients' pain. He liked helping people. And he was a brilliant clinician. He could take one look at a patient and know exactly the approach to take, the length their treatment should be, and the right words to use."

Anne tried to imagine Steven Hillyard hypnotizing her mother. She pictured him confidently raising a gold pocket watch, swinging it back and forth in front of her mother's troubled, panicked eyes. *You are getting sleepy. You are getting sleepy.* But, of course, it wouldn't have been so simple, so cartoonlike. Not to mention the fact that Hillyard had owned a Seiko.

"Would hypnotherapy have benefited an Alzheimer's patient?" Anne asked.

"Perhaps initially. It tends to have a calming effect on most people. But in the long run?" Stuart Hillyard spread his hands wide and shrugged dismissively. "Let's put it this way, it probably did her no harm."

Good, Anne thought. If Steven Hillyard had been able to relieve her mother's pain, even for a little while, Anne was grateful to him.

"What about your father's relationship with Philip Reynolds?" Anne asked. "They were partners in the clinic, weren't they?"

"Initially, yes. But they had a falling-out. Right before my father disappeared, he accused Reynolds of siphoning money from the business."

"Was it true?"

"I have no idea. Reynolds came over to our house one night and they had a big row about it. The partnership was dissolved and my father took over the clinic. I heard later that Reynolds had gone into hospital management. He renounced hypnosis completely. Claimed it was for charlatans and quacks."

Anne made a mental note to have Trasker look into the nursing home's financials. Something wasn't kosher there. How was Reynolds able to raise money to build more homes when Sunnydale was in such godawful shape?

"For what it's worth," she said, "when I came to see you I was serious about working together. I thought hypnosis could clarify some things for me."

"Your fear of commitment? The problems you're having with your fiancé?"

"Yes."

"And now?"

"I don't think it's necessarily the right way for me to go. But I appreciate your input and your help."

Hillyard nodded. He appeared to be softening slightly. "And I appreciate your honesty. Try playing the tape I gave you. You may find that your resistance to your fiancé lessens with repeated . . ." His voice trailed off uncertainly.

Anne looked up and saw Jack standing in the doorway, his eyes blazing.

"Don't mind me," Jack said sarcastically. "I can't wait to hear what comes next."

Chapter 18

*To repair damaged
hardwood floors, use a
wood-patch compound. (It
looks like wood-tone Play-
Doh.) First, remove any
dirt or wood splinters from
the damaged area and
smooth on the patching
material with a small putty
knife, so it's level with the
floor. When the material
dries, sand the patch with
fine sandpaper.*

For the next few seconds, there was dead silence
in the room. Anne didn't know what to say, what
words she could use to erase the hurt, angry look
on Jack's face. She should have just come clean with
Stuart Hillyard in the first place. Then none of this would
be happening.

"Jack," she began. "I'm sorry."

But even as she spoke she could see his face hard-

ening, shutting her out. Loyalty meant everything to him.
By discussing their relationship with a perfect stranger
she'd broken the code. She'd betrayed him.

"Hey, Doc," Jack said icily. "Did she tell you what an
overbearing perfectionist I am? How I planned a big
black-tie wedding without even consulting her? Twenty-
piece orchestra. Five kinds of wine. River view. I must
be a real jerk to want to give the bride a fairy tale ending.
That is, if she even bothers to show up."

Stuart Hillyard got to his feet awkwardly, looking embarrassed to be caught in the crossfire. "I would never
knowingly betray a doctor-client relationship," he said
stiffly. "I think this is something the two of you need to
work out in private."

Anne showed him to the door and closed it behind
him. When she went back into the living room, Jack was
standing at the window with his back to her, staring at
the ocean. The silence was so thick you could slice it
with a steak knife.

She walked over and stood beside him, though his
flinty body language warned her to keep away.

"Listen," she said. "I went to Hillyard's office to try
and get some information. I needed a reason to be there."

"So?" he said. He made it sound like a four-letter
word. "Why not tell Dr. Hypnosis you have trouble meeting deadlines, like you told me? Or that you're afraid to
fly? Or you're petrified of jellyfish? You could have lied
to him, told him anything. But instead you lied to *me*."

"Because I didn't want to hurt you."

"Gee, thanks." He swung around to face her. His jaw
was set. She could hear him breathing through his mouth.
"You thought a tape was going to fix things? If you have
a problem with who I am or what I do, you talk to me."

"It's not about you, Jack. It's about us."

"What about us?" he shouted. "You stood there on the
beach forty-eight hours ago and told me you wanted to
marry me."

"I know."

She could feel her cheeks burning. Her heart was somersaulting all over the place. What was this about, really? Why couldn't she commit to Jack? *Because something's not right.*

"It's really easy, Anne. Either you love me or you don't. Which is it?"

His cornflower blue eyes were focused on her, waiting. She felt dizzy, muddled, like a punch drunk boxer who'd been knocked against the ropes. "I think we both need some time," she said slowly.

"Like hell we do. You're the one who's stalling for time. I guess that's my answer."

He turned on his heel and strode from the room. The front door opened then slammed shut. Through the window, she watched him take the porch steps two at a time, get into his red Corvette, and gun the engine. The car shot down Ocean Avenue. And then he was gone and the only sounds she heard came from the ticking of the grandfather clock and her own wild heart.

Every time Anne dozed off, the phone would ring and the person on the other end, calling from a newspaper, radio, or TV station, would want to interview her about the skeleton. No, she told them all. Not interested. Nothing to say. She didn't care that Halloween was two weeks away and the buried bones would make a good news peg for the holiday. All she wanted was to escape into sleep.

In the middle of it all, Jennifer Joan called. It took Anne by surprise. She'd been communicating with the home repair guru by e-mail and fax, so it was strange to hear her voice on the phone, a voice that was not angry exactly, but laced with disapproval and concern.

"You're behind in your work," Jennifer Joan scolded. "You haven't sent me anything on repairing hardwood flooring or patching drywall."

Repairing hardwood floors. Anne searched her brain, trying to remember. Oh, right. Jennifer Joan had faxed her a drawing of what to do, but she couldn't make heads or tails of it. There was flooring and then there was subflooring, and Jennifer Joan hadn't bothered to distinguish between the two. Anne had meant to call her and clear everything up, but it had slipped her mind. The storm seemed to have drained her interest in the home repair book. What good was all this advice when her own house was falling apart?

"I'm tackling the floors right now," Anne fibbed.

Maybe she'd really blown it with Dr. Stu. Maybe she should have been working on her tendency to procrastinate this entire time.

"I thought I could count on you," Jennifer Joan said tartly. "We have a contract. We have a deadline. What's going on up there?"

Just a couple of murders, Anne felt like saying. *It's nothing compared to clogged gutters and cracks in foundation walls.*

"There's been a really bad storm," Anne said. "Maybe you heard about it."

"No, I haven't. I don't have time for TV or newspapers. Business is booming. There's my radio show and I must have sent you at least a hundred pages of notes."

"Uh huh."

Anne wished Jennifer Joan had better handwriting. Or a smaller ego. It would probably make things easier. "Look," she said. "I know you're swamped right now. But I'd love to set up a time to go over some of those notes with you. How about Wednesday afternoon?"

"I can't do it till five-thirty."

"Fine. Why don't you call me then."

Triple Star Publishing didn't pay for expenses. Anne would rather have it be Jennifer Joan's dime.

"About that storm of yours," Jennifer Joan said, right before she hung up. "A claw hammer can be your very best friend."

Anne lay on her bed under the eiderdown quilt, trying to empty her mind. No dice. The crash of the waves, usually so soothing to her ears, had the monotonous effect of a dentist's drill. Every time she closed her eyes she saw Maggie Zambini's face. God, how could Mrs. Z be dead? Anne had seen her just yesterday. And now she couldn't stop seeing her. Those china blue eyes. The white tufts of hair shooting from her scalp like newly mown grass. The way she'd handled the photograph of her dead lover—gingerly, carefully, as if it were a holy relic.

When a police officer rang the bell and announced he was installing a wire tap on the phone, it almost came as a relief. Anne let the cop in, called Trasker, who was out, and left a message on his machine. The autopsy would prove whether Mrs. Zambini had died of natural causes. If not . . . well, Anne hadn't a clue as to who would want to kill her. A harmless old lady who copied famous paintings. *People keep dying here.* Fourteen deaths in three months. Sunnydale, where the body count kept mounting.

Anne thought about phoning Teri to offer her sympathy, but instead, she ate the overpriced picnic lunch she'd bought for herself and Jack, and wrote Teri a condolence note. Someone on the staff would surely get around to mentioning that Mrs. Zambini's "niece" had visited earlier in the day, and Anne didn't want to be within spitting distance of Teri when that happened.

Questions tumbled inside her head like ping-pong balls in a lottery jar. Who had made that strange phone call? How had that person known Mrs. Z was dead? Who was driving the white Ford? Who had stolen Hillyard's picture? Was it Katie Crowley, the nurse Mrs. Zambini didn't trust? Anne took out Katie's phone number and dialed, trying to figure out how she was going to play it. She couldn't exactly come out and ask whether the nurse stole things from the dead. The phone rang four times before a machine answered. Anne hung up on it. If she was going to invent another lie, she'd need time to devise a whopper.

She glanced at the clock. Almost one. She wondered

where Jack had gone and whether he was coming back. She wondered what he was thinking right now. She could see him visualizing their relationship in terms of a business deal: Lay the groundwork, present the ring, seal the deal. Had two sessions with Stuart Hillyard constituted a deal breaker? But then, she wasn't being fair to Jack. He was a great guy. And he loved her. (Although neither of them was big on saying the L word very often.) Jack wanted to spend the rest of his life with her. Why? she asked herself. The question popped into her mind unbidden. Why did Jack love her? There were dozens of women he could date in New York. Beautiful, successful women who would adore being Mrs. Jack Mills.

Women were always coming on to Jack. Anne had seen waitresses flirt with him on countless occasions. And Jack himself joked about women at his gym or his apartment building or women he met through work who asked him out on dates or slipped him their home phone numbers on the backs of their business cards. Why had he singled her out for his attentions? Why had he spent the past year driving sixty miles on alternate weekends to a home town he'd rather never see again?

When you got right down to it, they were more different than alike. Her life was chaotic; he couldn't stand loose ends. He was obsessively neat; she hated to clean. He was the life of the party; she preferred spending Saturday night curled up with a Jane Austen novel and a cup of jasmine tea. He divided things into black and white; she viewed the world as a multitude of grays. True, they'd become friends, then lovers, then had settled into a pleasant pattern of spending two or three days and nights together. But when you were considering being with somebody for the rest of your life, shouldn't there be something more between you?

Anne looked at the diamond ring on her finger. She thought about what the ring meant, about why she had told Jack yes. She'd never done well with ultimatums, with making major decisions quickly. Her mind tended

to get slightly fuzzy around the edges when she was under pressure. Not her finest hour. But she knew now why
she'd agreed to marry him. It was because she didn't
want to say goodbye.

She let the cop out, picked up the phone he'd tampered
with, heard its bland reassuring dial tone, and put the
receiver back in the cradle. Then she got out her keys,
locked up the house, and drove back to Sunnydale. The
sky was still overcast, threatening rain, through it seemed
a shade warmer because the wind had died down. There
were several people strolling beside what used to be the
boardwalk, forging a rough path among the shards of
scattered driftwood. The sand dunes had shifted again,
appearing slightly lower, as though the tops had been
sheared off.

Workmen were boarding up the remaining broken windows on the Church by the Sea and doing more repair
work on the roof. Several ladders had been propped
against the building and the main double doors were
thrown open. As she drove past, Anne took a quick
glimpse inside. It didn't look too bad. The pews were
intact, though the soaked red carpet was the rosy brown
hue of dried blood. She cut through town and pulled into
the Sunnydale parking lot at twenty-five past one.

When she walked into the lobby, seven patients were
assembled at the far end. Anne recognized a few of them:
Andrew Deretchin, the man with Parkinson's disease, and
the woman who suffered from Alzheimer's. Greta Koch
and a plump dark-haired nurse were writing the patients'
names in big red letters on square tags, then sticking the
tags onto the patients' chests.

"In case they should get lost," Greta explained, as
Anne approached. "It's never happened yet. But fore-
warned is forearmed."

Despite all Greta's talk about respect, Anne noticed
that the nurse talked about the elderly patients in her care
as if they weren't there and couldn't hear every word she

was saying. She listened as Greta mapped out their route—exactly how many minutes it would take to get to the library, how much time they would spend there, and how much time it would take to walk back. Plotting out the afternoon seemed to take half the fun out of the trip. But Anne paid attention and nodded her head a lot, so Nurse Koch would know she was going to make a first-rate volunteer.

She'd spotted these nursing home excursions before— at flea markets, art fairs, or book bazaars—but had never given them much thought. There was usually a small contingent of frail old men and women shepherded by a few nurses. In the summertime, a group of them would appear from time to time on the boardwalk or on one of the fishing piers, the old people hunched in their wheelchairs, their heads shielded from the blazing sun by visors or floppy hats. The tourists smiled as they paraded by, a little slice of local color, another reminder of the down-home folksiness of the Heights. You'd never find this same scene on the boardwalk at Wildwood or Belmar, where on hot summer afternoons most passers-by were teenagers who cruised in and out of the tacky souvenir shops and greasy food stands, like lemmings.

Now, as she grabbed the handles of Andrew Deretchin's wheelchair and guided the chair out the double glass doors and onto the street, Anne couldn't help thinking about her mother. When Evelyn was locked up in nursing homes all those years, had she ever gone on an outing? Ever felt the wind on her cheeks as red and golden leaves tore loose from the trees? Not that Anne could remember.

The sky was still overcast, thunderclouds hovering ominously to the west. Anne had a sudden vision of the procession caught in a downpour—soaked, shivering, an unnecessary hazard for people already in such fragile health.

She eased the wheelchair over a crack in the sidewalk and fell to the rear. Greta Koch was in the lead, pushing the woman with Alzheimer's. Three of the patients had motorized wheelchairs and they cruised along by themselves, single file, engines humming. The plump nurse was about twenty feet in front of Anne, pushing the man who had Parkinson's Disease.

Deretchin was slumped forward in his chair, his chin practically resting on his chest, so that Anne thought he was sleeping. But when the wheels caught on a rough spot in the pavement, he jerked upright.

"Sorry," Anne said, maneuvering the wheelchair around the bump and easing it forward. "I didn't see that coming."

"Margaret is dead," he replied. His voice was low, barely above a whisper.

"I know. I was here early this morning, but they'd already taken her away."

Deretchin gripped the arms of the chair. He wore a tan raincoat, loosely belted at the waist, and dark gray trousers. Though the raincoat was dirty, it looked expensive. "I saw her last night, right before she went to sleep. She wasn't feeling well. Headache, upset stomach. I didn't think it was anything serious."

"What time was that?"

"About nine-thirty."

They turned right at the light and continued down Stockton Street, past one-story bungalows with low-pitched roofs and narrow Colonial Revival houses that had porches on both the ground level and the second story. Anne noticed that people had started to decorate the outsides of their homes again in the wake of the storm, hanging flags over doorways, and setting out pumpkins and plastic trash bags imprinted with ghosts and black cats.

"Did you see or hear anything unusual last night?" Anne asked. "Anyone going into or out of Margaret's room?"

Andrew Deretchin turned his upper body and craned his neck to look back at her. Away from the nursing home's harsh fluorescent lights, he looked and seemed more vital.

"I did see something," he said softly, his courtly drawl tinged with concern. Anne slowed her pace, to make sure the others wouldn't be able to hear. Deretchin was staring at her with a strange expression on his face. "I woke up to go to the bathroom at around one o'clock in the morning," he continued, "and I saw that sneaky blonde, the one Margaret doesn't like, coming out of her room, carrying a tray."

"Nurse Crowley?"

"Yes."

"Could you see what was on the tray?"

"A couple of small white paper cups. It's what they use to hold our meds. It struck me as peculiar; why would Katie be checking on her? But I was half-asleep at the time. Now I wish I'd gone in myself."

"Hey, there." Greta Koch had stopped at the corner and was waving them forward. "Get a move on. You don't want to get separated from the rest of the group."

As Anne picked up the pace, Deretchin turned around to face forward. Katie Crowley again. Was the nurse somehow connected to the spate of deaths at Sunnydale? Anne couldn't imagine how. But why the late-night visit to Mrs. Zambini's room? From everything Anne had seen and heard about Nurse Crowley, it was hard to picture her being solicitous—checking on patients and tucking them in.

The procession turned down Beechwood Avenue, where the houses were bigger and fancier: Queen Annes and Victorian Gothic buildings with spool-shaped balusters and projecting bay windows. They were only a few blocks from the beach; the scent of the ocean was clean and exhilarating. On Olin Street, they made a right and stopped in front of the library, a quaint sky blue building decorated with gingerbread and enclosed by a picket fence, also painted blue.

Delia Graustark, the town librarian, was waiting on the

front porch, wearing a long-sleeve, violet print dress. "Welcome. Do come in," she exclaimed, patting her snow white hair. "Mint tea is being served in the front parlor."

Delia ushered the wheelchairs up the entrance ramp. When she spotted Anne, she waved gaily.

"I didn't know you'd be here this afternoon," Delia said, pulling Anne aside. "I've been trying to get hold of you for days."

"I know. We keep missing each other."

After Helen, Delia was Anne's closest friend in the Heights. At the age of seventy-three, she still ran the library single-handedly and managed to know everything about everyone who lived in town. The locals had long ago dubbed her the Hedda Hopper of the Heights, and she did her best to live up to her namesake. Delia stored and processed information better than a computer. She could tell you everything that had happened within the Heights's square mile since the 1930s: who had cheated on their spouse, had a baby out of wedlock, drank on the sly, beat their kids, played the ponies, didn't file income taxes, stole from the Mini-Mart, and on and on. The news wasn't relayed maliciously or triumphantly, but matter-of-factly, as if it were Delia's civic duty to be the Heights's chronicler—the unofficial town crier.

"First of all, congratulations," Delia said, planting a kiss on Anne's cheek as the last wheelchair rolled into the library's front hallway. "Let me see the ring."

Anne held up her left hand for inspection. "Lovely," Delia pronounced, peering at the diamond through her wire-rimmed spectacles. "I heard the reception is going to be at the Water Club. Sounds divine."

"Nothing's been settled."

"Oh, but Jack said . . . I ran into him yesterday. Didn't he tell you?"

"He forgot to mention it."

"Men!" Delia said, in mock horror. She stepped inside the library and Anne followed, shutting the front door behind her. "Well, you'll have to bring Jack to the grand opening of the museum tomorrow and show him off. There are some girls in this town who'll be positively sick with envy."

Anne shrugged. Museums weren't Jack's strong suit. Besides, he'd told her he'd have no interest in viewing the boring minutiae of his hometown.

Everyone had assembled in the front parlor, a cozy, walnut-paneled room with two window seats upholstered in a pastel brocade fabric and several comfy floral print armchairs. It was known as the "reading room," a place to curl up with an armful of books and munch Delia's homemade pecan squares, which were offered to anyone Delia deemed a "lover of the word." Today, three small tables had been set up in the parlor. Each was covered with a snowy white cloth and set with bone china, silverware, and linen napkins. Scones and muffins were arrayed on tiered silver trays and each table had its own teapot, kept warm by a flowered tea cozy. Cheerful looking cutouts of black cats and friendly witches adorned the mantel.

"Delia, this is wonderful," said Greta Koch, admiring the room. "A real treat."

Anne, Greta, and the nurse spent several minutes getting people settled, taking off coats, pouring tea, serving food. Delia had set a tape player on the mantel and the lilting strains of Vivaldi's "The Four Seasons" gave the little party a festive air. The librarian was in high spirits, regaling her guests with stories about the library's current exhibit, a show on nineteenth-century military books.

Anne was seated with two women from the nursing home. She had to cut their scones into bite-size pieces and smear the cakes with butter and jelly. Both ladies had voracious appetites and pushed food in their mouths quickly, as if they were afraid it would disappear without warning. Outside, coppery leaves drifted lazily to the ground, carpeting the front lawn. The heat was on in the library and Anne could feel hot, dry air rising from the grates in the parlor floor. She settled back in her chair, listening to the hum of voices around her. At the next table, the woman with Alzheimer's was talking to herself. Anne wondered if she had family and how often they visited. There came a point with the disease where relatives were handed a choice: acceptance versus pretending. Anne had tried pretending for a very long time. Pretending that everything was still the same, that her mother was going to get well, that both their lives weren't shattered forever.

Anne sipped her tea. The heat was making her drowsy. She was glad she'd been spared the trouble of telling Delia about the engagement. Delia would make a fuss and start spinning plans. With a start, Anne realized she didn't really want anyone to know about her and Jack. But she felt too tired and confused to figure out why. She stared out the window at the autumn tableau. Her life seemed as chaotic as the falling leaves, whirling through the air and landing at random. There was no rhyme or reason to anything these days. The skeleton. Jack. Maggie Zambini's sudden death.

She shifted her gaze back to the parlor and noticed that Andrew Deretchin was no longer at his table. Rising, she pushed her chair back and left the room. The exhibits Delia mounted every few months were always displayed at the rear of the library, in a space devoted to books on history and science. There wasn't enough money for special display cases, so Delia arranged the books on tables and posted large signs warning viewers: LOOK, DON'T TOUCH. Deretchin was ignoring the advice. He'd pulled his chair up to one of the sturdy wooden tables and was leafing through a thick gray tome filled with old photographs. His back was to the door and the window to his left was partially open. Just as Anne was about to enter, a gull alighted on the windowsill and let out a piercing cry. Startled, Deretchin dropped the book. Then, to Anne's amazement, he clambered effortlessly out of the chair, knelt to pick it up, climbed back in, and continued reading.

It happened so quickly Anne almost couldn't believe she'd seen it. But she had. And she didn't quite know what to make of the fact that Andrew Deretchin could walk.

Chapter 19

To discourage squirrels from scampering down your chimney, fill a large flat pan with ammonia and position it inside the hearth so the fumes can waft upward. Cap the chimney as soon as possible.

When Anne walked into the room, the floorboards creaked. At the sound, Deretchin eased his chair around, his expression registering surprise and guilt.

"You caught me," he said, brandishing the book. "Don't tell the librarian. She's no pushover. She'll probably make me sit in a corner and write 'I will not touch the antique books' a couple of hundred times."

"I saw you just now," Anne replied, slowly and deliberately. "When you dropped the book, you got out of your chair and picked it up."

Deretchin managed a tight-lipped smile. "Sometimes this old body of mine surprises even me. Instinct, I guess. Old reflexes die hard."

"What gives, Mr. Deretchin? I thought you couldn't walk."

"I cannot." He reached out and gingerly set the book back on the table.

"It didn't look that way to me."

"Miss Hardaway, I am not a doctor. And as far as I can tell, neither are you. I have a degenerative nerve disease that makes walking an impossibility. Now unless you can tell me about a scientific breakthrough I'm unaware of, I suggest we both rejoin the rest of the group. Frankly, it's been an upsetting day. I've had quite enough excitement."

With that, he rolled his chair past her and through the arched doorway. His eyes were cast down, so she couldn't see his face. She went over to the table and picked up the book he'd been reading. *Firearms in the Civil War.* She leafed through it, pausing to study the pictures of muskets, Spencer rifles, and Colt revolvers. The first true machine gun, she read, was designed by a Confederate soldier in 1861. It was capable of firing sixty-five rounds per minute with fair accuracy.

She put the book back and gazed out the window. Many of the leaves on the ground had already turned brown and were curling at the edges. It made her think of winter, of death. If Andrew Deretchin could walk, why was he pretending he couldn't? What was he hiding?

When they got back to Sunnydale, it was a little after four. Anne's volunteering stint was officially over, but she told Greta Koch that she had time on her hands and asked if there was something else she could do. Turns out there was. She could sit at a desk in the office and answer the phones while the receptionist took a forty-five minute break.

Fine, Anne said. Glad to do it. And she was—especially when she noticed the office was lined floor to ceiling with metal filing cabinets.

For the first fifteen minutes, she manned the phones (which thankfully didn't ring very often). Then she got up, went to the door, locked it, and started nosing around. The first file she pulled out was Andrew Deretchin's. He'd been admitted two years earlier and had lived in Florida before that. He had some kind of nerve disorder Anne had never heard of, plus bursitis, a bleeding ulcer, and heart palpitations. There were a bunch of charts in the folder and lots of test results. Her eye scanned each page, trying to decipher the spidery, rambling scrawls. Why did doctors have to have such terrible handwriting?

She examined the medication he was receiving, his monthly progress reports, and his physical therapy regime. Everything seemed to be in order. She put the file back and located the one on Maggie Zambini. Apart from the after-effects of her stroke, Maggie had suffered from osteoarthritis. Her eyesight was failing and she had experienced bouts of depression. Anne turned to the last page of the report and found the cause of death: congestive heart failure. As she read the words, she could feel her own heart start to beat faster.

Working as quickly as she could, Anne pulled out the files of everyone whose obituaries she'd seen in the paper. The cause of death was the same for each of them: congestive heart failure. It was an unsettling coincidence. As she was reading the last file, she heard a sharp pounding at the door.

"Just a sec," she called out. She stuffed the file back in the cabinet, rummaged around the receptionist's desk, and found an unopened package of Marlboros and a book of matches. The pounding on the door was getting louder. Anne lit a cigarette and walked around the room, exhaling smoke. Then she stubbed the butt out in an ashtray and opened the door.

Greta Koch stood on the threshold, an angry expression on her angular, horsey face. "What's going on?" Greta shouted.

"I was grabbing a quick smoke," Anne said, injecting a note of apology into her voice.

"That was unwise," Nurse Koch said sternly. "There's no smoking on the premises. It's against the law."

"I'm sorry," Anne replied. "It won't happen again."

"You're absolutely right," another voice interjected.

Anne stared past Greta and saw Claire Hillyard standing in the hallway, her arms crossed over her chest.

"Anne won't be doing any more volunteering," Claire said to Greta Koch. "We can't have people working here who deliberately flout the rules."

"Yes, Ms. Hillyard," Greta said. Her attitude was so subservient that Anne almost expected her to curtsy.

"That will be all, Greta."

"Yes, ma'am," Greta said again, beating a hasty retreat.

Claire Hillyard stepped into the office and shut the door behind her. As usual, she was elegantly attired, in a smart-looking gray pants suit, an ivory silk blouse, and gray suede pumps. A triangular silver pin was attached to her lapel and her hair was adorned with a delicate silver comb. The woman knew how to dress, Anne thought. And she could turn on the charm when it suited her.

"You just can't seem to stay away," Claire said coldly. "Now why is that, exactly?"

"I'm trying to find out why so many of your patients are dying, including Maggie Zambini, who seemed pretty healthy as recently as yesterday."

Claire's gaze slid to the file cabinets, then flicked back to Anne. She took a step closer. "I heard about the stunt you pulled here this morning. If you try anything like that again, I'll have you arrested."

"There seems to be a congestive heart failure epidemic at Sunnydale. It's strange, don't you think?"

"I think you'd better back off," Claire said evenly.

"Your son came to see me yesterday afternoon," Anne said, changing tacks.

For a second, Claire dropped her guard. A stunned look appeared on her face. But the next moment it was gone. She stared at Anne with pure hatred in her eyes.

"Stuart told me your husband was cheating on you when he disappeared," Anne said. "He told me you knew all about Steven's affair."

"What if I did?" Claire demanded with a sneer. "What right do you have to pry into my life?"

"I'm going to find out who killed him and why. It's only a matter of time."

Claire took another step forward. She and Anne were only a few feet apart. The office seemed to have gotten smaller. The tension in the air was nearly palpable.

"Now you listen to me and you listen good," Claire said, her voice barely above a whisper. "If my husband wanted to run off with a hysterical, conniving viper that was his business. In fact, I should have seen it coming. The man started cheating on me six weeks after we got back from our honeymoon. You asked me before what my husband was like. He was the kind of man you shouldn't marry."

Claire took a deep breath, as if she'd just expressed sentiments she'd been storing up for years. "I hated him. But then so did a lot of people. I didn't kill him, if that's what you're thinking. I actually hired a private detective to find him, that's how worried I was. But as it turned out, when he vanished into thin air, my life began. It was like getting a second chance. And now, here you are stirring everything up again."

Claire spat out the words angrily, almost in spite of herself. Then her features hardened into a frozen mask. She walked to the door and flung it open. "I want you out of here, for good. If I see you on the premises, I'm calling security and having you thrown out."

"Suit yourself," Anne said. Claire Hillyard didn't scare her. In fact, she felt a little sorry for Claire. It was painful when your past began intruding on the present. Anne had learned that lesson all too well.

"Oh, and one more thing," Claire added. "I checked around. If your grandmother ever does get sick and needs a nursing home, pick one out of the Yellow Pages. She's not welcome at Sunnydale."

When Anne got home, Jack still hadn't returned. She went upstairs to the bedroom to see if his things were still there. They were. His clothes, his shaving kit, his suitcase—all exactly where they'd been that morning. She felt a flash of relief. She didn't want Jack to walk out of her life. Not like this. She wondered where he could be, what he was doing. She doubted he'd gone to see his father. Well, he had to come back at some point, if only to get his stuff.

She sank onto the window seat and stared into space. Three nights of sleep deprivation had taken their toll. She was having trouble concentrating; her head felt like it was packed with cotton.

The cat darted between her ankles, making plaintive feed-me noises. She went into the bathroom, splashed cold water on her face, then went downstairs and refilled Harry's food and water bowls. He purred at her gratefully and proceeded to chow down on Purina. If only the rest of life could be this easy. Ask and you shall receive.

When she checked the answering machine, she found three messages. One was from Helen, wanting to hash out the wedding plans. The second was from Jennifer Joan Klapisch, who asked to reschedule their phone interview for tomorrow afternoon. Where was the chapter on pest control? What about furniture repairs? At this rate, Jennifer Joan complained, they'd never be able to meet the deadline. But Anne was way too tired to think about that. She needed about nine solid hours of make-up sleep before she could face problem squirrels and wobbly table legs.

She played the last message back. Trasker. Telling her to call him as soon as possible.

"What's up?" she said, when she got the detective on the line.

"For starters, there's not going to be an autopsy on Margaret Zambini."

The news filled Anne with dismay. "Why not?"

"The husband won't allow it. Says it's totally unnecessary. The funeral's the day after tomorrow at one o'clock."

"Even after you told him there could have been foul play?"

"Uh huh. He's a tough nut, that one. Mad at the world. Just wanted the whole thing over with."

Anne paced around the living room with the cordless phone pressed to her ear. "But now there may be further evidence that Mrs. Zambini didn't die of natural causes." She told Trasker what Andrew Deretchin had said about Katie Crowley.

Trasker let out a sigh. "Unfortunately, Deretchin's not the most reliable witness."

"Why not?"

"We ran a check on him, like you wanted. Turns out he used to be an accountant for a children's clothing manufacturer in Tampa. The head of the company was accused of stock fraud and disappeared two years ago. Deretchin was left holding the bag, claiming he hadn't cooked the books."

"What happened?"

"The case was turned over to the Attorney General's office. They launched a full-scale investigation. It was in all the local papers."

"And?"

"They couldn't prosecute because Deretchin's doctors claimed he was too sick to stand trial."

"A degenerative nerve disease, right?"

There was silence on the other end. Then Trasker said,

"Have you been snooping around that nursing home again, Hardaway?"

"Sort of."

"I thought we agreed that would be unwise."

Anne went over to the living room window and looked outside. The ocean was choppy, the surf crashing against the shore and sending up tall plumes of spray. "Want to know what I discovered today?"

Trasker sighed. "Do I have a choice?"

"Andrew Deretchin can walk."

"That so?"

"He denied it when I confronted him. But in light of what you just said, I think he's faking his illness."

"Could be. I'll alert the Feds. In the meantime, I want you to steer clear of him and those other two you asked me about."

Anne could feel her heartbeat quickening. "What else did you find out?"

"That Philip Reynolds is a two-bit crook who's been hit with a number of nursing home violations."

"How's he managing to expand his operation?"

"He's got some heavy hitters backing him. Two of them are under investigation by the FBI for drug trafficking and money laundering."

"What about his connection to Steven Hillyard?"

"They were business partners. They had a falling-out over money. Happens all the time."

"And Katie Crowley?"

"Only one prior. In June of last year she got tagged for speeding. When the cops pulled her over they found narcotics in the trunk. Claimed she had no idea how the drugs got there. It was a first offense, so the judge let her off with a warning."

Anne's mind was racing. Was that how patients at Sunnydale were being killed? With narcotics? Maybe Philip Reynolds was bumping people off and scooping up their life savings. Maybe Katie Crowley was murdering people in her care. But why? To steal from them?

Their possessions weren't worth much. It didn't make sense.

"Anne, you still there?"

"Yup."

"I'll go over and talk to that nurse when my shift ends in an hour. See what she has to say for herself. In the meantime, have you gotten any more disturbing phone calls?"

"No."

"Good. Do me a favor. Stay away from Sunnydale for awhile. I'll do what I can on this end."

"Any word on the skeleton?" she asked.

"*Nada*, Hardaway. We haven't got a murder weapon. Or anything solid on the wife or Reynolds. I'm afraid we may never be able to find out who killed Steven Hillyard."

After she got off the phone, she thought about that for awhile. It didn't sit right with her. She had to know what had happened to Hillyard. She had to be absolutely certain. Otherwise, she'd never feel comfortable living in the house again. Ever since Chester had found the skeleton, she'd felt things were spinning out of control. Sure, life was unpredictable. You could wake up one day and find your mother had completely changed. Or you could be engaged to a man you weren't sure you knew. Or find a human skeleton buried beneath the floorboards of the house you'd grown up in, a house you'd come to love. She didn't expect the course of events to be smooth or even easy. She didn't believe in five-year plans. But this was different. Someone had shot Steven Hillyard at close range right here, in *her* house, and had gotten away with it. It felt like a violation. She couldn't ever change that. It would always color her experience of living in the house, growing up, getting older, oblivious to the dark secret festering beneath the floorboards. Finding out who killed Hillyard was the only way to make peace with what happened—to accept it and move on.

She paced around the living room aimlessly, trying to

sort it all out. Something tugged at the corner of her mind, a piece that didn't fit. But she couldn't quite grasp it.

She checked on the cat, who was dozing happily on the kitchen floor. Then she got out Katie Crowley's address and left the house. It was a little after six. The sky had cleared and light was just beginning to seep from the sky. Far out over the ocean, a thick bank of clouds hugged the horizon. The cool sea air made her feel slightly less exhausted. She took a few deep breaths, drinking in the cold, and climbed into the Mustang.

Katie Crowley lived on Bath Avenue, about a ten-minute walk from the beach. The cube-shaped house was known as a foursquare or a "classic box." It had two stories and a pyramidal roof with a large front dormer. Stout classical white columns adorned the porch, which extended the full front of the house. The first story was constructed of gray clapboard, while the second story featured white shingles. It was a simple, ordinary-looking house, not one of the Heights's Victorian gems. Anne wondered if Katie owned it or rented. She parked across the street and took stock of the damage caused by the storm. The gutters had come loose and one of the second-story windows had been boarded up. On the tiny front lawn, the wind had uprooted several box hedges. Two of the white shutters were gone and many of the shingles looked like they could stand to be replaced. Not too bad, all things considered. It had probably helped to be farther inland.

She crossed the street, rang the front bell, and waited. The lights were on. Music was playing. She tried peering through the window, but the shades were drawn. Could Katie be avoiding her? She rang the bell again and rapped on the door. Thirty seconds passed. Nothing. Oh, what the hell, she thought, turning the knob. The door opened and Anne found herself in a small living room, decorated in early grad student. A futon, a half-dozen milk carton crates that doubled as shelves, a rag rug, and a couple of mismatched chairs. On the mantel, a bunch of half-dead daisies languished in a blue ceramic vase.

"Hello," Anne called out. "Anybody home?"

There were no pictures on the wall, no photos on the mantel, no sign that anyone had settled in and turned the house into a home.

Anne followed the music—Bruce Springsteen singing "Hungry Heart." She passed a small bathroom and what looked like an office. At the door of the den, she pulled up short.

Katie Crowley was sprawled in an armchair, her legs splayed out in front of her. Her head was slumped forward, but her lifeless eyes were wide open and she was staring down at the carpet. In death, Katie Crowley looked smaller, almost childlike. She wore jeans, sneakers, and a pink Angora sweater. No makeup. Her blond hair was pulled back from her face in a loose pony-tail. Her mouth was half-open.

Anne came closer, her heart hammering a mile a minute. On the table next to Katie was a bowl of black olives, squares of triangular Laughing Cow cheese still wrapped in foil and arranged on a paper plate, a glass of red wine, and some white powder laid out neatly in two lines on a tortoise-shell hand mirror.

Anne tore her gaze away from the body and glanced around the room. A plaid couch, four metal chairs pulled up around a card table, and another armchair covered in a dirty yellow velour fabric. No sign of a struggle. Nothing appeared to have been disturbed. It looked like your basic overdose. On the CD player, Springsteen was just launching into "Born in the U.S.A."

Anne looked around for a phone to call 911 and spotted Katie Crowley's answering machine. Two messages flashed. Anne reached out, pushed the rewind button, and waited. She checked her watch. Six-thirty. Reaching out a tentative hand, she touched Katie's arm. It wasn't cold or stiff. But then Katie didn't look like she'd been dead very long.

The first message on the machine was from someone named Sue, a nurse at Sunnydale, who asked Katie if she would swap shifts with her next Saturday night. The second was from a man who didn't bother to identify himself. He had a sharp, nasal voice and he placed a long, elaborate drug order—Seconal, Dilaudid, Valium, Halcion, Benzedrine—specifying how many pills of each he wanted and how many milligrams they should contain. It sounded like Katie Crowley was running her own personal pharmacy out of her house. It made Anne wonder whether the staff at Sunnydale ever bothered to take inventory.

When the message ended, Anne reached for the phone. As she was about to pick it up, it rang. For a moment, she considered letting the machine answer. But curiosity got the better of her.

"Hello," she said softly into the receiver.

There was silence on the other end. Then a strange, hollow-sounding voice said, "Katie's dead."

Anne's heart began skipping as if she'd just been running a race. "Who is this?" she demanded. But she already knew. She'd recognized the voice immediately. It was the same person who'd called before, the person who'd told her Maggie Zambini had died.

Anne listened to the breathing on the other end. She felt flushed, skittish. "Who's there?" she whispered into the phone.

"Don't you know?"

The voice was faint, metallic sounding, like it had been altered, piped through a machine.

"What do you want?" Anne said.

The breathing grew heavier. Anne listened tensely. She was starting to sweat. Her right hand ached from gripping the phone.

"Justice. The wheel of justice finally turns," the voice cried, with a hollow, echoing laugh. It was the most chilling, soulless sound Anne had ever heard. And it was close by. Too close. She spun around, her eyes darting past the dead body. She was being watched. She was sure of it. Just like at the nursing home. And suddenly she knew the killer was still in the house and she had to get out. Now. She flung down the phone, her heart pounding wildly, and bolted for the door.

She ran out into the hall, past the office and the bathroom. She'd only taken a few steps into the living room when something hard struck the back of her head. She felt a sudden burst of pain, followed by something cold and wet, and then the floor rushed up to meet her and the whole world went black.

Chapter 20

There are certain home repair jobs you can't tackle yourself. You won't get brownie points for being a hero. If something looks beyond your reach, consider hiring professional help.

The first thing she saw when she opened her eyes was Mark Trasker kneeling over her.

"You okay?" he asked. "You had me worried there for a while."

"Yeah," she managed to mutter through the pain.

She was flat on her back staring up at the ceiling. Her back ached. So did her right shoulder. But it was nothing compared to the fire raging in her head.

She reached up and gingerly touched the place that hurt most. "Ouch!" she yelped, recoiling. She looked at her hand. It was streaked with blood.

Trasker reached out to steady her. "Maybe you shouldn't move just yet. The medics are on their way."

"That's all right," Anne said shakily, easing herself up slowly on one elbow. As she raised her head, the pain seemed to elongate, pressing against her skull. She rested her back against the wall.

"What hit me?"

"This." Trasker pointed to the blue ceramic vase, which was now broken into five jagged pieces. The daisies were scattered haphazardly on the floor. "Lucky for you you're hardheaded. What happened?"

"The nurse was dead when I got here, but whoever killed her was still in the house. He called me. It was that same voice, the same person who told me about Maggie Zambini."

"How long ago was this?"

Anne didn't answer. She was gazing at the living room. What she saw made her feel like Alice in Wonderland peering through the wrong side of the looking glass. The place was a mess. Chairs overturned. Futon on its side. Books and papers strewn on the floor. Rag rug bunched up in a corner.

"Did you do this?" Anne asked, gesturing at the room.

Trasker's eyebrow shot up. "Whoever conked you on the head did this."

Anne glanced at her watch. Seven fifteen. She wondered how many minutes she'd been unconscious. "It didn't look like this forty-five minutes ago," she said.

Trasker stared at her. "The whole place is trashed. The bedroom. Office. Den. Even the medicine cabinet."

"A robbery?"

"Maybe. Or a drug deal gone sour. Looks like the nurse was in over her head." A siren wailed once, twice. "Tell me about the phone call," Trasker said.

Anne thought back to the voice on the phone. Cold, metallic, inhuman. *Justice*, it had intoned. If the dead could talk, that's the way they would sound. Through the drawn shade, she saw arcs of red neon, twirling in a circle. Two uniformed cops burst through the front door.

Trasker motioned them toward the den, then turned back to Anne.

"The phone call?" Trasker prompted.

"I'm not sure. The only thing I know is it feels personal."

"Personal. I'm not following."

"It's like he's taunting me somehow. Like he wants me to know he's responsible. He *wants* me to be afraid."

The cops had left the door open, causing the brisk autumn air to blow in. It made her head ache even more. A knot of curious neighbors clustered on the sidewalk, tongues already wagging. You didn't see many drug-related deaths in the Heights. Statistically speaking, it was the safest town on the entire Jersey shore. She knew what the mayor would think: Thank God this hadn't happened during tourist season.

"I don't get it," Trasker was saying. "What's the connection? You barely knew Katie Crowley. And Mrs. Zambini. Didn't you say you hadn't seen her in years?"

"My mother knew her. She used to be my mother's closest friend."

Suddenly, Anne thought of the dream she'd had the other night. Her mother dressed in velvet and diamonds, drowning. Her mother. Her house. The skeleton. Mrs. Zambini. The nurse. There was something Anne had missed in all this, something that would make the numbers add up.

The emergency medical technicians headed up the front walkway carrying a stretcher. When they reached the living room, they set it down next to Anne.

"That's really not necessary," she protested. Her head felt like a watermelon about to split open, but her legs worked okay.

"Yeah, it is," Trasker said. "I'll call you later to see how you're doing. In the meantime, take care of yourself."

As the technicians strapped her on the stretcher and hoisted her in the air, she caught a glimpse of the place where her head had rested against the wall. It was smeared with blood.

Thank God for Percodan, Anne thought. The emergency room doctor had sewn twenty-two stitches into the back of her head, but she was feeling no pain. In fact, she was in pretty good shape. She felt a little like she was floating. Like she didn't have a care in the world. The doctor had cautioned her not to drive. But he needn't have bothered. Her car was still parked across the street from Katie Crowley's house.

She called home, got Jack on the phone, and was waiting in the hospital lobby when he came to pick her up.

"How are you doing?" he said, when she climbed into his Corvette.

Normally, she'd be tense about seeing Jack again. But the Percodan took the edge off. The fight they'd had earlier in the day seemed like it had happened a lifetime ago.

"I'm starving," she said, with a faint smile. "I can't remember the last time I ate."

"You want to hit the diner?"

"Sounds like a plan."

The Ocean Diner, on Route 35, was a fixture in Monmouth County. Built during the Depression, it was designed to resemble one of the Pennsylvania Railroad dining cars and had achieved some notoriety by continually feuding with a restaurant in Trenton about which of the two establishments was the first to feature Jersey cheesesteaks. Open twenty-four hours a day, it served Italian subs, frozen custard, and scrapple, and had a seven-page menu (one of which was devoted solely to the specials).

On the way over, Anne told Jack about everything that had happened in his absence. When she'd finished, he shook his head ruefully. He looked mad and upset at the same time.

"I'm sorry I took off the way I did," he said. "But that quack doctor made me furious."

"I thought I was the one who'd done that."

He studied the road and the car accelerated. "I think we're both under a lot of stress right now. I mean, here I am proposing at one of the worst moments in your life. With the storm damage to the house. The skeleton. And now, getting bashed on the head by some lunatic." He pulled into the diner's parking lot and eased the car into a vacant space by the front door. "You know what we should do? We should take a vacation. Hop a flight to Bermuda for the rest of the week. How does that strike you?"

Anne considered it for a moment. Pink sand beaches. Tropical breezes. Frozen daiquiris by the pool. The biggest decision she'd have to make was what number sunscreen to use. Actually, it sounded pretty darn good, especially if you were into escapism.

"Sounds wonderful." She unfastened her seatbelt and it snapped quickly back into its holder. "But I don't think I should go anywhere just yet. Not until I figure out what's going on around here."

She opened the car door and got out. A chipped white moon hung low in the sky. The clouds had lifted; the sky was pierced with hundreds of stars. Inside, they settled into a booth by the door. Anne plopped down on the crimson Naugahyde seat, which had been patched with tape, and ordered the Number Three breakfast special for dinner: pancakes, sausages, home fries, and orange juice. Comfort food. It had been a tough day. She could use a little comforting. Jack stuck to his diet, choosing an egg-white omelet with a small side salad and a seltzer with lime. A plump waitress in a pink uniform who addressed them both as "hon" scribbled down the orders.

When she headed for the kitchen, they both sat staring at each other as if they were strangers on a train who happened to be sharing the same compartment.

"So," Anne said, breaking the silence. "How was *your* day?"

"Not as eventful as yours. I drove down to Atlantic City. Went to Harrah's, played a little blackjack and roulette."

"You win anything?"

"Nah. I broke even."

He was rearranging the stuff on the table, placing the sugar to the right of the salt and pepper shakers, plucking napkins out of their black metal holder, and studying the paper placemat showing cocktails no one drank anymore.

Anne leaned her head back against the seat and closed her eyes. The jukebox was playing Frank Sinatra singing "I'll Be Seeing You." For some reason, it struck her as incredibly sad. If she could just have one good night's sleep, everything would be clearer in the morning. She touched her hand to the back of her head. The doctor had taped a bandage over the wound. She tried to imagine what the scar looked like: a thin ragged line sloping toward her neck. *You're lucky*, the doctor had said. *Your hair will cover the wound. No one will ever see it.*

Like the skeleton, Anne thought suddenly. Secret. Hidden.

"You okay?" Jack asked. "Does your head hurt?"

She opened her eyes and looked at him. He was wearing a light blue cotton shirt, jeans, and sneakers. His concern showed in his eyes, in the way his mouth tightened ever so slightly. He cared about her. Well, of course he did. He'd asked her to marry him, hadn't he? You didn't do stuff like that unless you were in love, unless you were sure.

She wanted to open up to him—to tell him how scared she was of the future, about loving someone so much you agreed to be together forever. She couldn't think about forever. She barely knew what she was doing next week or next month. She wanted to confide in him, just like she always did. But something held her back. Jack was one of her closest friends. But now that they were engaged, it was almost like they were strangers again, trying to chart the waters of a choppy new relationship.

"My head's better," she said. Well, only if you didn't delve too deeply inside it.

The waitress came back, setting down the food. Anne ate quickly, slathering the pancakes with syrup. They made small talk all through dinner, which was just as well. Underneath her Percodan haze she felt a sliver of anxiety. She didn't want to have to think about the future.

When they got home, she changed into her pajamas, brushed her teeth, took another Percodan, and crawled into bed. She fell asleep minutes after her head hit the pillow. It was a deep, heavy sleep, where not even dreams could touch her.

When she woke up, the morning light was filtering through the room and the back of her head was sore. The pills had worn off. She rolled over gingerly and glanced at the clock. Seven-fifteen in the morning. Hallelujah. She'd slept through the night. It was a delicious feeling. She lay there for a few seconds, watching the ocean crest and ebb, before she realized Jack wasn't beside her.

She got out of bed and padded downstairs. It was a beautiful fall day, with the ocean blue and calm. She could hear scraping and tapping noises coming from below. The door of the linen closet was ajar and the trapdoor leading to the basement was half open. She headed down the concrete steps, stopping short when she saw Jack. He was attacking the far wall with a chisel and hammer. Much of the paint was already scraped off. His tools were spread out on the ground: an electric drill, a handsaw, tape, and a carpenter's hammer. The cat was sitting on the bottom step, glaring at Jack with suspicion.

"Hey!" Anne cried out.

Jack swung around.

"What on earth are you doing?"

He wiped his hands on his sweatpants and came toward her. His skin and clothes were covered with a powdery white dust. "Trying to find the bullet."

For a second, Anne's mind went totally blank. Then she remembered. The bullet. Right, the 23-year-old bullet that had killed Steven Hillyard.

"So far, no luck," Jack said. "But I'm going to keep at it."

"Shouldn't the cops be doing this?"

"You tell me. That detective is a friend of yours, right?"

His voice had an edge. She should have expected it. Nothing had been resolved between them, nothing at all. Underneath last night's small talk lay an undercurrent of tension.

"I'll talk to Trasker about it. But in the meantime, this is a crime scene. I think we should leave it alone."

"Fine," Jack said, with an angry shrug. "Whatever you say."

He threw down the hammer and chisel and marched past her up the stairs.

"Jack," she called after him. "Wait a sec."

She caught up to him in the kitchen, where he was splashing cold water onto his hands and face.

"I didn't mean to sound ungrateful," she explained. "I really appreciate all your help. With the house, the skeleton—everything. It's just that the police are conducting an investigation. And I'm not sure we should disturb anything down there."

"Fine. You made your point." He turned off the water and dried himself off with a dishtowel.

Anne watched as he moved silently around the kitchen, fixing himself tea, cereal, pita bread, and juice from organically grown oranges. In just a few months, she could be Mrs. Jack Mills. They could be eating breakfast, talking or not, side by side in the breakfast nook of his two-bedroom apartment overlooking Central Park West.

Jack wasn't particularly open about his feelings. They were friends, sure, but they didn't have many heart-to-heart talks. Maybe that was par for the course. The whole men are from Mars, women are from Venus thing. When you considered how different men and women were, it was a wonder anyone ever got together.

She washed down two Extra-Strength Tylenol and tried to ignore how much her head hurt. She still had some Percodan left, if the pain didn't start to subside. "I really think we should talk," she said to Jack. He was spooning up a health food cereal called Protein Plus! that he'd brought from the city. Anne automatically distrusted any product with an exclamation point tacked on the end.

"We need to iron stuff out," she said. "About the wedding. Our future."

"Up to you," he said curtly.

At heart, she knew it was pointless. They could serve and volley all morning, and when they'd finished, she still wouldn't be sure where they stood. Maybe he was the type of guy who'd go out for a package of tofu one day and never come back. Maybe they'd end up with the kind of marriage her parents had had, the kind that dissolved like chalk in a rainstorm.

She wasn't cut out to do all the heavy lifting in a relationship. She was someone who didn't always say what was on her mind, who could nurse a grudge with the best of them, and who didn't know what she wanted half the time.

Was she wrong to have told him to stop destroying the wall? Hell, if she knew how to dig up a missing bullet, she'd be down there doing the work herself.

"I'm having trouble with the home repair book," she said, apropos of nothing.

He made a noise that she guessed was supposed to be sympathetic and took his pita bread out of the toaster oven.

"How's your head?" he asked.

"Better," she lied. "Anyhow, part of the problem is I can't understand Jennifer Joan's directions. She faxes me all this material about draft-proofing your home or filling cracks in concrete and I can't make heads or tails of it."

"You want me to take a look?"

"If you wouldn't mind."

He spooned cottage cheese onto his pita and took a bite. "So basically, I can do hypothetical repairs, but I can't help you fix this place up. I can offer you theories about Hillyard, but I can't find out how and why he was killed. I can ask you to marry me, but I can't set the wedding date. Have I got the rules about right?"

"There are no rules," she said hotly.

"Are you kidding me? You practically wrote a whole playbook."

He threw his napkin on the table and left the kitchen. She heard his footsteps on the stairs, then the sound of the water blasting in the shower.

It was progress of sorts.

At least this time he hadn't left the house.

Chapter 21

When it comes to home repairs, treat your house the way you would your car—checking the oil, washing it, and keeping it in smooth working order on an ongoing basis. Remember, maintenance is next to godliness.

The Oceanside Heights Museum was newly ensconced in what used to be Bea's Kite Shop, on Pitman Avenue. The museum had been in the works for years, with bits of the collection formerly housed in the library, in the offices of the historical society, and in the backs of garages and attics all over town. Its scope was ambitious: Trace the history and popular culture of the Heights since its founding in 1896. The inaugural exhibit was supposed to have opened right after Memorial Day, to cash in on the tourist trade. But the kite shop was still being renovated last summer and the grand opening had to be postponed until October.

The museum's director, Bill August, had been collecting Heights-related memorabilia since the early 1980s. Now, he had more stuff than the museum could contain and was busily trying to renovate a lower level of the store to be used for rotating shows.

Anne had been planning to go to the grand opening. In fact, she'd donated a few items to the museum and was wondering if they'd made it into the exhibit. She asked Jack if he wanted to come with her, but he shook his head and said he had work to do. Since he'd stormed upstairs, he'd been avoiding her and she didn't quite know what to do about it. Now she popped her head into the living room, intending to make up.

"I should be back in about an hour," she said. "Do you want to eat lunch out?"

"Fine by me."

He was sitting on the couch, flipping through a trade journal, pretending all was right with the world. The way she knew he was pretending had to do with his eyebrows. They knit together when he was in a sulky mood.

He flashed her a quick smile. "See you later."

"I'd love you to come."

It was true. Museums were always more fun when you had someone to share them with. Besides, she wanted the old Jack back. Her friend. Her confidante. The guy who wasn't always mad at her.

As he glanced up, his cornflower blue eyes had a serious cast. "Next time, okay?"

Across the room, near the window, Harry had found a patch of sunlight on the floor and was basking in the warmth. The cat and Jack appeared to have established a wary détente. They could tolerate one another if neither got in the other's way. Maybe that's how good marriages survived. Life lessons from a cat. It sounded like a book title. She should call Triple Star right now and pitch it. Team up with one of those cat lovers who feel kitties are better company than humans.

She stood in the doorway, fumbling through her bag

for her sunglasses, hoping Jack would change his mind, knowing he wouldn't. He'd put down the journal and was spreading out pages of architectural blueprints on the coffee table.

"See you later," she called, trying to inject a note of gaiety into her voice.

"Annie," he called after her.

She turned back. "Yeah?"

"About the basement. I was just trying to help."

"I know."

She wanted to say more, to talk about what was happening between them, but she couldn't find the words.

His head was bent over the blueprints.

"Have a nice time," he mumbled, dismissing her with a wave.

Right, she thought, as she headed out the door. As if she could forget about their problems. As if the events of the past few days would evaporate like wood smoke if she ignored them for an hour or two. Well, maybe she should give it a try. She'd had enough death and destruction to last a lifetime, thank you very much.

The weather improved her mood a bit. Another gorgeous fall afternoon. The wind had died down. The sky above the ocean was a searing shade of blue with nary a cloud in sight. She decided to walk to the exhibit. She hadn't run in a couple of days and she figured she could use the exercise. The beach was lovely this time of year. Private, serene. She preferred the off-season, actually. No tourists with skin the color of boiled lobsters. No waiting in long lines at the cash machine and the Mini Mart. No trouble finding a parking space.

Even the storm's aftermath was striking. The dunes were wild-looking now. Without the fence separating the sand from the street, the beach looked less perfect and more the way Anne imagined it had looked a hundred years ago when a group of Methodist ministers thought they'd discovered paradise on earth.

She walked down Ocean Avenue for a few blocks,

taking in the view, before turning west on Pitman. The curved Victorian streetlights had been righted and most of the sand had been removed from people's front lawns. The town almost seemed restored to its old self.

Outside the museum, a flock of pink and blue balloons bobbed a festive welcome. Anne peered through the plate glass window. Five past noon and the place was packed. She opened the door and threaded her way through the crowd. It appeared as though the whole town had shown up to celebrate. She saw Bill August, dressed in a tweed vest, tie, and jacket, surrounded by a cluster of reporters. Across the room was Delia Graustark. Anne waved, but couldn't catch the librarian's eye. She looked around, hoping to spot Helen. Members of the Ladies' Auxiliary were carrying trays laden with mini quiches, pigs in blankets, and cups of soda. Anne reached out and grabbed a glass. Tepid Coke, no ice.

She edged closer to the far wall, peering over a line of heads to try to see the exhibit. High up was a large wooden sign: *Welcome to Oceanside Heights. Where Summer Never Changes*. Yup, Anne thought. They got that right. People jostled her, some smiling a greeting, and she found herself caught in a sea of elbows and chins.

The museum walls were plastered with old photographs, newspaper clippings, shop signs, advertisements, and old-fashioned memorabilia, like a Christmas ornament decorated with one of the swan boats that used to glide on Wesley Lake and blue seltzer bottles from a time when the area was prized for its "restorative waters."

There was a whole section devoted to the lakes and the boardwalk. Anne had to grin when she got close enough to see the pictures. On the "bathing grounds" at the turn-of-the-century, women strolled the beach in ankle-length bustled dresses, shading their faces under parasols. Men splashed in breeches and short-sleeve shirts.

The 300-foot-wide Wesley Lake was freckled with ca-

noes, ferries, and gondolas that shuttled summer vacation-
ers between the Heights and then-fashionable Landsdown
Park. On the boardwalk, young ladies bunched their skirts
up and rode bicycles with brio. Boys pushed lovestruck
couples in high-backed wicker conveyances, while girls in
pinafores clung to their mamas' hands and gazed longingly at the waves. Wealthy travelers from New York were
delivered to their hotels in covered horse-drawn carriages.
Once they disembarked, they were treated to music from
an elevated bandstand and "the prettiest stretch of ocean
east of the Mississippi."

The scenes were calm, tranquil, laced with an air of
unshakable innocence. You couldn't imagine inclement
weather, disease, or human nature disturbing the stolid
serenity, the placid resort atmosphere.

Anne inched her way around the crowded museum,
taking in the past—covered wagons loaded with ice; mer-
chants who sold sheet music, bristle goods, notions, and
elixirs; a sign from Campbell's Barber Shop, sturdy
Roseville pottery, commemorative plates of the Church
by the Sea; the pristine rows of tents near the church,
like a peaceable scene from an old Western.

Have you ever tented 'neath the church above
Where each one dwells in perfect love
Where each one tries his best to do
Where God's Holy Spirit is shining through

That was only one of the ads for the "Christian seaside
paradise." It was a distinctive marketing campaign, actually. *Oceanside Heights. Where the Lord Reigneth.*
Cape May and Atlantic City may have been grander once
upon a time, but they never claimed you'd find Jesus in
the salty sea air.

There was an entire section devoted to the Heights's
rules and regulations that used to be in effect each Sunday, including: No sunbathing on the beach until after

twelve noon—the only town ordinance to have survived into the '90s.

She craned her neck, searching for the commemorative ashtray she'd given the museum and spotted it sandwiched between a ruby glass vase and a flyer announcing a 1930s gospel sing. In front of the ashtray a card read *Donated by Miss Anne Hardaway*.

She turned and saw Teri working the crowd, smiling and nodding like she was hostessing the event. Apart from being a shade or two paler, she exhibited no signs of grief. No one would have guessed that her mother had just passed away. A little behind Teri, to her left, stood Dominick Zambini, clutching a plastic cup. He too gave no sign that he had lost his wife. His face registered its customary angry demeanor, so that he seemed to glare at each person as they approached to offer their condolences.

Anne didn't get it. Was Maggie Zambini so unimportant to the two of them that they didn't experience her death as a loss? Were her past transgressions so severe that she could never be forgiven, even now?

As the museum grew more crowded, the noise inside the room swelled. Anne was pushed along by a tide of people and found herself in front of a pictorial display of the town's historic inns, many of which had been torn down or destroyed by fire. The word "inn" didn't really do the buildings justice. They were more like grand hotels, outfitted with broad wraparound porches, turrets, striped awnings, sweeping roofs, widow's walks, and the occasional elevator. Even the names were grand: the Excelsior, the Madison, the Waverly, the Fenimore.

She scanned the photos, smiling at how fashions had changed. Hoop skirts and parasols had given way to shorts and T-shirts as proper attire for porch sitting. She felt the crowd surge around her, then she came to a dead stop, staring at one of the pictures on the wall. The black-and-white photo showed a group of people enjoying afternoon tea on the front porch of one of the inns. The

porch featured a bird's-eye view of lacy white gingerbread, which Anne supposed was the reason it had been
selected for the show.

But she was more interested in the man in the left-
hand corner of the frame—the man holding a bone china
teacup and reaching for what appeared to be a scone.
Steven Hillyard was facing the camera, but not looking
into it, his eyes slightly cast down. His demeanor was
serious, apparently captured unawares, and his posture
indicated a formality at odds with the relaxed poses of
the other guests. She studied the accompanying caption:
Afternoon Tea, Oceanside Heights, 1973. The lender was
Anonymous.

Anne inched closer, studying the photograph. There
was something familiar about the picture, but she
couldn't place what it was. The people on the porch were
photographed from a distance, at an angle, as if the person who shot the photo was standing off to the side. The
lighting was soft and slightly hazy. Even the gingerbread
was blurry. Hillyard's was the only face Anne could see
distinctly. That commanding expression, always serious,
always in control. It seemed odd, as if whoever took the
picture was more interested in Steven Hillyard than in
the beguiling architectural details.

Anne made her way slowly across the room, to where
Bill August was standing. The museum director was in
his glory, and enjoying every minute of it. Press cover-
age, record attendance, a chance to outshine Cape May
for once, all because of his efforts.

"Bill, hi," Anne said, raising her voice to be heard
above the din.

"Hello, Anne. Great day, isn't it?"

"I wanted to ask you about one of the photos. *Afternoon Tea, 1973.*" She pointed to indicate where she
meant.

Bill August nodded. Anne could see he was only half-
listening, caught up in the room's hectic swirl.

"Who lent the picture?"

"Anonymous donor," Bill replied, reaching behind her to shake yet another hand.

"Right. But you must know who it is."

"I do. I just can't share that information. The donor is a private person who doesn't want folks to kick up a fuss."

"I understand. But this is extremely important. Whoever lent the photo could be a suspect in a murder investigation."

Her words were wasted on Bill August. He had already spotted the mayor and was moving across the room, a wide smile on his broad, ruddy face.

Anne turned away. How could she learn the identity of the anonymous donor? There must be records and transactions somewhere in the museum's office. Only it was too crowded to start snooping now. And she wasn't quite sure why it mattered.

The room was uncomfortably warm. She suddenly longed to be somewhere quiet and cool, somewhere she could hear herself think. She made her way to the front door, buffeted by the crowd, like a leaf in a windstorm. Once outside, she felt better. She breathed in the crisp October air with relief. After a moment, she took a few steps in the direction of the beach, then froze.

The rusty white Ford was now parked a few feet from the entrance to the museum.

Anne looked around warily. The car was empty. She didn't see anyone menacing lurking behind the bushes. Up close, the Ford was more battered than she'd thought. One of the rear doors was so badly dented it looked like it had been kicked in. The paint was scraped off the front right fender. And there was so much rust on the car it seemed to have been glazed. She jotted down the license plate, tried one of the doors, and was surprised when it opened, even though nobody locked their cars in the Heights. No need.

The inside of the Ford smelled like fried onions, stale cigarettes, and day-old beer. The upholstery was so worn and stained she couldn't tell what color it had been when the car was new. Anne opened the glove compartment, which didn't contain much of interest: a Jimi Hendrix tape, a battered map of Jersey, one black glove, and a couple of greasy napkins. There was no registration, no papers of any kind. A pair of sunglasses and some quarters rested near the gears.

Anne got out and opened the door to the backseat. Now this was more promising. There was tons of junk back here. She pulled aside a ratty old blanket that half covered the seat and started to sift through piles of·stuff. She found lots of clothes—sweatshirts, T-shirts, jeans, baseball caps, and a mud-caked sneaker—plus at least a week's worth of beer cans and food wrappers from McDonald's and Kentucky Fried Chicken. Did this guy live in his car?

Every few seconds, she peered out the window to make sure no one was looking. There were a couple of magazines—*Sports Illustrated* and *Playboy*—a half-deflated football, another pair of sunglasses (though these were broken, the frames bent, one lens missing), earphones, a paper placemat from Vic's in Bradley Beach, a yellow Frisbee, and enough dirty socks to fill a junior high school locker room.

She was just about to stop searching when she noticed a man in a baseball cap heading for the car. Without stopping to think, she grabbed the blanket and threw it over her. She scrunched down as far as she could, her nose pressed against a crumpled can of Michelob. She heard the car door open and slam shut. With the radio blasting, Baseball Cap turned the key in the ignition and eased the car out of the space and down the street.

Chapter 22

To patch drywall, cut out and remove the damaged section using a drywall saw or utility knife. Slip backer boards into the hole and secure them with 1¼-inch drywall screws. Tip the patch into place, securing it with the screws. Use the damaged piece of drywall as a pattern for this patch. Cover the seams with self-sticking Fiberglass tape, then spread a thin coat of joint compound and let it partially dry. Sand and apply two more broader coats, then sand until smooth.

 She couldn't tell where they were going, and didn't want to risk lifting the blanket off to see. Baseball Cap had rolled down the window, and from the way the wind was tearing through the car, she guessed they were doing seventy. He had the radio turned to an oldies station—WZVU out of Long Branch. Diana Ross was belting out "Stop in the Name of Love."

Each time there was a bump in the road, her nose smacked against the floor. This is nuts, she told herself. She should have gotten out while she had the chance. Baseball Cap couldn't touch her on Pitman Street, not with all those people a few feet away in the museum. Now it was too late. The smell of stale grease was making her nauseous. The back of her head was beginning to hurt again. She felt like she could barely breathe.

She wondered what would happen if she popped up and surprised him. The way he was driving he'd probably lose control of the car and plow into a tractor trailer. TWO DIE IN FATAL COLLISION. MORE NEWS AND TRAFFIC AT THE TOP OF THE HOUR.

She felt the car slow, then make a sharp turn that threw her against the seat. A couple of seconds later, the Ford rolled to a stop, cutting Diana off mid-lyric. The door opened and closed. Anne counted to twenty. Then she raised the blanket cautiously and looked around. They were in a Pizza Hut parking lot on Route 35, about five miles north of the Heights. God, this guy couldn't get enough fast food. If there'd been a drive-through window, she probably would have been covered in pepperoni and mushrooms.

She got out of the car, still feeling a little wobbly, and followed him inside. The place was half empty. A couple of mothers with kids in tow. A few office workers yukking it up. A fat guy seated at a table for four working his way through a large meatball pie. Baseball Cap was on line, with his back to her, looking at the menu like it was the Holy Grail. She slunk over to the condiments, keeping her head down.

Something about the guy looked familiar. He was skinny and slight, dressed in jeans and a brown leather bomber jacket. Even from a distance, she could see the jacket was cheaply made.

After what seemed like an eternity, he turned from the counter, carrying his tray. Anne stared at him in disbelief. The kid from the *Landsdown Park Press*. Mr. I've-Got-a-Scoop Cub Reporter. Jimmy Olsen with an attitude problem.

Anne walked over and slid into the plastic bucket seat opposite him.

"Howdy."

He looked up, startled, his mouth dripping cheese.

"Oh, hey," he said, trying to engineer a quick recovery and failing.

"I don't know much about how newspapers work," Anne said, smiling. "But I can't imagine your editor would be pleased to learn you've been staking out my house at all hours. Not to mention what the cops are going to think."

He dropped his slice as if it burned him, his eyes as round as his Styrofoam plate.

"The cops?" he echoed. His voice was a high-pitched squeak.

"I have to tell them you've been harassing me, don't you think?"

She could tell by his stricken expression that he wasn't going to bother denying it.

"Look," he said, pushing his pizza away. "I'm sorry about that. The truth is I'm an intern." He paused and stared down at the floor. "Well, a copyboy, actually, which is worse. You have to get people coffee and sandwiches from the cafeteria. You have to come when they shout 'Copy!' Even though there's no live type anymore. That skeleton piece was my first break. If I follow it up with something big, maybe they'll make me a real reporter."

"What about the other day, when I saw you on Main Street photographing the storm damage?"

"The paper was short staffed during the storm. So I

got to go out. Do some man-on-the-street reaction stuff. Take some pictures. I phoned in what I had to the rewrite guy."

She resisted the urge to steer him toward another profession. One that paid better, with saner hours. She'd been a small-town newspaper reporter herself a while back. Lots of grunt work, no glory.

"So you're not Bart Mendinger?"

"Bart's about seventy years old. My name's Dan Hemp. Like the rope."

He stuck out a greasy hand, which Anne reluctantly shook. She couldn't believe she'd let this kid scare her half to death.

"Are you going to eat that?" she asked, pointing to the pizza.

He pushed the pie toward her. "Have as much as you want."

"Thanks." She bit into a slice. It wasn't all that warm and the crust was a little doughy, but otherwise it tasted excellent.

"So, Dan," she said, wiping her lips with a napkin. "What'd you manage to find out?"

"Nothing," he said, averting his eyes.

"I don't think so. You wouldn't be sitting outside my house at six-thirty in the morning on a whim. You wouldn't waste your time."

Dan Hemp swallowed hard and studied the paper napkins on his tray. Anne tried to put herself in his shoes, to imagine what it felt like to be on the verge of a career breakthrough. She'd been writing self-help books so long, she'd nearly forgotten her dreams of becoming a famous novelist. That was the thing about dreams. If you didn't take care of them they died on the vine, like blighted tomatoes. As Dan began shredding the napkins into strips, Anne sat back and folded her arms. She'd gotten this far. She could wait.

After a while Dan said, "I got a buddy works over in

the M.E.'s office in Newark. He showed me a copy of the forensics report."

"And?"

Dan licked his lips. "There was something funny about it."

Anne helped herself to a second slice of pizza. She noticed that Dan appeared to have lost his appetite.

"Funny how?"

"One of the hands had a finger missing."

"Rats could have gotten it."

Dan shook his head. "Not according to the forensic anthropologist. The report said someone had sliced the finger clean off at the base. Most likely with a kitchen knife."

Anne put the pizza down. Why hadn't Trasker mentioned this to her? It seemed like an important detail to overlook.

"Which finger?" she asked, feeling a twinge of apprehension she couldn't explain.

Dan grabbed hold of her hand. The gesture was so unexpected that Anne flinched. He squeezed the finger that wore Jack's engagement ring. "This one."

Anne pulled her hand free. "But I saw the hand," she protested. "It was in the dirt, before they dug the skeleton up."

"You must have seen the right one. This was the left."

Anne stared at her ring and shuddered. So whoever murdered Steven Hillyard had cut off his ring finger before burying him. There was no wedding band under the stairs because the killer still had it.

She looked up and met his gaze. "You think my mother murdered Hillyard, right? You think I'm covering up for her."

He didn't need to answer. She could see it in his eyes.

"Who else would bother to cut off the man's finger?" he said nervously. "I mean, he must have been dead then right? What was the point? Except if it was a crime of passion." He swallowed hard. "I did my homework. Your mother had been behaving erratically for months. She'd been having marital difficulties, memory loss, whole days she couldn't account for. Hillyard was treating her in her own house. And he was six feet away from whoever shot him. If it was me, I'd probably do the same as you. Cover up evidence. Get friends on the force to keep quiet about stuff. The dead guy's wallet, his watch, the stuff your mom wrote in her diary."

Anne's mind was racing. This put a whole new spin on things.

"Let me get this straight. You've been sitting out in your car, watching my house, in hopes I'll what? Destroy important evidence? So you can catch me in the act?"

"Hey," he shot back. "I read a lot of true crime. Believe me, it happens."

"What else?" she said suddenly. "What else do you have?"

Dan Hemp took a sip of his soda. The straw made a faint slurping sound. "That's it."

"Dan, I wasn't fooling about the police. You seem like a good guy. An ambitious guy. You don't want to blow your career by holding out on me."

He slumped a little in his seat, weighing the possibilities. He looked a little sick. Finally, he said, "Well, there *is* one more thing. I got a buddy over at the Motor Vehicle Bureau."

"You've got friends all over the place. Is that how you knew about my mother's diary? From a 'friend' at the sheriff's office?"

He ignored the question. "My buddy ran a check on Hillyard's car. A 1972 green Volkswagen Beetle. It disappeared around the same time he did. Turned up a year after he disappeared, in an abandoned lot in Landsdown. It was totally trashed. Stripped for parts, no license plate, seats slashed."

"How'd they identify it?"

His eyes slid away from her face. "There was a torn picture of Hillyard and your mom in the glove compartment. Their names were written on the back. The cops checked it out. Your mom was in a nursing home at the time. She'd had her license suspended, and besides, the car wasn't hers. Which brought them to Hillyard. His wife had never even filed a missing persons report."

"It's a little too pat, don't you think? The car's wrecked, but the photograph manages to survive? Come on."

"Whatever you say. Anyhow, that's it. That's all I know. So you won't call the cops, right?"

"I won't call the cops."

"Great." Relief showed on his face like the sheen on a newly waxed coffee table. "Anything you want. Just name it."

"I could use a lift back to the Heights."

"Sure. No problem."

He wiped his hands and stood up. "Maybe we could work together on this. Figure out whodunnit. I'd appreciate any suggestions."

Anne got up. "I do have one," she said, as they headed out the door. He gazed at her expectantly. "You should really take better care of your car."

Jack was sitting on the sofa when she got back. There was a stack of blueprints on the coffee table, next to a large bottle of Perrier, a half-empty glass, and the crumpled remains of a peanut butter Power Bar.

"I found it," he announced, when she walked into the living room.

"Huh?"

"The bullet."

He held something out to her. She went over to him and took it. A small metal fragment, about half the size of a lima bean. She stared at it like it was alive.

Jack said, "I know I promised not to look anymore. But I realized I was going about it the wrong way. Hillyard wasn't killed in the basement. I mean, think about it. He comes over to treat your mom. She's not here. The door's open. So he walks in. Where's the most likely place for him to wait? Here." Jack thumped the sofa cushion. "In the living room."

She looked around the room as if seeing it for the first time. On the far wall, the oil seascape painting had been removed. In its place was a hole about the size of a hard-cover book. Plaster had fallen like dirty snow on the wood plank floor.

"Sorry about the mess," Jack said. "I'll patch the dry-wall and repair the hole myself. I borrowed old man Klemperer's metal detector and ran it over all the walls. Worked like a charm."

Anne sat down heavily in the armchair. Her head was doing loop-de-loops. She felt slightly dizzy.

"Don't know why your detective pal missed it," Jack said. His tone was triumphant. "Once I ruled out the basement, the rest was pretty obvious."

Anne went over to the phone and dialed Trasker's number. One, two, three rings, then the machine came on. Her message was on the curt side. She was mad at Trasker. He hadn't told her everything he knew, not by a long shot. It was like he was trying to protect her. But she could have told him that was an impossibility. The truth would come out. It always did in the end.

She sank down in the chair again, still holding the bullet. The heat of her palm had made it warm to the touch. "Thanks, Jack. For being so tenacious. I guess a part of me didn't want to believe he'd been killed here. Even after all the facts said otherwise."

She realized it was true the instant after she'd said it. That's why she hadn't combed the basement herself. She hadn't wanted to know.

"If this had happened in New York," Jack was saying vehemently, "the cops would have found the bullet the first day out of the box. But these Jersey detectives are strictly Mickey Mouse. Your friend should stick to tick-eting cars."

Anne looked at Jack's face. It was tense with anger.

His eyes were like cold blue stones. She realized Jack felt threatened by Trasker. That's why he was acting like this. She thought of her parents' marriage. When she tried to analyze what had gone wrong, as she had so many times over the years, it came down to her father abandoning her mother. It was a betrayal of sorts, of their vows, their life together, anything they had ever meant to one another. Being unfaithful didn't only mean having affairs. There were dozens of other ways to opt out.

"What?" Jack said. "What are you thinking?"

Whether we can be happy together. Whether what we have is enough.

Anne stood up, trying to decide how to answer. "I have to talk to Claire Hillyard," she said, switching gears.

"Why?"

"Because parts of her story don't add up."

"From everything you've told me, that woman doesn't want anything more to do with you. Maybe you should call, instead of going over there."

"All right."

She dialed Sunnydale and waited to be connected.

Claire wasn't in her office, the operator said. As Anne waited for Claire to be paged, she studied the hole in the wall. The bullet had lain there untouched all these years, like the skeleton. It was the perfect crime. If not for the storm . . .

"This is Claire Hillyard. How can I help you?"

"Claire, it's Anne Hardaway."

"I have nothing to say to you," Claire said icily.

"Just listen a minute. You told me you hired a detective to find your husband. But now I understand you never even filed a missing persons report."

"I've had it up to here with you badgering me," Claire said. Her voice was shrill.

A question popped unbidden into Anne's head. "Did you take the photos that are up at Sunnydale? The black-and-white ones of the patients?"

"Leave me alone."

Anne heard a click, then the line went dead.

"I'm going over there," Anne said to Jack.

"If you can wait about forty-five minutes, I'll come with you. I'm expecting an important fax from the city."

"I'll be back by then. You know what? Let's go out to dinner. To Vic's or The Blue Marlin. Someplace nice."

"Sure. We'll celebrate."

Anne stopped to think. Then she remembered. Right. The engagement. That's what they were going to be celebrating. With all the commotion, it was the last thing on her mind. She went into the kitchen and slipped the bullet into her silverware drawer, in the small compartment that held loose nails and screws.

"See you in a bit," she said to Jack.

She walked outside and got behind the wheel of the Mustang. It was late afternoon, and the sun was just starting to slip in the sky. Seagulls circled lazily over the beach. The wind smelled of salt and brine. She looked up at her house—at the faded paint, the torn shutters, the missing shingles, the windows that were desperately in need of washing—and felt a surge of affection. In a short while she'd be leaving all this behind to move in with Jack. She could make a new life for herself in New York. Start her novel. Take up t'ai chi. Join a book club. Spend her lunch hour exploring museums.

But even as the car pulled away from the curb, she knew it wasn't true. She belonged here, by the shore. She rolled down the window all the way and let the air wash over her. This place had worked its way into her blood. It wouldn't be the same, coming back on the occasional weekend or on a one-week summer vacation, like a tourist.

She gazed through the window at the sand dunes rising and flattening out again, tawny shapes that shifted with the uncertain forces of nature. She didn't like change. She wasn't nearly flexible enough.

Chapter 23

*If a bulb flickers but works
fine in another lamp, try
cleaning the socket.
Unplug the lamp, wipe the
socket interior with fine
sandpaper or scrape it with
a screwdriver until it
shines, then bend up the
metal tab at the bottom
to improve contact with
the bulb.*

There were two wheelchairs parked outside the nursing home. The old ladies in them were bundled in coats and hats and had the dazed, confused look of drugged winter birds. They slumped in their chairs, their feet barely touching the footrests, their hands curled inward like tiny cabbages. Anne entered the building and walked quickly by the guard in the lobby. She didn't really believe Claire would have her thrown out, but it didn't hurt to look like a woman with a mission.

In front of the elevators, she paused to study the black-

and-white photos on the wall. That's why Hillyard's picture in the museum looked familiar. They reminded her of these, which were shot at an angle, in soft focus, perhaps with a filter, so the patients looked a little younger and healthier than they really were. Anne scanned the captions: *Dorothy, Knitting. Herbert, Tossing Salad. Estelle, At the Saturday Sing-a-Long.* She wondered if the same person who had taken them had photographed Hillyard, at afternoon tea.

When she came to the end of the hall, Anne turned left and went into Claire Hillyard's office. It was empty. The pumpkin had been removed from the windowsill. The desk looked like it had been hastily straightened. Files were stacked in untidy piles. A coffee mug had leaked a brown ring onto a yellow legal pad. Anne touched the mug. Still warm.

"May I help you?"

A young nurse with heavily made up eyes stood in the doorway, smiling perkily.

"I was looking for Claire," Anne told her.

"She's left for the day."

"When did she leave?"

"About ten minutes ago."

"Do you know if she was heading home?"

"I really couldn't say. I saw her for a moment in the parking lot as I was coming in. She was in a big hurry."

"Thanks."

"If you'd like to leave a note, I'm sure she'll get back to you first thing in the morning."

"That's okay."

Anne brushed past the nurse and dogtrotted back down the hallway. She had Claire's address in West Long Branch. It wasn't more than a twenty-minute drive. This time, Claire wouldn't be able to elude her. She would finally be able to get some answers. She'd almost reached the lobby, when she heard someone call her name.

Greta Koch was sitting alone in the solarium drinking a cup of tea. At an adjoining table, a small, wizened man in a wheelchair sat napping, his chin nearly touching his chest.

"Anne," Greta called out. "Do you have a minute?"

Anne stood in the doorway. The late afternoon sun streamed through the windows, illuminating a flurry of dust motes hovering above the long row of plants. "I'm actually in a bit of a hurry."

"This will only take a minute. It's about yesterday. I wanted to apologize."

"For what?"

"That business in the office. For not standing up to Claire. She overreacted, don't you think?"

For an instant, Anne detected a gleam of hatred in Greta's dark eyes. She walked over and sat down beside the nurse. This could prove interesting. Maybe Greta had some dirt on Claire. Maybe she knew something.

"Would you care for tea?" Greta said. "I just made a fresh pot. And there's some butter cookies."

"Sure."

Tea and cookies sounded great right about now. She was suddenly starving.

Greta got up and walked over to a plywood table where the hot water urn was plugged in. "I heard Claire threaten you. Don't take it personally. She enjoys throwing her weight around. Lording it over the rest of us."

"You sound as though you don't care for her."

The nurse emitted a low-pitched laugh. "Hardly. But neither does anyone else at Sunnydale."

When Greta returned to the table, she was carrying a plate of cookies and a steaming cup of tea in a cobalt blue mug. Anne took a sip. The tea was dark and strong. She could feel it coursing through her.

"What's Claire like?"

Greta stirred her tea idly with a spoon. "She's a good administrator," the nurse said grudgingly. "But she hasn't a compassionate bone in her body. Claire's a number cruncher, pure and simple. She doesn't care about the quality of people's lives, if they're in pain or depressed or lonely." Greta's voice was laced with anger. "The only thing that interests her is whether somebody foots the bills."

"I noticed she collects vintage cocktail shakers. Does she have any other hobbies?"

"I wouldn't know. We're hardly close friends."

"I was wondering if she took those photographs in the hallway."

"Why do you ask?"

"I was just curious. They remind me of a picture I saw today at the new historical museum."

Greta bit into a cookie and chewed it thoughtfully. "I hardly think Claire has time for photographs. She's much too busy entertaining her latest boyfriend."

"Boyfriend?"

"Philip Reynolds. Our illustrious commander-in-chief. They're an item. Or hadn't you heard?"

"No," Anne said, as she tried to process this new information. Her head was swimming. Her stomach gave a sharp heave. The sleep deprivation was catching up to her. She knew from past experience that if you missed enough shut-eye, you could feel like you had a twenty-four hour bug.

She drank the rest of the tea, hoping the sickness would subside. The old man at the next table was snoring softly. The plants were so green, they almost looked artificial. It was bright in the solarium, too bright. The light hurt her eyes.

She took a deep breath, released it, and turned back to Greta. "That nurse who was killed, Katie Crowley. Were she and Claire friendly?"

"Not especially. Katie was a loner—kept to herself. Rumor has it she was stealing from some of the patients."

"What do you think?"

"It's certainly possible. There's hardly any security here. I suppose Katie could have pinched a few trinkets without anyone becoming suspicious. Of course, it's an awful thing to do to poor defenseless people who haven't got many worldly possessions."

Anne nodded weakly. Her stomach lurched again and she felt a sharp, stabbing pain right below her sternum. Her head hurt. A wave of dizziness passed through her.

"Are you all right, Anne?" Greta Koch asked. The nurse was standing over her.

"Must be the flu." She'd broken out in a cold sweat and had started to shake uncontrollably.

"Could I fix you another cup of tea?"

"No, thanks. Actually, I'm not feeling well." An understatement if ever there was one. She felt like she wanted to crawl in a hole and stay there for a week. "I should really get going. If you could just help me to my car."

Anne stood up, lost her balance, and stumbled. The room spun round and round and round. Plants, wheelchair, table, Greta. And then, for the second time in less than twenty-four hours, she blacked out.

When she opened her eyes she was flat on her back on a narrow hospital bed. The room was stuffy and dark, the shades drawn. She heard voices coming from a long way off, in a half-forgotten dream. She was tired and sick, and she could feel herself slipping back into sleep. But she forced herself to open her eyes and keep them open. She was exhausted, weak. It felt like all the energy had been sapped right out of her. Maybe Jack's right, she thought hazily. Maybe it was time to start taking vitamins.

Time. What time was it? Anne lifted her arm weakly and saw that it was attached to an IV drip. A pole next to the bed held a bag of fluid. Her watch was gone. So was Jack's engagement ring. She looked down and saw she was wearing a blue-and-white cotton hospital gown. Where were her clothes? Where *was* she? She looked around the room. A chest of drawers, sink, closet, nightstand, chair. She tried to get up and sank back, over-whelmed with dizziness. She was in Sunnydale, that was it. She'd fainted and now she was lying in one of the rooms she'd seen on her tour.

She felt more tired than she'd ever been in her life. If she could just get some rest, she'd feel better. The diz-ziness and nausea would go away. She closed her eyes and turned on her side. The pillow felt cool against her cheek. But she couldn't sleep, couldn't shake the sickness spreading inside her. She slid in and out of conscious-ness, twisting from side to side in the bed. Her mouth was dry. Her limbs ached. She seemed to be floating above her pain-ridden body, watching herself try to get some relief. Her head felt hot and swollen, like an over-sized balloon attached to her neck.

Time passed. After a while, she heard the door open. Greta Koch walked to the side of the bed and stood over her.

"How are you feeling?" Greta asked.

"Not good."

"The doctor was in to examine you. Did you speak with him?"

"No. Must have slept through it." It was an effort to talk. It made the pain worse.

"You've got Asian flu. It's been going around. If you'd like, I could call your regular physician. But the best thing to do is stay put for now. When your fever breaks, you'll feel a lot better. In the meantime," Greta pointed to the IV drip, "we're forcing fluids, so you don't get dehydrated."

"Could you call my fiancé? Tell him I'm here?"

"Certainly. What's the phone number?"

"555-6797." She tried to say the numbers, but they came out slurred.

Greta scribbled it down on a piece of paper anyway.

"My things," Anne said. It was getting harder to talk. "Where?"

"Right here." Greta slid open the drawer of the night stand. Anne's ring and watch were nesting on a sheet of tissue paper. "Your clothes and shoes are in the closet. We considered sending you to the hospital, but the doctor felt we should try to treat you here. You should feel better soon."

Only she didn't. Sweat formed a sheen on her face. Her stomach felt like it was broiling ever so slowly over an open fire. "Is there something . . . for the pain?"

Greta plumped the pillow slightly. "I'll go ask the doctor now. Try and get some rest."

Greta turned and walked noiselessly across the room, shutting the door behind her.

Anne closed her eyes again, but it made the dizzy feeling worse. She threw back the covers. The nausea was like a giant wave, cresting and falling ceaselessly against the pit of her stomach. She wanted to be home, in her own bed. She wanted Jack to rub her back and bring her a glass of flat, warm ginger ale. She sat up and swung her legs over the side of the hospital bed. Reaching into the drawer, she took out the watch and the ring, and put them on. She could hear herself panting from the effort it took. Her breath came in short, rapid gasps. She felt her heart fluttering in her chest, like an animal trapped in a small, locked cage. She was drenched in sweat, the hospital gown stuck to her skin.

She stood up slowly. As soon as she did, she was sorry. The room swung in and out of focus. There was a dull ringing in her ears. Her arms flapped wildly as she tried to keep her balance. Her legs felt thick and heavy as tree trunks. *Focus*, she told herself. *Focus*. Taking baby steps, she inched across the room, dragging the IV pole behind her. The closet was only about fifteen feet away, but it took over a minute to get there. She tried to ignore how sick she felt, tried to ignore everything but the door to the closet, which slid open when she finally reached it. Her blue cotton shirt was hanging next to her jeans. Good. She'd get dressed, call Jack, and go home. Everything would be better at home.

She put her hand on the wall and groped for the light switch. She felt lightheaded, like she might faint. Her legs were wobbly as Jell-O. Her hand found the switch and the naked light bulb hanging from the ceiling lit up and began to flicker. Anne let out a sharp gasp. There was something wrong with her eyes. The entire room had a yellow tint. She blinked, shut her eyes for a few seconds, then opened them, but the room was still yellow, like the afterimage from a flashbulb. She felt like she was about to puke. An angry rash was creeping up her arm. She stared at it for a long moment, then ripped the intravenous tube out. No way could she get better in this dump. Enough was enough. *Adios* Sunnydale.

She lunged for the door handle and pulled. Nothing. The handle was stuck. She tried again, tugging as hard as she could. And again. The effort sent her sprawling backwards. She lay on the cold, hard floor, feeling sicker than she'd ever been in her life, and realized with sudden clarity that she was being put to death. Like Maggie Zambini. And Myra Stanton and Ernest Kamber. And all the other patients at the nursing home who had died before their time. Bad medicine. Poison. Chemicals racing through your veins, delivered by injection or through an intravenous tube. She wondered if the drugs would cause her heart to stop. Congestive heart failure. That's what the death certificate would say, just like the others.

She tried to get up, but couldn't. She could barely keep her eyelids from closing. The pain was so bad it had taken over her whole body. There was nothing else left.

"Help," she called out. "Help me." But the words sounded no louder than a whisper. She felt herself losing consciousness and pinched her arm hard. Through the nearly closed shades, she could see the mangled branches of the big elm tree, wrecked by the storm. If the window was by the tree, it meant she was on the north end of

Sunnydale, in the old wing of the nursing home. She could scream her head off. There was no one around to hear.

Why? The word caromed through her fevered brain. *Why? Why? Why?* Images came and went: Claire Hillyard's icy gray eyes. Margaret painting tiny Degas ballerinas. The gold ball and chain in Stuart's office. Jack's face when he asked her to marry him. Steven Hillyard on the porch of the inn, so serious looking, so in control. It all began with Hillyard. This whole crazy dance that ended with her writhing on the floor, feverish, pain-ridden, gasping for breath.

The door of the room swung open.

"What happened?" exclaimed Greta Koch. "What are you doing out of bed?"

Why would the nurse pump poison into her veins? Why? Why? Why?

"Bathroom," Anne whispered. "Fell."

Greta walked toward her. "You were trying to get to the bathroom and you fell down?"

Anne nodded her head weakly. She needed to get out of this horrible place. She needed to get out now.

"What about your IV?"

"Out."

Greta frowned. "You don't want to get dehydrated. Doctor's orders. Here. Let me help you." Greta gathered Anne in her arms and set her gently back on the bed. She did it easily, as though Anne were no heavier than a sack of ashes.

"Call . . . fiancé." Her thoughts were getting muddled. Greta's face was a round white blur. White moon. Stars. Bones.

"I tried your house," Greta said. "No one picked up. I'll call back later, if you like."

"Marcus," Anne whispered.

"What?"

Dr. Marcus, she wanted to say. My doctor. Call Marcus. But she couldn't form the right words. Her heart was beating way too fast, galloping along at breakneck speed.

"Everything's going to be fine," Greta said. Her voice was strangely soothing. "The wheels of justice grind exceedingly slow."

Anne shivered through the pain. *Wheels of justice*. The same words she'd heard on the phone. She saw Greta grab the end of the IV tube. Summoning all the strength she had left, she tried to speak. "Steven."

It came out faint, but Greta heard.

"What?" Greta bent over her.

"Bullet," Anne gasped. "Killed . . . him."

Even in her hazy state, Anne could see the consternation on Greta's face.

"What did you say?" asked Greta sharply.

"Found . . . bullet."

Anne's head rolled to the side. There was a sudden tightness in her chest and then a crashing sound in her ears. Everything seemed to stop. It was as though she were diving into a big wave headfirst. She looked up and the nurse was gone. Her heart was bursting, like an overblown peony crushed underfoot. She thought her life would flash quickly before her eyes, the way people claimed. But it didn't. There was no big revelation, no insight on what it all meant. Instead, a flurry of thoughts came and went: her unpaid heating bill, the chapter on pest contol, whether Jack would get his ring back or not. She wondered if she'd remembered to buy enough food for Harry and why she hadn't made arrangements for somebody to look after him if something ever happened to her.

In her mind's eye, she saw her house, before the storm hit. She saw herself walking along the beach, in a long, flowing white dress she didn't own. She was by the water's edge at twilight, staring out to sea. The water was a deep, lovely green, smooth as polished jade. It was oddly peaceful. Anne closed her eyes. It occurred to her that dying wasn't as awful as she'd thought it would be.

The pain was farther away now. It hardly touched her. She imagined herself floating up out of her body, like mist rising off the beach. She wished she'd had more time. She wished she wasn't leaving this world in a blue-and-white checked hospital nightgown. Damn you, Hillyard. Why couldn't you rest in peace?

She felt something prick her arm hard. A bee? A nail? She opened her eyes and saw Greta had come back. The nurse was holding an intravenous tube that was plunged halfway into the crook of Anne's elbow.

"This should perk you right up," Greta said, with a smile.

The smile scared Anne more than the syringe. It was sinister, demented. Greta's eyes were two black holes that swallowed up all available light.

Anne felt her body go limp. The tightness in her chest began to let up, the pain decreased by a few decibels. She still had as much energy as a wet dishrag, but she was definitely in the land of the living.

Greta pulled a chair over to the bed and sat. "Now then," she said, smoothing the sheet back, "you were saying something about a bullet."

Anne licked her dry lips. Her heart was still racing, but the vise that had gripped it relentlessly was gone. "Found it. In living room wall."

"The bullet that killed the man in your basement?"

Anne nodded.

"Where is it?"

"My house."

"Where exactly?"

"Kitchen."

"In a drawer?" Greta prompted. "One of the cabinets?"

"My head hurts. Can't remember."

Greta's expression was disapproving, like a school-teacher whose star pupil had just failed the big exam. "You're scatterbrained. Like your mother. Well, there's only one thing for us to do."

Greta got up and opened the door of the closet. She pulled out Anne's shirt and jeans and flung them on the bed. She was smiling again, that same creepy smile.

"We need to go get it."

Chapter 24

*Respect your power tools
because they can be
dangerous. Read the
manuals carefully and pay
strict attention to safety
tips. A little diligence and
patience goes a long way.*

It was surprisingly easy to leave Sunnydale without being seen. Greta simply led Anne down the stairs to a side door in the back of the old wing, then out to the empty parking lot. Anne was still feeling woozy, but whatever Greta had pumped into her at least allowed her to walk without feeling like she was going to collapse. Any thoughts she harbored about making a run for it were quickly put to rest by the handgun Greta concealed in the pocket of her navy blue sweater.

The parking lot was deserted, lit by streetlights and a faint ivory moon pasted to the sky. They took the Mustang. Anne drove. Greta sat in the passenger seat and pointed the gun at Anne's heart. On the floor by her feet was a black medicine bag, like the kind old Doc Fisher had brought to the house when Anne was sick as a girl, in the days when doctors still made housecalls.

The car swung onto the road and headed for the Heights. Anne was the first to break the silence. "You were his lover, right?" Her voice sounded small, unfamiliar.

"I was his one and only," Greta corrected.

"What about Claire? And Mrs. Z?"

"Steven never loved his wife. He only married her because she was pregnant. As for Maggie Zambini, she never meant a thing to him."

"I thought they were going to run off together."

Greta scowled. "Is that what she claimed?"

"Yes."

"He would never have gone through with it. He would never have left me for that mousy little snip."

"But that isn't what he told you the day he died. The day you followed him to our house."

Greta shifted the gun in her lap. When she spoke, her voice was low and girlish sounding. "Steven and I shared a special bond. No one could ever love him the way I did. *No one*."

It was all fitting together—the hysterical phone calls Greta had made to Hillyard, the way his wedding ring had been sliced from his hand. Dan Hemp was right after all. A crime of passion, from start to finish.

Anne tightened her grip on the wheel. She was driving as slowly as she could, but Greta didn't seem to notice.

"You didn't know Mrs. Zambini was the other woman, did you?"

"Not until Sunday. I have you to thank for that, I suppose." Greta turned toward her and Anne saw the glint of the gun barrel out of the corner of her eye. "I wonder how Maggie managed to keep it a secret all these years. Her long-ago love affair." Greta's tone was sarcastic. "You saw the way she looked, the way her husband can't bear to be around her. Do you think she could hold a man for more than five minutes?"

Anne slowed at a stop light. For a split second, she considered opening the door and running. She wasn't wearing her seat belt. Maybe she could make it. She breaked and the car rolled to a stop. The street was dark, devoid of life. The nurse would shoot her dead if she ran. She knew it with the same certainty she knew her own name. Greta was so close Anne could hear the faint rumbling of her stomach.

The light changed and the car cruised down Main Street. It was surreal to pass familiar landmarks—Moby's Hardware, Baby Face, Quilters, while a deranged woman was training a gun at your chest. Most of the Victorian houses were dark. There was no one on the streets. The Heights closed up early. All her neighbors were tucked in their beds, safely asleep.

"What was in my IV bag?" Anne said.

"Digitalis. It's used to treat congestive heart failure. Only the dose that cures is very, very close to the dose that kills. We have to be so careful when we administer meds." Greta smiled again, her lips stretched over her big, crooked teeth. "Wouldn't want to risk an overdose."

"But how?" Anne stammered. "You can't just medicate people at will. There are doctors and nurses. Charts. They'd know."

"Not necessarily," Greta reprimanded. "Digitalis is administered in liquid form. It can be obtained pharmaceutically, of course. In Digoxin. But there are other means."

"Like what?" Anne rolled her window down. She was still feeling headachy and nauseous and the salt breeze rolling inland from the ocean had a soothing, restorative effect.

"Plants," Greta murmured.

Anne pictured the row of plants in the solarium. Ferns. Spider plants. Cacti. Herbs. Tall leafy plants. Squat, bulbous plants. Plants with narrow, grassy leaves and thick, tubular roots. Silky, grayish plants, the undersides hairy along the veins. Fragrant plants. Plants leaking milky sap.

Plants she didn't recognize, with downy stems, tiny spangled flowers, and peculiar black berries.

Of course, Anne thought. She'd read about Digoxin when she was researching heart failure on-line. She just hadn't made the plant connection.

"Digitalis is found in foxglove leaves," Greta explained cheerfully. "In the nineteenth century, it was used to treat dropsy. Doesn't taste too bad. Especially in tea."

"Why?" Anne whispered. "Why kill all those innocent people?"

She'd spotted a car in the rearview mirror and had slowed down even more, so they were crawling through town at ten miles per hour.

There was a dreamy look in Greta's eyes when she spoke. Her voice was pitched low, laced with genuine sadness.

"They're all alone," Greta intoned. "Do you know what that means? Do you have any idea? To be old and sick and lonely?" Anne glanced in the rear-view mirror again. The car behind them was tailgating the Mustang, its headlights glaring. "You start to lose things," Greta continued. "Dignity. Hope. Respect. Until all that's left is a shell of your former self. Until you cry out for release from pain, for death to wrap you in its warm embrace, gently, tenderly, like a lover."

She really believes she's saving them, Anne thought. Nurse Greta Koch. Patron saint of the aged and infirm. It was another kind of passion, actually. Greta crusading through the corridors of Sunnydale.

The car in the mirror swerved to the left, crossed the yellow line in the center of Main Street and gunned its engine, speeding past them into the night. Anne felt her heart plummet. There was no one else on the road.

"What about Katie Crowley?" she said to Greta. "Katie wasn't a lonely old lady."

"Katie was a druggie. And a thief. She stole jewelry, heirlooms—anything she could get her grimy little hands on."

"Katie told you about Maggie's affair, didn't she? I caught her eavesdropping outside the door."

Greta's laugh was bitter. "A little too nosy for her own good. If she'd spent more time tending to her patients and less time hovering in doorways, she'd be alive today."

Anne thought back to what Andrew Deretchin had seen: Katie skulking out of Maggie Zambini's room. The nurse could have recognized the digitalis, could have guessed something wasn't right.

"How much money did she want?"

They had reached Ocean Avenue. Above the beach, the sky was strung with a necklace of stars. The lifeguard towers cast long, thin shadows like tentacles on the sand.

"Twenty thousand," Greta said. "I don't have that kind of cash."

"But you knew she was stealing."

"And I knew she was a drug addict. Didn't matter. She threatened to tell Claire about me. She figured out Maggie wasn't the first. Just like you. Snooping through those medical records. I can't have that," Greta scolded. "No one must interrupt my work."

"What were you searching for in Katie's house?"

"Her *proof*. Do you think anyone would believe a coked-out little druggie unless she had evidence? She got hold of some original medical records before I had a chance to doctor them. But she was stupid." Greta spoke dismissively, her voice laced with derision. "Didn't even have the sense to keep them in a bank vault."

Anne peered down the road, trying to see her house. She prayed Jack was home. But the Victorian cottage was completely dark. As if reading her mind, Greta said, "Your boyfriend called the hospital earlier. One of the nurses told him you'd left hours ago. She remembered you'd been looking for Claire. You know where Claire is right now? At a quiet B & B in Spring Lake with Reynolds. His wife thinks he's attending a medical conference in Philly. That should keep your boyfriend busy for awhile."

"What did you do to Katie?"

"Poor girl. She was a little too fond of cocaine. But she never considered herself an addict. Not our Katie. She never smoked crack or freebased. Just a quick sniff through a rolled-up dollar bill. Very genteel, wouldn't you say? She used to bring it to work in a Ziploc bag, inside her purse. Not very bright of her. Anyone could have tampered with it, cut the stuff with other drugs, made a few slight alterations."

Greta motioned for Anne to stop. They were at the house. Anne pulled up to the curb and cut the engine. She was weak and sick and dizzy. She opened the car door and got out. She saw the bulge of the gun under Greta's blue sweater. The black medical bag swung jauntily in Greta's other hand.

"Get moving," Greta ordered. "We haven't got all night."

Anne forced herself to walk up the stone path to her house. *This can't be happening. This can't be real.*

At the front door, she fumbled in her bag for her key. She felt the gun poke her lower back, prodding her to be quick about it. A wave of nausea passed through her as she turned the key in the lock and the door swung open. Inside, she flicked on the hall light. The cat loped down the stairs, a reproachful look in his one eye. It had probably been hours since he'd last eaten.

Do something, Anne silently beseeched him. *Pounce. Attack.*

"Well, aren't you sweet," Greta purred to the cat. "Good kitty. Pretty kitty."

Harry walked over to the nurse and rubbed against her ankles.

Doesn't this beat all, Anne thought. *Here, I have the most antisocial, stay-off-my-turf cat in the universe, and the one person he chooses to befriend is an insane killer with a savior complex.*

"Don't you ever feed this poor animal?" Greta said reproachfully.

"In case you haven't noticed, I've been out of commission."

Greta's gaze was wrathful. She shook the gun like it was her fist. "The kitchen," she commanded.

Anne led the way, trailed by Greta and the cat. The kitchen was spotless, but the scent of herbs and garlic lingered in the air. Jack must have fixed himself another gourmet meal. Normally, Anne would practically be salivating. But tonight, as sick as she was feeling, the smell made her stomach give a violent heave.

She leaned heavily against the wood countertop. Her vision was starting to blur. The light in the kitchen was taking on the same yellow cast as the room at Sunnydale.

"Where do you keep the cat food?" Greta asked.

Anne gestured weakly toward a cabinet near the sink.

"Go on then," Greta said, waving the gun.

Anne dragged herself through the motions of pouring cat chow in Harry's dish. With an appreciative glance at Greta, the cat began to eat. So much for feline loyalty.

"Now, the bullet, if you please."

Anne's head was spinning. She felt as if her legs were about to give out. As soon as she gave Greta the bullet, the nurse would have no reason to keep her alive.

"I can't remember . . ." Anne said.

"Just like your mother." Greta's eyes were glassy with hatred. "Weak, confused. She loved him, too. It was pathetic, the way she threw herself at him. But I knew . . . I knew one day I'd make her pay. And I have. Through you."

"The wheels of justice," Anne murmured.

At that moment, she wanted to hurt Greta Koch more than she'd ever wanted to hurt another living soul. This deranged witch, this lunatic, had tried to frame Evelyn for murder. She knew it as clearly as if she'd been in the house that August night in '74. She could see Greta firing the gun, dragging Hillyard down to the basement, digging his grave, and hiding his wallet and watch where her mother was sure to find them. Later, planting the picture of Evelyn in his car. It was a miracle Evelyn Hardaway was never arrested and convicted—a miracle she didn't spend her final years in jail.

"The bullet," Greta snapped. "Get it."

"No."

"If you don't give it to me immediately, I will shoot this precious little kitty in the back of the spine." Greta trained the gun on Harry, who was happily eating his dinner. "Death may be instantaneous. If not, the bullet will lodge in his spinal cord and cause excruciating pain."

Through the fog that was beginning to envelope her, Anne caught a glimpse of Greta's clinical, flat expression. The nurse was dead serious.

"Wait!" Anne cried out. She stumbled over to the silverware drawer and removed the bullet fragment. It felt tiny and cold in her hand.

She held it out to Greta, took a step forward, and overwhelmed with dizziness, collapsed in a heap on the floor. Her head was pounding. And something was wrong with her heart. It was beating all jagged, like it was about to burst. Greta faded in and out of view. Anne was dimly aware that the bullet had slipped from her fingers. The room was suffused with that awful yellow light. The cat had stopped eating and was circling her in frantic arcs.

From a long way away, Anne heard water streaming from the faucet, saw Greta wipe her hands on her white nurse's skirt.

Greta's voice pierced the fog. "I see the potassium chloride is beginning to wear off."

Anne's heart was thudding unevenly. Each breath had become a struggle.

Greta opened her black medical bag. "This will ease your pain, dear." The hypodermic sliced the air, silvery thin.

"Wait," Anne gasped, struggling to raise her head.

"They'll figure it out." Her voice was thick. "They'll find me. They'll know."

Greta laughed in genuine surprise. "Find you?" she echoed. "My dear girl, no one's going to find you for a very long time. By then, there'll be no trace but the whiteness of bones."

Like Hillyard, Anne thought wearily. Swallowed by the earth, left to molder and rot. She heard a phone ringing in the distance. Thoughts careened through her mind like pinballs ricocheting through a broken down machine. Where was Jack? Where was her mother? Her mouth tasted bitter, her pulse hammered its wild tattoo. Harry let out a sharp wail and darted from the room.

As if in a dream, she saw Greta move toward her, holding the needle. Closer, closer. There were three Gretas, then four, hovering just above her. Anne thrust her knees out and kicked with all her might. She heard a cracking sound, followed by a thud. Greta howled in pain, and hopped back on one foot, clutching her sore ankle.

Anne rolled to her left, her hands pinwheeling like a blind woman, her fingertips scrabbling over the cold, hard floor. As she grabbed the gun she felt the needle jab her calf. She found the trigger, squeezed. The first shot sounded and out of the corner of her eye she saw Greta leap away. Something liquid and cold under her skin. Her heart skittered wildly in her chest and she struggled to stay conscious. Then Greta was looming over her, reaching for the gun. Anne fired again and Greta slumped back against the refrigerator door. The nurse moaned. Anne saw the room spinning like a carousel, faster and faster. Everything bathed in that strange yellow light. Her ears were ringing, her vision so blurred that the kitchen had become a swirl of indistinct shapes. She heard her breath coming in short, choked gasps.

With a last desperate attempt she staggered to her feet, nearly falling again as she stumbled across the kitchen to the phone and dialed 911.

* * *

It was a singularly unpleasant experience to have your stomach pumped, but Anne supposed it was a lot better than the alternative. She sat on her front porch the next morning, recovering from the experience, drinking in the ocean air as thought it were champagne. The day was raw and cold. A stiff wind blew from the east. The ocean was an angry shade of gray, with choppy waves that roughed up the shoreline. Fall seemed to have vanished overnight, leaving the first hint of winter in its wake.

Anne pulled her jacket closer and took another small sip of her hot chocolate. She still felt a little weak and disoriented. She sat in the wicker swing across from Jack, who'd made Belgian waffles topped with low-fat frozen yogurt to welcome her home. She'd been the one who'd wanted to eat out here, even though he'd set two places in the dining room, with her lace placemats and the good silver.

"I'm so sorry," he said, for the umpteenth time. "I can't tell you what an idiot I feel like."

"Don't. It wasn't your fault. If I were you, I'd have been out searching for me too."

She thought of Trasker, who hadn't said he was sorry—not in so many words. But she could see it in the hospital, in the way he looked at her while he took down her statement, in the way he pressed her hand when it came time for him to go. Greta Koch had confessed, he'd told her. In all likelihood, they would be able to retrieve the bullet Greta had washed down the kitchen sink and use it as evidence. As for Greta's shoulder, the doctors said it would heal quite nicely, after a few months. Trasker dispensed his information quietly, without fanfare. Andrew Deretchin was leaving Sunnydale. Heading back to Florida for a new trial. And there was going to be an audit of the nursing home's books, one that Trasker was sure would land Philip Reynolds in jail.

"What a wild goose chase," Jack was saying. "When I finally tracked them down in Spring Lake, Reynolds threatened to have me arrested. Did I tell you that?"

"Mmmm."

Actually, he'd told her three or four times. It was part of the same litany he'd been repeating since he'd picked her up at the hospital: What he'd done. Why he wasn't there. How sorry he was. It seemed pointless, really. When you thought about it, she was the sorry one, the one who needed to be forgiven.

"I made dinner reservations at The Breakers," Jack said. "Seven o'clock tonight. It'll be a real celebration."

"I don't think I'm up to it," Anne said quietly.

"Okay then. I'll cook. I need to drive to Red Bank to pick up a few things. Salmon maybe. And new potatoes."

"Jack . . ." she began. She looked out toward the beach, where ring-billed gulls were circling the sand for food. A wave crested and dashed against the shoreline, sending up a tower of spray.

"What?" he said. "What's wrong?"

"We can't keep on pretending this is going to work when we both know it's not."

He stopped eating and looked at her.

"Let's face it," she continued, wishing she'd practiced what she was going to say ahead of time. "We're too different to spend the rest of our lives together. You like the city, I like it here. You have these gourmet dinner parties and I'm happy with the chicken special at Roy Rogers. You spend money like it's water and I live from hand to mouth. We don't even have the same ideas about vacations. Exploring the outback of Peru is great, if you're a llama. But I'd rather be exploring America. I've never been to San Francisco or New Orleans or even Chicago, for that matter."

"We'll go."

"I wish it were that simple, but the fact is, I'm not ready for a major commitment. We enjoy spending time together. We get along, for the most part. But if you really look at the situation, you'll realize there's other stuff going on, reasons why we're together that might not have anything to do with either one of us."

"What stuff?"

"Your brother, for one. Do you realize how many times you tell me how grateful you are that I helped you figure out how he died? I think that's a big part of this whole equation. Why we started going out in the first place."

"Anne . . ." He held both hands out in front of him. But she could see by his face that she was right. She'd sensed he'd been having his own doubts.

"Now we're even. You helped me. More than you realize. You're the one who found the bullet. And without that, Greta would still be free. And I'd never know how that skeleton got there."

"Why were you with *me* then? Why were you in this?"

"Because for a while, it was great. *You're* great, Jack. You are. And someday you're going to find someone who's absolutely right for you." She slid the diamond ring off her finger and held it out to him. "When that day comes, I think you should have this."

Without a word, he took the ring and slipped it into his pants pocket. He stood up. "I should head back to the city," he said. "I've got a lot to do at work." He didn't sound angry or sad or surprised. His face reflected a certain resignation that she'd seen there before. When the blueprints weren't right, when his floor plan wasn't going to work.

She almost said something about still wanting to be friends, but the words died on her lips. It was the ultimate kiss-off cliché. Besides, the friends thing didn't work unless both people had found someone else, and by that time, there was usually no point in trying.

She watched him walk back into the house and shut the front door behind him. She was going to miss him. Probably more than she realized. She looked at the Victorian cottage, at the torn shutters and faded yellow paint, the roof that needed patching, the weather-beaten porch. It was an old house—a pain in the neck sometimes. But it was hers. And it was skeleton-free. Cleansed of violence, past sins, buried bodies.

She turned back to the beach and listened to the muffled roar of the waves. It was a soothing melody. And she sat there for some time, watching the sun glint off the water, gulls, driftwood, dunes, the way the ocean looked like a swatch of gray velvet. She was aware of the cool, sea air filling her lungs, her entire being. She thought it smelled like hope.

Murder Is on the Menu
at the Hillside Manor Inn
Bed-and-Breakfast Mysteries by
MARY DAHEIM
featuring Judith McMonigle Flynn

Discover Murder and Mayhem with
Southern Sisters Mysteries
by
ANNE GEORGE

MURDER ON A GIRLS' NIGHT OUT
78086-0/$6.50 US/$8.50 Can
Agatha Award winner for Best First Mystery Novel

MURDER ON A BAD HAIR DAY
78087-9/$6.50 US/$8.50 Can

MURDER RUNS IN THE FAMILY
78449-1/$6.50 US/$8.50 Can

MURDER MAKES WAVES
78450-5/$6.50 US/$8.50 Can

MURDER GETS A LIFE
79366-0/$6.50 US/$8.50 Can

MURDER SHOOTS THE BULL
80149-3/$6.50 US/$8.99 Can

And Coming Soon in hardcover
MURDER CARRIES A TORCH